O God, I could be bounded in a nutshell
and count myself a king of infinite space,
were it not that I have bad dreams.

William Shakespeare, *Hamlet*

1

The day Nik Wallenda crossed Niagara Falls on a tightrope, Zoltan Beck lay in a private room in palliative care at St. Cecilia's Hospital. He hated Jell-O, so his son Ben had brought him a jar of blackberry jam and a spoon. When Ben's wife, Lucy, had asked about the jam, Ben said that, if his father couldn't have straight jam now, when would he get another chance?

Three tubs of uneaten Jell-O, one red, one yellow and one green, lined up miraculously on the windowsill like a recumbent traffic light. Zoltan slurped purply and rapidly on the jam, and while it was not a full-blown Prince concert, Ben had to sit back to avoid the purple mist falling around them.

Zoltan told his son that he hated eating now, but he finished off the jam quite nicely, then handed Ben the jar and spoon. He moaned as he settled back on his pillow. The colon cancer had blown through him like an underground wind.

Zoltan looked up at the clock hung too high on the opposite wall. It was stopped at 11:07, but he didn't seem to mind. Ben stared at it too and found it calming. Like a sleeping cat. All that potential bottled up—calming for that reason, he thought.

A single potted plant sat pouting on the nightstand. Lucy had brought it to cheer up her father-in-law, but now it was having the opposite effect. Though she watered it often, it looked more concerned than cheerful.

"Dad, do you want me to arrange for a TV to be brought in? Nik Wallenda is going to cross the falls later today."

He didn't answer Ben, or even look at him.

"Why don't I do that?" Ben said. "I'll arrange for a TV. Would you like to read now?"

Ben handed him his book, *Hitler's Mistakes*, which Zoltan was reading for the second time. His father didn't take it, so Ben placed it by Zoltan's side, along with his reading glasses. He wanted to take his father's hand in his own and say to him that, if he wanted to, he could still battle this thing that was raging inside him. *Some* people managed to beat the odds. Ben looked at that hand, almost touched it, but he and his father did not touch, or rather they only shook. Even when Ben's mother died, his father shook Ben's hand and said it would be all right. Touching his hand otherwise, covering it with his own, was not the same. It was not what gentlemen in suits did. That was always their benchmark: gentlemen in suits.

Zoltan looked past Ben at the window, at the blue carton of sky, which he might have wanted to have and to hold, even if not to open.

"I'll go ask about a TV," Ben said again, and stood up. Zoltan was still looking as Ben slipped quietly out of the room.

When he got back, his older brother, Frank, the accountant, was there, sitting by the bed, flipping through *Hitler's Mistakes*. Their father was staring at the clock again. The afternoon sun warmed the room.

"What's he been up to?" Frank asked, as if their father weren't there.

Ben rolled his eyes at him. "The doctor's coming in later this afternoon to give us an update. Are you going to be around?"

"No can do," Frank said. "I'm flying to Las Vegas in a couple of hours." He held up his fingers to the light. "These babies are going to roll us a fortune."

"Frank, anyone who says 'no can do' generally loses at craps. It's a proven fact."

"And do you know what else is a proven fact?" Frank said. "That you're a dick."

Frank got to his feet, glanced up at the clock for a moment, then at the mount on the wall for a television. "We should get him a TV," he said.

"Good thinking."

"I'll pay for it," Frank said, meaning, I'll pay for it. You arrange it.

He was about to touch their father's hand too—Ben could see it—but he also thought better of it.

Zoltan did not budge as Frank departed. For Ben, it was all good. Frank was best taken in small doses. Or no doses.

He sat again on the chair beside his father. Zoltan's eyes did not move. Ben was afraid he was dead. But then something did move behind the eyes, like something stirring on the floor of a pond.

Ben waited. The air in the room was too thin to hold an odor. The walls were drab and blemished, as if they too were ailing. How was it possible to stare at these walls or at the clock with its stopped heart, or breathe in the thin air, without reaching for significance? A room like this near the ocean would smell salty. A room like this in the mountains would be too bright. You could look out the window to search for the place where the sky ended and heaven began. But here there was nothing to distinguish this room. It was in a building in the center of a city where tall trees must once have stood, where the buffalo roamed and where songs were still written.

But maybe that was the point for Ben's father and him. Maybe this was the right setting after all. Ben could feel his thoughts loosening, the knot of them untangling. He was here with his father, but he was not sure Zoltan had any need of him.

Zoltan had said once that the last days of life were still life. Death was simpler.

Ben could hear his own voice coming on, the pulse in his ears. "Dad, let's not wait for the TV guy. There's a lounge at the end of the hall with a nice TV in it. Let's go down together and have a visit. We can watch Nik Wallenda cross the falls. I'm not sure what time he's on."

An answer was hatching in his father's mouth but never quite broke through. Ben stared at him, at his mouth, his face. All the days of his life were clamped in him now and sealed. The flight from the Russians. The triumph over Nazism. The arrival at Pier 21. The smell of sweet noodles with walnuts and plums. The cat that came mysteriously to their house one day and never left. The reading of Alexandre Dumas, especially *The Three Musketeers*. The last of the melting snow. The mad magnetism of a streetlight to a moth. The keeling over of a top-heavy coat-tree that stood in the vestibule. The tasting of a piece of grilled lamb chop to see if it was done.

Did he not want to pat his first great-grandchild on the head, see where his own line might be going?

Were there unexploded fireworks still in him? Zoltan was normally such a noisy man that the plump silence grew big enough now in the room to bounce, if you let it. How pointless it seemed suddenly to see the summer smiling in from the window.

"Come, Dad," Ben said. "When are we ever going to see a guy crossing the falls again?"

Zoltan let his son help him up and put a robe on him. Ben expected him to trudge down the hall the way people did on this floor, but his father was not a trudger, so they walked briskly, almost broke into a trot.

They could hear the TV clanging and dinging from a good distance. "Come on down," said Drew Carey. Someone was watching *The Price Is Right*. A young, cheerful girl and her grandfather were quite caught up in it. They were both dressed in street clothes. Visitors, like Ben.

The grandfather was clapping, and the girl was jumping like mad from side to side.

Beside them on a small round table was a carton of chicken-wing bones, the lid marked Wing Ding. It was as if a whole flock of birds had been snatched out of the air and laid to rest there.

Zoltan took a seat on a leather lounge chair beside the girl and Ben sat on a wooden chair on his other side. Ben clapped along with the girl's grandfather. A tall woman called Ryta, according to the name tag pasted on her bright pink T-shirt, was about to guess the price of a sailboat, plus a trip to the South Seas. The girl stopped jumping and chewed the ends of her shiny brown hair.

A few minutes later, when the announcer called on Thelma to "come on down," the girl began jumping all over again, but straight up and down this time. Suddenly, she sensed Zoltan was watching her rather than the TV.

"Do you have jumping people?" she asked him.

"Pardon me?" he said. Ben could hardly hear his father.

"I mean people who jump for you in the back when the man says, 'Come on down.'"

"Is that what you are?" Ben asked. "Are you a jumping person?"

"Yes," the girl said. "But I also have jumping people. And if I get to be on the show, I want to take my jumping people with me."

Zoltan's eyes ripened, his ears closed. Ben knew him well. His father had reached that moment in the eye when seeing everything and seeing nothing met.

He kept expecting his father to vanish, the borders of him to dissolve.

The little girl was wearing white-and-black saddle shoes, and now she was leaping outright to show everyone what she'd meant. She was raising her arms high in the air too, hoping to hit the ceiling.

2

The day, some eight months earlier, that Ben's father was to have his colonoscopy, an autumn sleet was falling hard, mincing the air. For whatever reason—probably because Ben had internalized Zoltan as much as he had—the weather made him as anxious as his father was sure to be.

Plus he was having the procedure. One would think that someone who'd spent his declining years worrying about how he was going to clear himself out would welcome the prospect of a colonoscopy. But Zoltan couldn't drink the whole prescribed gallon of Expulsor. He said he was sure the stuff tasted worse than the crap that was in him. Besides, he said, after downing four and a half glasses and dashing to the can repeatedly, he could tell that his innards were squeaky clean up to the neck.

He'd managed to avoid two previous appointments, for reasons he claimed were legitimate, but when his youngest son, Sammy, the doctor, insisted, Zoltan realized the time had finally come. Still, Ben and Lucy agreed that Ben would have to take his father to the hospital to ensure he didn't slip out of this one too. Ben's brothers were not available that day, though they were rarely asked to help out anyway. If Ben couldn't manage the appointment, the next in line would have been Lucy, and next likely would have been Leah or Anna, their daughters, if either was in town and available.

Ben took time off work to get Zoltan to the GI clinic at St. Cecilia's Hospital in North Toronto. Ben had told his father that, since his appointment wasn't until 11:45 A.M., he'd pick him up at 10, even though the drive took only a half hour. By the time he got to his parents' place, at exactly 9:40, it was overcast but nothing was falling.

He nearly ran his father down at the end of his driveway. Zoltan liked to arrive for his appointments several hours early, but he was especially keen on this occasion. The man was a tiger, pacing back and forth, and, to emphasize the point, he was wearing an open jacket and his tiger sweatshirt, though luckily not the matching bottoms.

"Hey," he yelled, as he jumped out of the way. He gave Ben a fierce look through the windshield, as if his son had wanted to hit him and he knew it.

Zoltan stepped into the car. He was a small man but agile for his age, and his hair was still quite a bit more black than silver. His eyes were grayer than his hair, he liked to tell people, though really they were hazel and seemed to like to change color depending on what he wore. He pulled his jacket closed and his Panama hat down too tightly on his head, or it might just have been that his head had shrunk a little. The Panama had the usual dome top and a perfectly flat brim, giving Zoltan's head the look of Saturn.

He said, "Your mother would have joined us, if she was still with us. You know that, don't you?"

"Of course I do."

"She could have come and relieved you, so you wouldn't have to wait through all this."

"It's no problem, Dad. I took the time off. I'm yours."

Ben's parents didn't like to put people out. They were as self-reliant as could be. But times had changed. Hannah had been gone for two years now, and Zoltan lived on his own.

As the two sat at the stoplight, waiting to turn onto Lawrence Avenue, Ben watched his father's face redden. Zoltan took on a diabolical look, contradicted by the over-sized Panama. As they crawled along in traffic on Lawrence, dark shadows rolled over Zoltan's face like film. Then the sun powered through a cloud and lit up his head. Sunrise on Saturn.

They got to the hospital at 10:05. Ben slowed near the main entrance, and his father threw open the door and leapt out, even before the car had come to a full stop. "See you upstairs," he said, and he bashed through the door like someone who mistook glass for clear air.

Ben parked and walked into the hospital. A statue of Saint Cecilia stood just inside the main doors, her bronze wings outspread, and Ben paused to read the inscription at the base, from John Donne:

> You, to whom love was peace, that now is rage;
> Who did the whole world's soul contract, and drove
> Into the glasses of your eyes
> (So made such mirrors, and such spies,
> That they did all to you epitomize)
> Countries, towns, courts: beg from above
> A pattern of your love!

It was barely 10:10 A.M. when he got to the clinic, where his father was holding up his health card and pacing again like a cat in front of the woman at the desk, who was on the phone.

"I don't know now," he was saying, "I don't know," scraping and flicking the card under his chin as though it were a razor. He had removed his Panama hat and was slapping it against his leg.

The woman at the desk looked at Ben, at Zoltan, looked at the clock up on the wall, ticking audibly, then went on with her phone conversation. A thorny red rose in a thin white vase stood guarding her desk.

Ben put an arm around his father's shoulders to steer him toward the chairs. Zoltan shrugged himself free. The half dozen other patients peered up from their magazines and books and watched as Ben escorted his father to sit among them. A woman moved three chairs away as they approached. They sat near a couple who didn't move. Zoltan didn't notice a thing and wouldn't have cared if he had.

"Dad, give me your card. I'll be sure the woman at the desk sees it in the next few minutes."

He didn't answer.

"Dad?" Ben reached for the card.

"Oh," Zoltan said, still clutching it.

Ben eased it out of his hand. "It's okay," he said. "We're a bit early."

Zoltan let out a strangled breath. Ben handed him a magazine, *Cottage Life*, but he didn't open it. Instead, he rolled it up in his hand, turning it into a bat.

"I wonder if Sammy will look in on me," he said.

Sammy worked in the same hospital. He was an ophthalmologist, specializing in retinas. Their parents had taken every single one of their friends to see him to have their eyes examined. Frank once said it was a good thing Sammy hadn't become a proctologist.

"I don't know if he has time today," Ben said to his father. "I think he's performing surgery all day, remember?"

Zoltan nodded. "I don't know why he couldn't just prescribe glasses," he said. "A nice, quiet, steady business. Who needs all this horror of blindness and shrapnel in the eye and these macular degenerates? Just prescribe glasses in a mall. Would that have been so awful?"

Ben shrugged.

"Oh, well," Zoltan said. Then he looked his son dead in the eye. "If something should happen to me today, Ben, I'd like Sammy to be my medical power of attorney. You know, pull the plug and so on, if it comes to that."

"Of course," Ben said.

"And Frank should be my financial power of attorney."

"Okay." Ben sighed audibly in his father's direction. He was the middle son, the teacher. "Would you like me to be the educational power of attorney?" he said. "If you drift into a coma, I could tell them to stop the geography lesson right away."

His father waved the batty magazine at him. He was about to say something to Ben but didn't. Instead, he snatched back his health card.

Ben did not feel unloved. There was enough love to go around, in his mother's case especially, for six children and two husbands, let alone three and one. If anything, he was *over*loved. Frank used to say that he was breastfed for so long that, in later years, he'd go out afterward for a smoke.

The woman at the desk hung up the phone, not realizing she was doing so at her peril. Zoltan bolted over. Ben beamed a smile at their companions in the waiting room, each of them looking a bit crazed, no doubt as a consequence of all that Expulsor they'd imbibed and the violent visits to the toilet. The waiting room smelled faintly of what the Irish fondly call shite, or maybe it was all in Ben's head.

His father said to the receptionist, "Are these people ahead of me?" He looked all around him, then down at the belligerent red rose. He was slapping at his sides again.

"Yes, they are."

"Who is?"

"All of them."

He surveyed the room again. He had a look of contempt for each of them, holding them responsible for what he was enduring, holding Ben responsible. Was all this really necessary?

Zoltan returned to sit with his son, and they spent a time not talking. He even looked at an article in *Cottage Life* about how to build a dock, though he'd never built anything in his life. *Handy* was not a word anyone who knew Zoltan would have used to describe him. He had tools at home, wrenches and C-clamps and chisels, but he wielded them recklessly. Once, when Ben was young, his father took a saw to one of the kitchen cupboards because he hated noise at night. He thought the fridge made too much of a racket, though the rest of the family agreed it was the normal noise fridges made as they went about their business. But he wasn't having it. He'd sometimes woken Ben in the night and asked him to lift a corner of the fridge so that he could slide rolled-up newspaper underneath it to muffle the beast. When that didn't work, eventually he decided the noise came from the top, with the fridge clattering against the cupboard above it. It was no wonder with all those wads of newspaper underneath.

One afternoon, while everyone was out, Zoltan removed the dishes from the cupboard and took a saw to the cabinet, crudely cutting out the bottom altogether, leaving gashes and zags in the wood and a rainfall of sawdust.

When Hannah got home, followed by the boys, Zoltan had gone. The boys and their mother were aghast. It was as if an army had invaded, a dumb and feckless army, confused about its mission, or forgetting it halfway through.

When Zoltan returned home, Hannah screamed at him, "What did you do here?"

"The fridge was making too much noise. I did the manly thing."

"This is not a manly thing. It's not even a beastly thing. It's the work of a maniac."

In the waiting room, Zoltan told Ben it was time to go.

"It is not time to go," Ben replied. "Do you have an appointment elsewhere that you have to get to?"

"I have a little life left to live," Zoltan began to say—and then he was called, still five minutes before his appointment time. By then, Zoltan looked defeated. When a nurse wearing a top with Crayola crayons printed on it, as if she worked in a children's hospital, came to get him, he trudged off with her like a prisoner to the gallows.

Ben read about docks for no more than a half hour before the nurse with the crayon top returned. "Mr. Beck," she said. "Ben Beck?"

He sprang to his feet, relieved.

"Your father needs you," she said.

"Is the colonoscopy done already?"

The nurse shook her head. As he followed her, she told him, "We couldn't complete the procedure. Your father was all plugged up."

"Oh, no. Where is he now?"

"He'll need to recover from the sedative we gave him."

She led Ben to a door. "He's in there. Feel free," she said, and continued down the hall.

Ben walked in and found his father lying down but fretting.

"Now, now, what's going on now?" Zoltan said.

"Stop the algebra quiz," Ben called out to no one at all.

The room smelled like a sewage plant, and he soon saw why. Zoltan had on a diaper, and it was overflowing. Ben breathed just through his mouth.

"What's going on?" his father said again.

"You're full of shite," he said.

"Oh," Zoltan said. He started to get up.

"What are you doing?"

"I'm starving. Let's get some grub."

Ben felt faint. He looked for an alarm button of some kind, but the nurse came back and asked to be left alone with Zoltan.

"Of course," Ben said.

On his way out, he glanced back at his father, half tiger, half creature of the brown bog. This man could have authored *The Art of Shitting*, so bent was he at all times on clearing out every single morsel that passed through him. He could have led seminars on the many good ways to prepare prunes, on the serene pleasure of drinking Senokot tea, on the wonders to be found in Metamucil. Yet when he was given a magic potion that would have given him and his students a gleaming smile, he did not have the fortitude to finish it off.

In less than half an hour, miraculously, Zoltan and Ben were downstairs, mowing through the cafeteria line. Polite Canadians had never really been a match for this wild Hungarian man. He'd been to the Swiss Chalet station, gotten his quarter chicken dinner, plus some soup, plus rice pudding, tea and orange juice, all before Ben had poured himself a coffee. Ben waved to the cashier as his father pushed past her to indicate that he would pay up for both of them in a minute.

When he caught up with his father, Zoltan was sitting in the first booth he could find, opposite a stunned woman, his tray awash with tea and soup that floated his sugar wrappers and the empty packets of ketchup to and fro. He had clearly opened the ketchup with such violence that arcs of it had colored the corners of the unsuspecting woman's tray.

"Why don't we leave the nice woman alone to finish her lunch?" Ben said.

His father looked up at him, the juice of his torn prey trickling from his mouth, as Ben eased his lunch out from under him. Zoltan followed Ben, his swamp eddying over the lip of his tray. They found another booth in a far corner, and Ben watched him finish. He had to hold up a napkin like a shower curtain to shield himself from the storm.

When Zoltan was done, he took the tray to the conveyor belt and returned with a swath of liquid cutting diagonally across the tiger stripes of his top. He was dabbing himself with a napkin, but what he really needed was a beach towel.

Outside, he smiled and said, "Ah—that hit the spot."

"It hit the whole building," Ben said.

Zoltan glared at him. "You know, I should just have driven myself."

"You don't have a proper driver's license anymore."

"So what would they do if they stopped me? Imprison me?"

It was Ben's turn to stare. Here was a man who couldn't even eat without harming himself and others. When he was downtown once, in the days when he did drive, he pulled over on Bay Street, flung open his door as he reached back for his briefcase and a truck took the door clean off. He came home that night and at first wouldn't tell anyone why he looked so windblown. Ben knew as soon as he looked out the living room window at the car.

One afternoon more recently, they were pulling into the lot of a mall, and a man had dropped a bag of groceries. There were oranges and grapes and olives and pepperoni sticks scattered all around. The man saw them coming and waved frantically but had to jump out of the way to save himself as Zoltan drove straight ahead over the man's groceries, squashing the fruit and meat all over the lot.

As they drove out of the hospital parking lot, Ben asked his father, "Do you want to swing by the cemetery to visit Mom? I have time."

To his surprise, his father said, "Yes, for a few minutes." Though he had brought her up in the waiting room, Zoltan didn't like to be reminded of Hannah, much less of death.

He sat calmly as they drove, his hands clasped in his lap. Ben sometimes stared at those hands, remembered years ago how warm and dry they'd always been when his father took him across the street.

On a school trip to Dublin, at the National Museum, Ben saw the bog people lying in glass cases. They were figures buried in a bog twenty-five centuries before and preserved well enough that you could see the hair on their heads—auburn red in one case—and their fingernails, and you knew then that they must once have run a crude comb through those red locks, might even have gnawed down their nails to keep them short, smiled to show their teeth.

Lucy had asked Ben only a week before if they should be thinking about getting themselves a plot. All this land Ben and his father now drove by way up north on Bathurst Street, land with some houses on it and many more yet to be built, the sales centers standing on the corners, their bright flags eagerly flapping, was just plots waiting to happen, plots with bog people lying far beneath them.

At Park Lawn Cemetery, Ben pulled over near his mother's grave and his father hopped out of the car before Ben switched off the engine. He glanced at the solitary tree nearby. It was a balsam poplar, a variety Ben knew his mother loved. Once, when he was in elementary school, Ben gathered a dozen of the beautiful flat, pointed leaves, pressed them in the pages of a small notebook and presented them to his mother on her birthday.

Zoltan pushed his hat down hard on his head, in order to warm his thoughts, Ben guessed. "Do you have the stones?" he asked over his shoulder, as if Ben were his assistant, the magician's assistant.

Ben was the family's stone collector. He didn't remember when his mania began, but since he was a child he had always been on the hunt for stones, looking down at beaches and on forest floors. He loved the contradiction in them: they seemed solid yet on their way to becoming something else— sand, water, dirt, dust, airborne particles.

"Do you want a red one and a white one?" Ben asked.

"The colors don't matter."

Ben handed him the stones.

"Do you have blue and white?"

"Not with me."

His father placed them on top of the gravestone beside three white ones, which were there from the last visit, when Lucy and the girls had visited. Zoltan was mouthing something to Hannah, probably something about the failed colonoscopy. Ben tried to read his lips. His father stepped forward onto the chrysanthemums still clinging to life at Hannah's feet.

Ben and his brothers had composed the inscription for her headstone.

HANNAH KOHN BECK
She gave more than she took. Good night, dear heart.

Zoltan didn't so much as glance at the left side of the double grave. What were the boys going to say about him on the stone? "Tyger Tyger, burning bright"? It was going to be tougher.

Zoltan looked straight up now, and Ben joined him, gazing at their puzzle piece of sky. Then Zoltan headed quickly toward the car. In the distance, a big fat cloud was muffin-topping itself over a ridge.

Ben remembered thinking that he didn't want to leave his mother here that first night. He tried to imagine the place at night, the mounds and stones darkening, all the sound that used to come from the people lying here, all the sound they used to make, all of them now muted, every last one as if they had entered a vast library. Ben closed his eyes. He strained to hear, until his father blasted the car horn.

During the ride back, his father said, "So what happens at the end? Do we simply stop counting the years, draw a line underneath, or do we reset to zero?" Ben looked over at him. His father was staring straight ahead. "It's either endless day or endless night," he said. "If you can tell me which, you get a cash prize."

"How much?" Ben asked.

"Two hundred and forty-two dollars."

They rolled along some more before Zoltan said, "Do you think I'll see your mother, after—"

"I think so, possibly, yes."

Zoltan looked out his window. It was a long moment before he said, "I don't believe it either."

When they got to Ben's parents' place, his father said, "Do you think there's a chance I could get my driver's license back?"

"I think there is a chance."

Zoltan opened the car door but paused before getting out. "Same chance as seeing your mother again." He was staring at Ben.

Ben took a deep breath. After a time, he said, "Dad, Saint Augustine divided people into two camps: those who are here merely to use the world and those who are here to leave something of value behind. What camp do you think you belong to?"

"Do you know what?" he said. "I brought you boys here to Canada. If I did nothing else, I brought you here. I'm leaving *you* behind."

Ben felt his face burning.

"I'm not saying it was an act of genius," Zoltan went on. "It was a guess, that's all, a toss of the dice, but every once in a while you guess right. That's what you owe me for guessing right." He added, "I wanted to bring you to a place where you don't have to squirm, you don't have to cringe to say, I'm here." He still wasn't done. "I gave you a predictable life. Do you know what that's worth? You should thank me for that."

"Thank you."

"A lot."

"Thank you a lot. You did extremely well."

"I didn't do extremely well, but I did well enough."

Ben felt that old, familiar feeling again, those early years here as a refugee, the strangeness of it, the strange language, the strange look of the place. Were they going to start a new subspecies here, *be* a new subspecies after a time, through language mutation, cultural mutation, hockey mutation, maple syrup? How could he be sure of anything? The memory of fleeing the Russians as a three-year-old, of crossing a dark border late one night to freedom, of gripping your grandmother's hand, stayed with you, even if you couldn't remember all the specifics. You could settle in in the new land, breathe out finally, take off your coat and stay for a while, but you always had one eye on the coat.

"Dad, can Lucy and I take you out for dinner tonight?"

"Lucille, Lucille," he was singing, "fair maiden of the dune." His eyes were closed. He was beaming. "Lucille, Lucille, your light shines even when the sun goes out."

"May we, Dad? We'd enjoy it."

"No," he said. "Let me take you. I insist."

"Okay," Ben said. "We'll pick you up around six."

"Five thirty," he said, and waited.

"Okay, how about three fifteen?"

Zoltan's eyes hardened. "I didn't have sons. I had critics." He got out of the car, closed the door, but was glaring at Ben still through the glass. "*Hodie mihi, cras tibi,*" he said.

Ben could hardly hear him. "What?" He rolled down his window as his father came around to his side.

"It's Latin."

"I know what it is."

"Today me, tomorrow you."

He then turned and was gone.

3

On a day not long after the Second World War had erupted, the world of Bela Beck and his younger brother, Zoltan—or Zoli, as he was then called—turned, and it would not turn back. At dawn, the boys had gone for their daily swim at the Palladium, one of the only places in Budapest with an Olympic-sized pool. Bela had made the national team, and now he was determined to make the Hungarian Olympic team. His younger brother was a first-rate swimmer too but, where competition was concerned, could only cheer Bela on from the sidelines and was glad to do so.

The two boys were in the dressing room with a few of Bela's teammates, including Bela's good friend Imre Horvath.

Imre had snatched Bela's towel away from him and was about to snap it at Bela to get a rise out of him. Zoli was doubled over with laughter. Bela, naked, tried to get the towel back from Imre, but Imre laughed too and held it behind him.

Zoli left to use the toilet, and when he returned, the coach was there. He didn't usually arrive until later, when the boys had warmed up in the pool. He was telling Bela it might not be a good idea to practice today. Bela smirked and Imre giggled some more, but the coach wasn't joking. "I'm sorry," the man said.

"No need to be sorry," Zoli said boldly. He was just pulling up his bathing suit. "We can manage without you today." He took his stopwatch from his satchel. "We're all prepared—see?"

The coach had not budged. He had not even turned toward Zoli.

"What do you mean?" Bela asked. "What are you sorry about?"

An officer entered behind the coach. He was dressed in the black uniform of the new special police. Imre got to his feet beside Bela. He offered his friend his towel back, but the officer slapped it to the floor before Bela could take it. Zoli ran to pick it up, but the officer raised his arm to bar him. The man looked Bela up and down. "Out," he told him.

"What do you mean?" said Bela. He glanced at the coach, who looked away.

"Out," the officer said.

Zoli began to dress again, punching his way through the damp sleeve of his shirt.

"What are you talking about?" Imre said. He stood in the man's face, but the officer pulled the towel off Imre's waist and looked at him too. Then the officer put his hand hard on Imre's shoulder and sat him down again. "You have one minute," the man said to Bela. "Don't come back." He pointed at Zoli. "And take him with you."

"Don't come back at all, or today only?" Imre asked, and the officer slapped him hard with the back of his hand and he almost fell off the bench. Zoli rushed at the officer and took a hard slap too. It made his lip bleed.

Bela scrambled to get his things. He trembled with rage. He helped his brother out the door and was gone, not once turning back. The two marched straight over to the Ferenc Liszt Academy, making quick work of the long walk across town. They hardly said a word to each other. They knew what this was about. Their father had told them these days were coming. He knew before most. Yet here they were. How could they have prepared?

When they arrived, another black shirt stood in front of the door. Bela's first thought, strangely, was how quickly they had manufactured these uniforms. Was it during the friendly conversations between Horthy and Hitler, or was it even before? The Hungarians had once again sided with Germany, as they had in the First World War.

"What do you think?" Zoli whispered. "We could take him, the two of us. We could punch him senseless."

"Are you crazy, Zoli? This is a music academy."

The guard at the door had a softer look on his face than the man at the pool. He seemed younger, possibly Bela's age. Bela and Zoli stepped forward. "Excuse me," Bela said. He had a key in his hand.

"What do you want here?" the guard asked in a boy's voice.

"I practice music here," Bela said. "This is my brother. I *teach* music here. I have a student this morning. I know it's early—"

"Not today," the guard said.

"Yes, today. I'll show you my schedule."

"You won't be having students today."

"Then I'll just practice for a short time."

"Not here," the man-boy said. "Not today."

Zoli was breathing hard, panting. Bela looked the guard in the eyes, and the guard looked away, then down, but he stood his ground. How did he even know who Bela was? Had he been warned to expect him? Bela wanted to take his brother and back up. He wanted to wait on the other side of the street, stare at the guard, make him squirm a bit, see if he turned others away. But then what? Was Bela going to call the police? Was he going to storm the building with his brother? Bela filled his lungs with blue Danube air, and Zoli followed suit, waiting for his brother's lead. But Bela took his brother by the shoulder and turned toward home.

When they got there, Bela pushed through the door into the foyer. He took his mother's face in his hands and kissed her on each cheek. The housekeeper, Vera, was right behind her, but she sensed something and withdrew. "No swimming today," Bela told his mother quietly, "and no music."

"What's going on?" she asked. "Has something happened? Is it a national day of mourning?"

Now Zoli took his mother's face in his hands too. "Not national," he replied. "Local. *Very* particular." He too kissed her, but her eyes followed Bela. The two boys went to Bela's room and slammed the door behind them. Of course, their mother asked through the door what had happened, but Bela said, "Later." His mother asked if she could get them something, but heard nothing back.

A few hours later, a girl called Izabel stopped by. She was Zoli's age, sixteen, and pretty, with white skin, black hair tied back and cobalt blue eyes, but with something warm behind the eyes, feverish. She'd come to ask if she could have her piano lesson with Bela here since he wasn't at the academy.

The Becks had a beautiful rosewood Bösendorfer grand piano in their front room. They'd had it shipped from Vienna. One evening, Bela entertained a room full of his mother's friends, and when he turned to Schumann's *Kinderszenen*, Adel Toth, who was sitting by Bela's mother in the front row of chairs, sighed audibly and then toppled like a soft boulder to the floor.

Bela was the first one by her side.

"Has she had a heart attack?" his mother asked. Eugenia was trembling. She called out to her husband in his study. "Vilmos!"

"No, she's just swooned," Bela said. He was patting Adel's hand.

"And now you're a doctor too?" his father asked. Vilmos *was* a doctor. He knelt by his son. Adel was coming around already. Without looking at Bela, his father said, "Yes, it's a little fainting spell."

"It was the Schumann," his mother said.

"No, it was the playing," Adel said, as she struggled to sit up with some help and with a grunt.

Adel had not had children of her own and had always admired Eugenia Beck's. She showered them with gifts every time she saw them. "What gentlemen," she once called them, "and beasts," she added, growling.

Now young Izabel, who'd come for her lesson, was led by Eugenia to the front room. Izabel immediately took her place on the piano bench. Only Zoli exited Bela's bedroom to sit with Izabel. While he tried to make conversation, Eugenia went to see about her other son.

By the time Eugenia joined the two in the front room, Izabel looked uneasy. Zoli was making a small speech about music, how important it was, good for the soul. He was looking down at his hands as he spoke, the spread fingers thrusting out, as if he were about to play something to show Izabel what he meant. He wanted to comfort the girl, reassure her, but his comforting look turned to panic, which infected the girl with panic too, until finally she rose to say she thought she might go.

Zoli rose as well. A clump of sound came out of his

mouth, but nothing more. Izabel smiled at him but turned and departed quickly.

It was not until Imre came by that evening that Bela showed his face. Imre began to tell Eugenia what had happened that morning, but Bela interrupted him. "Let's go out," he said. He took a jacket and was outside before he'd got both arms through the sleeves.

A minute later, he returned to ask his brother if he wanted to join them. Zoli was thrilled. He grabbed his jacket out of the front closet and followed. Bela smiled at his mother. They headed off on foot to a favorite haunt, Tamas's Tavern and Schnitzel House, near the Oktogon, on Andrassy Avenue.

Zoli told his brother that Izabel had been anxious about her lesson.

"Did you give her one?" Bela asked with a smirk.

"I bet he did," Imre said.

Zoli's face flushed a hot crimson.

The three boys drank plum *palinka*, a specialty of the house, then tried to mop it up with some food, but they quickly returned to their bottle and ordered a second. Imre slurred something about the swim team and the water polo team. He said he wouldn't stand for what had happened and was going to talk to his father, Laszlo Horvath, who was the well-known minister of the interior in Horthy's cabinet.

Bela was tracing the rim of his glass with his finger. He looked as if he might cry. He didn't answer. He downed his drink, and his brother followed suit.

It was late by the time the boys emerged onto the street. They had to pause to right themselves at the Oktogon. Imre was about to hail a cab when a young Gypsy girl approached them. She reminded Zoli of Izabel. She had the same coloring and might even have been the same age, his age.

"What are you boys up to?" the girl asked in a growly voice that didn't seem to suit her. It was as if she'd been fitted with the wrong voice by mistake.

Zoli stepped up. He looked into the wet light of the girl's eyes. He was about to close his own eyes, lean forward, when someone shoved Imre from behind.

"Hey!" Imre said.

Two soldiers were upon them. They were not black shirts but regular army. One shoved Bela and Imre pulled the man back by the shoulders. The shover stepped between Zoli and the Gypsy girl and kissed her hard on her red lips. He was grinding himself against her when Zoli grabbed a clump of the man's hair and yanked him back. When the soldier turned toward him, Zoli slugged him in the jaw so hard that the man fell back on some bushes.

The girl cried out. Her scarlet lipstick was smeared. When the other soldier drew his pistol, Imre said, "Do you know who I am? My father is Laszlo Horvath, and I will have you court-martialed before you see a day of service, you pathetic rodent."

The soldier didn't know what to say. He bent over his friend to help him up, and the two of them slouched off down Terez Street, not once looking back.

The girl was crying now. Bela stepped up and handed her all the money he had in his wallet, more than she'd earn in a week. Zoli took her in his arms. She sniffed back her tears, gave him a kiss on each cheek, and then she kissed the other two boys. Imre offered her his handkerchief. "Just go home," he told her. "Sleep for a change."

It was at least ten years later that Imre recalled the details of this incident to Eugenia and Zoli's young wife, Hannah. It was after all the trouble had passed, and they were reminiscing. "I could have sworn Zoli was in love," Imre said, chuckling. Hannah smiled at him. "It was that time in our lives," Zoli said, and he smiled too.

4

Lucy and Ben arrived at 5:15 and were surprised that Zoltan was not outside. Lucy was suddenly worried, and Ben used his key to let them in. His father was frantically searching for something upstairs.

"I'll be right there," Zoltan said. They could hear him banging around, dropping things on the floor.

"What are you looking for?"

"Never mind," he said, and grunted.

Ben looked at Lucy and said to her, "I can imagine."

"Leave it," she said.

"Just wait. Let's see what it is."

Now things were quiet. "Is everything all right?" Ben yelled up.

His father didn't answer but came hurtling down the stairs like an athlete, right by them, not even glancing at them. He was wearing white cloth gloves.

"What are you doing?" Ben asked.

Zoltan ignored him.

"Dad, why are you wearing those gloves?"

"I don't have to tell you."

Ben glared at Lucy.

"Leave him," she said.

"You see?" Zoltan said, turning toward her. "Lucille is the daughter I never had." He caressed her cheek with his gloved hand.

"Is everything okay?" she asked.

Zoltan hated questions, but he tolerated them from Lucy. "Yes," he said. "I have a rash on my thumb, and I find that colorless gloves help with the symptoms."

"Those aren't colorless," Ben said. "They're white. White is a color too. Those gloves weren't born white."

Lucy said, "Do you have the rash on both hands?"

"No, but I can't very well go out with a single glove, can I?"

"You can make like Michael Jackson," Ben said.

"It's fine," Lucy said.

Lucy gave her front seat up to Zoltan and got into the back. He put his gloved hands on his knees. "It's the same rash I have on my feet: athlete's foot," he said. "I think it has spread." Ben looked down to see if his father was wearing white socks. He was.

Before Ben pulled out, he said, "Dad, we have to stop at Velda Kerbel's on the way. She's been calling us. She's called twenty times. She wants to give you something."

"She's left me a number of messages," Zoltan said. "I don't want anything from Velda."

"She has your mother's handwritten recipe book," Ben said. "Mom lent it to her years ago, and Velda doesn't feel it's right for her to hang on to it."

"What would I do with a cookbook?"

"That's not the point," Ben said.

"No, I'm sure it isn't."

"I would like to have it," Lucy said. "It's a family heirloom."

"Then you pick it up sometime, dear," Zoltan said.

"Dad, she gave the Heart and Stroke Foundation ten thousand dollars in Mom's name."

"That was of little use to your mother," he said.

He was right. Velda wanted something else, and it wasn't difficult to guess what. Velda Kerbel had been a widow for fifteen years and had always had her eye on Zoltan, even before her husband, Saul, had died. She was at least ten years Zoltan's junior, but she acted and tried to look even younger. She was the heiress to the Kerbel pickle dynasty: Kerbel's Famous Kosher Style Pickles, Kerbel's Pickled Tomatoes, Kerbel's Pickled Sweet Banana Peppers, Kerbel's Smokin' Hot Banana Peppers and, of course, Kerbel's Pickled Herring

Tidbits in Wine Marinade. Every visit from Velda to your home earned you a case of one of the above. All you had to do was come get it out of the back of her Lincoln SUV. Nowadays, Velda was spending much of her time painting. She fancied herself undiscovered, though she made it difficult for anyone *not* to discover her.

"It'll take one minute," Ben said. "It's on our way down Bathurst. Lucy told her we'd stop."

Ben looked at his father's gloved hands fidgeting in his lap. He was always on high alert. He said, "If it's true all she wants to do is return our cookbook, then she should hand it to you and we can be on our way."

Ben was hoping that Lucy might change his father's mind, but not another word was exchanged. They turned down Velda's street and pulled up to her gates, which opened magically, then rolled along a circular cobblestone driveway that seemed constructed for horses and grand carriages. The immense white house looked much like the Hermitage in Saint Petersburg, meant to display Velda's art, and Velda.

Velda must have waved off the servants, because she came to the door herself as Ben and Lucy were getting out of the car. In fact, she came straight at her guests with a newly freshened pair of breasts beneath a tight top. They were like greeters. If they'd been any perkier, they'd have been chewing bubble gum. The breasts were fanned from above by an impressive set of false eyelashes. She looked out through the thicket at Zoltan and madly waved at him to come in. When he didn't open the door, she knocked on his window. He seemed to be staring straight at her chest. How could he not?

"Come on," she was saying. "Come *on*."

Finally, he relented and huffed his way out of the car. Ben wondered if she'd noticed his white gloves. If she had, she didn't seem to mind. She was beaming.

"I want to show you something," she said.

"I think I've seen enough," Zoltan said under his breath, but just the same he followed her into the house.

Velda took Zoltan's hand. "Close your eyes, everyone," she said, as she led them toward the great room. Lucy and Ben did as they were told, but they crashed into Zoltan, who was not cooperating. "Please," Velda said. "Humor me."

They continued. It was a longish walk, but soon they could sense the bright light of the great room. They walked a dozen more steps until Velda said, "Okay! One, two, three, open sesame!"

They opened their eyes and gazed up. It was impossible not to. Velda had recreated the entire Sistine Chapel ceiling in her own great room, complete with the creation of Adam at its center, with God reaching out to the first man. Velda had given Adam much more prominent genitals than Michelangelo had dared to. But it was all there: the creation of Eve; Daniel; Isaiah; Jacob; Joseph; the twelve prophets; the Flood and Noah; David and Goliath.

Ben leaned in close to his wife, who had her hand over her mouth.

"So, what do you think?" Velda said. The figures were spectacular if somewhat cartoonish. Ben's father was glaring at him, his white-gloved hands clenched. Everything was blasting out at them: Velda's greeters, her eyelashes, Adam's genitals, the room itself.

And here's what Zoltan had to say: "We're here to pick up our recipe book."

Zoltan got to the car first and sat in the back this time, clutching the recipe book and staring blankly out to the side, though Velda was waving and flapping from her front door. "Can I give you a case of pickles?" she was saying.

Ben could see now, in the sunlight, that Velda's nipples were spectacular too. They were like greeters in their own right—greeters-in-training. He wanted to ask Lucy if one could have new ones installed in order to achieve that level of nipularity.

Lucy looked at Ben as if she knew what he was going to say. "Velda has a lot of energy," she said, though faintly.

"I'm sorry, Dad," Ben said as they pulled out, but Zoltan didn't answer. Lucy kept looking thoughtfully at him. Ben wasn't sure that much of what they'd just experienced weighed on his father's mind, or even registered, other than to temporarily perturb him. What Velda didn't know about Zoltan was that he was so grounded he made no effort whatsoever to be loved. By anyone. If you grew up in his sphere, as his boys had, you sensed that you were there at his pleasure and were not unwelcome to be, but he didn't try to impress you even in normal ways. He often didn't even greet you as he came and went, and you came and went.

He didn't say a word all the way to Steve's Restaurant, but he still seemed willing to go in.

Ben couldn't say what was worse: going to a restaurant when his father was depressed or going when he was happy. Standing in line turned his father into a third thing altogether. The unsuspecting could never be ready for what was to come, so Lucy marched into the restaurant first, saw that fourteen or fifteen people were waiting for tables, turned and smiled.

Zoltan said, "Let's go."

"It's a big restaurant," Lucy said. "It should only be a short while."

"Let's go."

They didn't move. Zoltan went up to the young woman taking names and said, "We need a table," as if he were saying, "We need a defibrillator."

"It will only be a few minutes," she said. "May I have your name?"

He glared at her. "How long?" he said.

She turned to survey the tables around the dining room. Zoltan slapped at his sides. She looked back, noticed his white gloves. He was the tiger again, the tiger penned in, his prey loping calmly, unsuspectingly, near the pen. Hannah had always asked her boys, please, not to upset him more around mealtime, not to question him. On one occasion, he actually screamed out. On another, he punched the wall, and they had to take him to emergency for an X-ray. The boys tried, occasionally, to get as far away from him as they could. Frank and Ben would sidle up to another family. Young Sammy would bury his face in his mother's back.

No one could understand it. Ben thought maybe he'd lost it during the war and never quite got his sanity back. He'd come from a well-to-do family in Hungary until the Germans came, and then they had quickly become poorly-to-do. During the war, they didn't know where their next meal was coming from, if *ever*, where Zoltan was concerned.

Ben told the young woman his name, then returned to the back of the line, where Lucy was comforting his father. He was bouncing from foot to foot. "Do you want to go outside for a bit?" Lucy said. Zoltan didn't answer. "Do you want to go outside?"

"What's outside?"

"Some fresh air. It's sometimes nice just to get some air."

"It's not my lungs that need to be refilled," he said. "Why don't we go somewhere else?"

"Dad, we've been through this drill before," Ben said. "By the time we drive somewhere else and park the car, we'd have gotten a table here at Steve's. Besides, we might have to wait in line at the next place too, and the one after—"

"I've had it," he said. He was punching his sides and huffing. "Let's go. I'll boil a hot dog at home. Let's go."

"Ben," the woman called, and they were in! Like having a death sentence commuted.

He was Jekyll again the second they sat down, cheerful now. He wasn't even tearing at the menu. "Would anyone like to share a meal with me," he asked, "the pasta maybe?"

"I will," Lucy said.

"You see?" Zoltan said. He was beaming, beaming, searchlights beaming out into the heavens.

Ben studied his father's face. Maybe he was brain damaged. Maybe he'd taken a blow to the head. He would easily have attracted blows to the head from people who didn't know him as well as they did, and maybe some who did.

Lucy and Zoltan ordered seafood pasta slathered with tomato sauce, and Lucy divided it neatly, expertly, as she always did. Zoltan's half was more like two-thirds of the heaping order. But in a few short minutes he had snorkeled and splashed his way through it. A splotch had landed on Lucy, where her neck met the collar of her white blouse. A drop was on Ben's knuckle and another on his watch face. His father was glistening red. One of his white gloves was dyed scarlet; bits of onion and a shrimp tail were caught in the back of the other. Lucy was holding only her second or third forkful and marveling at him. She set it down and said, "Can I help you?" She offered him her own napkin.

"Thank you," he said, and smeared his face in an operation that spread the sauce up to one earlobe and into his hair. He said, "Excuse me," went to the bathroom to clean up and returned soaked in water from shoulder to shoulder and down one arm. He looked so satisfied, so pleased. He had parted the waters of the Red Sea, and he saw that it was good.

He sat back down at the table and then, suddenly, turned

grim. He held his red gloves up to make a steeple at his mouth before saying, "Am I even supposed to be here?"

"Where?" Ben asked.

"Here," he said. "What am I doing here? I thought I was supposed to be laid to rest six months after my dear wife took her leave. Isn't that the way it goes?"

"It's just an average," Lucy said. "You could be here for twenty-five more years." She knocked on the plastic table-top. "We need to keep you healthy."

"Why?" he said, but he wasn't really expecting an answer.

"Maybe he's not getting enough magnesium," Lucy said to Ben as if Zoltan weren't there. Lately, Lucy was on a magnesium kick. A dietitian friend had given her a book on its wonders. If she could have joined a magnesium cult, she would have. She would sit in blue vapors if that was required. Next month, it would be metabolic syndrome.

Lucy could barely look Zoltan in the eye. She said, "Ben tells me you went to the cemetery to see Mother." Ben loved her for calling her that. Lucy had a genius for saying just the right thing to Zoltan and by extension to Ben. She took Zoltan's damp, gloved hand, or at least the tips of the fingers of one of his hands. "Was it all right?" she asked him.

He looked straight at her, though she was still struggling with the directness of his look. He sometimes looked at you the way a child would, never averting his gaze. "Do you know what, my dear?" he said. "People are each alive in their own ways, whereas dead people are dead in the same way."

"Oh," Lucy said. She wasn't sure if she should be amused, if he was being Tolstoy or Groucho Marx. He carried both personae with him much of the time.

She said, "Did you take some flowers to the cemetery?" Neither of them answered. Lucy loved flowers—*adored* them. If she thought in flowers, they'd be in bloom all year long, some sirening out, some wallflowering, some opening their lips to receive the rain, some aspiring to become the perfect black rose. She always took some to Hannah's grave, along with the stones. She'd plant petunias in the spring, replace them with mums in August, and the chrysanthemums Zoltan stepped on.

After that, Lucy and Ben finished their meals quietly but quickly.

They walked Ben's father to his door and stepped into the vestibule, where he stood before the mirror. He was clutching his recipe book in his reddened gloves. "How many more times do I have to look at this face?" he said. "I'm sick of myself." And he turned to Ben with an expression that said, I'm sick of you too.

"You look very handsome," Lucy said. She took the recipe book and turned her X-ray eyes on him. He tried not to return her gaze, but Lucy was one of those people: you could feel her looking even when you couldn't see her looking. Like him, actually. Like the sun. "Why would you say such things?" she asked. He didn't answer. "It's not a rhetorical question," she went on. "I want to know why." She wanted Ben to step in, but he just shrugged his shoulders.

His father had met his match in Lucy. He was the Great Concealer, and she the Great Revealer. There was never enough communication for Lucy. All thoughts and feelings exited from her mouth. Nothing could stem their flow.

It was Lucy's most pronounced quality. She took an interest in everyone, and the interest was true and deep. She wanted to know people intensely, profoundly, as if she were an actor trying to get inside them, *be* them for a time, try them on. She was the opposite of Velda. It was you she wanted to turn inside out, you she wanted to deepen, to widen, to broadcast so she and everyone else could have a look at the good in you.

At her office, Lucy would feel the awkwardness of the temp, called Cindy, who was replacing the regular receptionist while the regular receptionist attended a wedding in Vancouver. Lucy brought Cindy coffee, learned that she was a fraternal twin but that her brother, Michael, would not speak to her on account of an "incident" the previous Thanksgiving. Besides, Michael's wife hated Cindy, hated the whole family, including a cousin, Amanda, who hadn't said a word to her ever.

Lucy and Cindy had lunch together, and Lucy spoke in italics: "*I can't imagine what that would be like. You spent nine months in the womb together. How sad, how desperate.*"

Lucy would hold the hand of the young boy in the waiting room at his first dentist's appointment while the boy's father read a magazine. "*Dentists want your teeth to be nice and strong,*" Lucy said. "*Like the rest of you. Nothing to be afraid of.*"

The trouble with Lucy's deep interest in everyone was that people felt she could be their best friend. They wanted her to be. No one had ever taken such an interest in them.

But Lucy couldn't be everyone's best friend. The time would come eventually, in most cases, when she couldn't realistically return all the calls she got, and she would disappoint people as completely as she had attracted and impressed them.

Of course, this outcome did not apply to family. Zoltan felt it. She had on the look now, the look of intense inquiry.

"Look at me," Zoltan said. He was staring again at his face in the mirror. "It's so much more exciting to become something." He pulled back on his temples, then up on his forehead. "Becoming is the thing." He took a deep breath, held it, then pushed it out, spitting slightly. "But before you know it, you're in the unbecoming phase. Ripening turns to rot. 'The darling buds of May' take their autumn exit. You can fool yourself. You can have everything tightened, or you can play it loose." He chuckled. "You can pull yourself in and puff yourself out. You can have your boobs stand to attention. You can paint the goddamn Sistine Chapel, spend so much time with it that it helps you to forget, slightly, that someone did this before you, because on some level, somewhere deep inside of you, you believe it should have been the Velda Chapel or the Kerbel Pickle Chapel or the Herring Tidbits Chapel." He turned to look at his own modest living room ceiling. Ben shuddered. If Zoltan simply sat under it with his dinner, he could do a Jackson Pollock in two swift minutes.

Zoltan had wanted his life to consist of a string of anec-dotes, but to his dismay each of the anecdotes had deepened into a story. And Lucy sensed it, knew it. She kissed his cheek but then examined the spot before gently rubbing it to remove some hardened tomato sauce.

"I have my driving test a week from Thursday, in the morning," he said, turning to Lucy. Zoltan's license had been suspended after his doctor sent a note to the Ministry of Transportation following an "incident." Three years before, Zoltan had driven off with Hannah's hand still stuck in the handle of the car door. He'd taken off the tips of her thumb and index finger. Luckily, it was her left hand. She was hold-ing grocery bags in the other hand. What Zoltan's doctor and the Ministry of Transportation didn't know was that he'd been driving that way since he was thirty-five. Age had nothing to do with it.

He had officially applied to challenge the suspension.

"Lucy's working," Ben said. "Frank said he might be able to go with you."

"It can't be with Frank," he said. "You know that. Do you teach Thursday morning?"

Ben shook his head.

His father smiled and said, "Thanks."

"Thursday," Ben said. "I'll be here Thursday morning."

5

To cheer Zoltan up, Lucy and Ben took him to a piano recital downtown at the Glenn Gould Studio. The program featured an up-and-coming Hungarian pianist named Attila Szabo. He was all of seventeen, yet he'd become known the world over, for his interpretations of Chopin in particular. He'd played the composer's two piano concertos accompanied by the London Philharmonic when he was just fifteen and a year later had recorded the concertos with the Vienna Philharmonic.

It had been a long time since Zoltan attended a concert. He used to enjoy going with Hannah. To make the evening extra special, at Lucy's insistence the three of them dressed up for the occasion. Ben's father wore a charcoal suit Hannah had helped pick out for him years before and his favorite burgundy tie. He even wore a satin pocket square with a swirling floral pattern, which Lucy had presented to him to go with the tie.

They took him out for dinner beforehand at a steakhouse called Archie's, which solemnly promised that the time of their reservation would be honored—there would be no standing in line—and that with much of the fare there would be no splashy sauces to worry about.

Then came the concert. Ben took a picture of Lucy and his father outside the concert hall with the bronze sculpture of Glenn Gould seated on a bench. They had seats right in the middle of the orchestra and got there early enough to find their places without having to climb over anyone. In short, all eventualities had been thought through and accounted for.

And then came the musician, the boy at the keyboard, and boy he was; he looked like an adolescent who had not yet started to shave. He wore red socks to offset the tuxedo. Zoltan said it out loud: "He's wearing red socks." The boy grinned from the stage. The two of them, the boy and Zoltan, seemed almost to rejoice, the boy pleased he could get such a rise out of someone. And even as he stood before them, there was a kind of violent delicacy to the boy, which was borne out in his playing.

When he sat at the piano, his hands loomed over the keys. He had the thinnest wrists, at the ends of which were freak-ishly long hands and fingers, hands that had surely never seen the sun but were hidden like turtles in their shells and coaxed out only when it was absolutely safe, hands that looked as if they'd been added on later by someone who wasn't paying attention.

And what music those hands wrought from those keys. What else would the music of loss and regret draw out but the feelings of loss and regret, lost opportunities, remembrance of lost times. Ben kept glancing at his father, who was sitting on the other side of Lucy, and she glanced too, her eyes puddling throughout.

When the young musician turned to the lovely Nocturne in E-flat major, Opus 9, Number 2, Zoltan was suddenly on his feet. "Dad," Ben whispered. Lucy tried to pull him down. "Dad," Ben said again. But Zoltan didn't so much as look at him. Instead, he went crashing over the legs and laps to the right of him to get out to the aisle.

Lucy looked mortified. The music played on. "Go find him in the bathroom," she whispered.

"He hasn't gone to the bathroom," Ben said.

"Where then?"

The person behind them told them to shush.

"He's gone," Ben mouthed. "In a cab, probably."

"What?" They were lip reading.

"Poof," Ben said.

The performance was lost to them. They had to wait another quarter of an hour for the intermission. Lucy was sure Ben was wrong, that his father hadn't left. They searched everywhere, beginning with the bathroom. They described

Zoltan to the girl at the coat check. She said he'd gone straight out.

They drove to his place and could see that the lights were on. Zoltan was already in his pajamas and having Alka-Seltzer. He told them when he let them in that he was too old to have steak. Chewing issues, he said, pointing at his dentures, then patting his stomach. He asked them if they wanted some, meaning the Alka-Seltzer.

"Maybe a little later," Ben said.

"Is that why you left the concert?" Lucy asked. "Because of your stomach?"

He didn't answer. He had the look, the one that said, I don't have to tell you, but he didn't dare say that to Lucy. They were expecting him to pat his stomach again, but he didn't. She waited.

Finally, he said, "Yes, it is."

"In the middle?" she asked.

"In the middle of one of the pieces?" Ben asked loudly.

Zoltan sat down in the living room and took another sip of his Alka-Seltzer. "Yes, the middle," he said.

"Did the concert upset you?" Lucy asked. "Did the Chopin upset you for some reason?"

He was rocking in a chair that didn't rock.

"Was it that Hannah loved Chopin? Did it remind you of Hannah?"

"No, it wasn't Hannah."

They listened to the fizzling of the Alka-Seltzer, watched the sparkle of it in the quiet light.

Zoltan set the glass down on the coffee table. "That Chopin nocturne was the very last piece I heard my brother play," he said. "It was the last piece Bela *ever* played, in fact, and I couldn't bear to hear it again tonight. It was the first time I'd heard it since then, since my brother—since—since then."

Without saying another word, Zoltan went upstairs to bed. Lucy and Ben didn't say anything either. They watched him go, then washed out the Alka-Seltzer glass, turned off the lights and locked up.

In the car, Lucy told Ben he had to take his father back to Hungary. It would be good for Zoltan. It would be good for both Ben and his father, for their relationship, she added. "He needs to go," Lucy said. "It would bring some kind of closure."

"He's had closure," Ben said. "He was in Hungary for years after the Second World War. I was born in Hungary, don't forget."

"Yes, but there are matters to settle. If not emotional ones—and we'll come back to those—then what about the matter of the payments?"

Ben's parents were receiving reparations from Hungary on account of Zoltan's service in the labor camp, and from Germany because of the murder of Hannah's parents and six siblings. An enterprising woman in Budapest named Szilvia Vukcsics had looked them up and told them she could arrange for these payments, as long as she could keep a small portion for herself. Zoltan had not agreed at first, but Szilvia Vukcsics was persistent.

Now, since Hannah had died and they had asked Szilvia to let the authorities know, the woman had gone silent.

"She's almost certainly keeping all the money for herself, including the money coming from Germany," Lucy said.

"My father doesn't care," Ben replied. "He'd tell you let her keep it. He doesn't want the money. He didn't in the first place. He wants nothing to do with Hungary. He wants to rid himself of it."

"But it's not right," she said, "and more importantly, he had a brother, Bela, who died, right? And he doesn't know why or how. There is more to find out about Bela, and it's eating away at him. You need to go with him, take him by the hand. He will be the happier for it, and so will you. He'll forever be grateful to you."

"If such a thing should come to pass, he should be grateful to you."

"That doesn't matter. I don't care about that." And she truly didn't.

"I'll look into it," Ben said. "I can't promise, but I will at least look."

"I'll make it easy for you," Lucy said. "I'll look into it."

6

When Zoli and Bela Beck were younger, a chauffeur drove them to school and maids picked up after them at home. And there was Hajnal, meaning "dawn," their grandfather's summer home, complete with a meerschaum pipe longer than a man's arm and a raspberry-marble pedestal table with a painting by Edvard Munch under glass on its top, as well as a dollhouse modeled after Hajnal itself.

The brothers summered there with many of their cousins, and Zoli often recalled the vivid colors of the place, the green rolling land, the blue pond and the great white house. The grandchildren always seemed to be running down the long corridors of the place or out over the fields to the tall grasses of the meadow. Hajnal gave Zoli a feeling of endlessness, end-less lines, endless day. It was a place where you could not only feel healthy but also magnanimous enough to confer good health on others, even your grandparents and great-aunts and -uncles, a place you could feel princely, confer equality on the servants and farmers. Always, in the back of his wintry city mind, there was Hajnal, the creamy, balmy green land where it was safe to be who and what you were and safe, especially, to fall in love. The summer before he was thirteen, Zoli fell in love twice at Hajnal, once with Timea Antal, the daugh-ter of the new kitchen assistant, until Timea was spirited away to her grandmother's place on the very morning Zoli had gathered wildflowers to present to her. And once with his cousin Mary, who implored him to play the part of the father and grandfather and husband in the toy house mod-eled on Hajnal. Before long, Zoli found himself playing the part of Mary's husband with more ardor than he'd expected. He would play it all that day, following Mary downstairs for meals, still in character, not noticing anyone else but her around the table, then following her back up, until finally they were called to bed. Even then he was still in character, falling asleep picturing Mary's chestnut eyes closing, her fra-grant golden hair spread out over her pillow and his.

The truth was, it was the real Hajnal, not the toy one, that felt provisional to Zoli. For him, Hajnal was the doll-house where he could act out a life with Mary unfettered by a past or future. Just a present. An eternal present. Or not even. Not in time at all.

Zoli was sixteen in 1939 when Germany attacked Poland. Bela was seventeen and already studying and teaching music at the Liszt Academy and, after skipping two grades in school, entering his second year at Eötvös Loránd University, majoring in archaeology.

As Germany's ally, Hungary was expected to adhere to the values and laws of the Third Reich, so Zoli and Bela fell under the *numerus clausus* restriction, as did all of Hungary's Jews. They could no longer freely attend university or pursue careers, and even those Jews who were long established in various professions, especially law or medicine or finance, had their licenses revoked.

Bela was barred from all public pools, and of course the Franz Liszt Academy remained out of bounds for him. Zoli had hoped eventually to enroll in law at the university, but he knew now that he would not be permitted to do so. He was already a great reader and persuader and was at the point in his life when he wanted to sit the world down to let it know what he had discovered: that we were all after the same things and running from the same things. We all wanted nothing more than security and peace and hope; and we all feared bullies and conquerors. We feared suppression. What surprised him was that these truths were not obvious to everyone.

Their father was well connected. He was a respected doctor and the federal minister of health until the war broke out, and, like Bela, he was so popular personally that the government allowed him to keep his cabinet office and secretary, though they stripped him of his title and rank. So he went to the office each day, sipped espresso and read the paper. And he tinkered with things. He was an inventor on the side, and he loved the miracle of how things functioned, ordinary things like zippers and complex things like flowers. He often held a safety pin or nail clippers or a whistle up to the light and turned it every which way to admire its design.

Although the war did not come to Hungary for five full years—not until 1944—on account of its alliance with Germany, the war on minorities began much earlier. Once the anti-Jewish laws were passed, Vilmos worried about his sons especially, and in 1942 he spirited Bela and Zoli off to a trade school as yet unaffected by the proscriptions. There they learned a skill, tool and die making, a trade that proved invaluable to the war effort. Bela was twenty-two and Zoli twenty-one in the fall of 1944—young men in the prime of their lives—when they were informed that they would be sent to a labor camp in Transylvania, where they would make munitions. It was not a concentration camp. It was one step higher, but only one.

When the call came, Vilmos met with the minister of war at a favorite haunt, the Gerbeaud Café, in the heart of the capital and asked that he intervene to keep his sons from having to go to a labor camp. The minister said he couldn't help. The times had changed. Vilmos said he knew it was a slave camp. The minister of war said he would see what he could do, but he did not look Vilmos in the eye when he said it. The man called over the waiter, quickly paid the bill and left.

Vilmos then spoke with a judge who had married a favorite cousin of his. The judge met with Vilmos at the cousin's insistence but told him he was not able to help. The judge said he was just grateful that his wife had converted to Christianity when they married. They were in a dark time, he told Vilmos. He said this as if he were reporting news. Everyone was saying it. Vilmos wanted to say there were degrees of darkness. The times were darker for some than they were for others. Still, the judge was obviously distressed about where the country was headed, and sad that he'd been stripped of some of his power, but he didn't even promise to ask around, even if only to reassure Vilmos.

Bela had his own meetings. He met with a friend of Imre's called Tamas Sotet in an alley behind the Liszt Academy—he was no longer permitted even to enter the building—and Tamas told him there was a chance he could arrange passage for one person to Palestine.

"What about two people?" Bela asked him right away.

"I said there was a *chance*," Tamas said.

"Is there a chance for two?"

"It's possible."

"I can get the money," Bela told him.

"I'll try."

"What if I could find the money for four people?"

"We started with one," Tamas said. "I don't even know if I can manage two. I don't know if I can manage *one*. Nothing is certain."

Bela started to press the man, but Tamas stopped him.

"It's not a question of money," Tamas said. "Money doesn't have the power it used to have. In a sense, money seems trivial these days, absurd even. My family had money. Now they have—what?"

That evening, over dinner, Bela told his parents that he and Zoli could make it out safely to Palestine.

His father laughed at him. "It's safer here than it is in Palestine," he said. "It's safer here than it is *getting* to Palestine. Do you even know what you're talking about?"

Bela slammed down his glass. "Don't patronize me," he told his father. "I'd rather take my chances and leave. I can't speak for Zoli. I can only speak for myself."

"Please," his mother said to Bela, getting out of her chair and putting her arm around his shoulder. "Your father is not patronizing you. He's trying to protect you. Your best chance is still with your father."

"My father has lost his influence. I don't know who's fooling whom."

Bela stormed out of the house and did not return all night. Vilmos paced between Bela's empty bedroom and the front room, where he repeatedly peeked through a gap in the closed curtain. No one slept, not his brother, not his parents and not Bela. Bela had gone to Imre's house. His friend was as distressed as he was. Imre offered Bela his country house on Lake Balaton where he and Zoli could hide out for a while, but both of them knew the idea was not a good one.

That was a Tuesday in late October. By Thursday of the same week, Zoli and Bela were taken by cattle car, along with a couple of hundred other young men, to Hernyo Camp. Hernyo, meaning "caterpillar," was so named because of its zigzag arrangement of old green army barracks around the foot of a mountain. On its other side, the camp faced a tall and ancient forest.

It could have been worse. The boys could have been deported to Auschwitz when Adolf Eichmann brought his "cleansing" army to Hungary because Germany's ally was not cooperating in the war effort as fully as Hitler would have liked.

At Hernyo, some of the men were sent to the small factory building near the camp to make molds for howitzer shell casings, and this undertaking required the special training Bela and Zoli had completed. Most of the other men were sent farther out to lay down rail tracks for a new railway line to be built in the river valley. The work was backbreaking, and the autumn days were getting shorter and turning colder. When one of the men, a small man named Denes Kis, developed a lower leg infection from a gash he'd suffered in the forest, he was told he could choose to either "work through the infection" or have his leg amputated. The infection spread quickly. Kis groaned through the night in his cot, until he began coughing, hacking without cease for days. Then one morning it became very quiet. The men crept toward Denes's cot and found him dead.

Though the work was less grueling in the factory, the men were pushed to manufacture as many units as possible to be shipped out. If you made a mistake, and Zoli was the most prone of all the men to make mistakes—even Bela did once—the attending sergeant ordered that you not be served your meager evening meal, or he slapped you, or knocked you over with the butt of his rifle.

Bela took enough of a blow with the rifle butt that first time—the only time—that he was knocked out cold and had to be taken to the infirmary. It was there, on that one occasion, that the commanding officer, Colonel Vad, happened to visit to see the camp doctor about a toothache. Dr. Fischer, a Jewish man and former professor of medicine at the university in Szeged, examined the colonel and told him he had developed an abscess. He said he could extract the tooth and to do so would ultimately be the most expedient and least painful option. But since he had no local anesthetic, the doctor said, he'd have to knock the colonel out entirely. "Or," he offered, "you could go into town and have the dentist there look after it."

"I don't trust him," Vad said. "He's a hack." So the colonel decided to take his chances then and there with the doctor, in the infirmary.

Still, the mistrustful colonel sent for Sergeant Zold, the one who'd struck Bela, to watch over things while he was out cold.

When Bela came to, he found Colonel Vad coming out of anesthesia in the next bed and Sergeant Zold standing guard. Dr. Fischer was not in the room. Bela rubbed the bandage on his head as he tried to sit upright.

The colonel groggily asked Bela his name and where he'd come from.

Bela answered the colonel, then added, "I was a student there. Of music and archaeology."

"I guess we put an end to that," the colonel said. He chuckled, and the sergeant laughed outright.

"Not an end," Bela said, "just a delay."

The sergeant took a step toward Bela, but the colonel put up his hand.

"I own you," the colonel said. He was smiling broadly.

"With respect, sir, you don't own me," Bela answered. "You're just borrowing me."

The colonel looked at Bela and burst out laughing. The sergeant didn't join him this time.

The colonel asked Bela how good a musician he was.

"Fair," Bela said. "I play piano. I used to teach piano at the Liszt Academy."

"Ah, the Liszt. Goodness!" The colonel looked at his sergeant. "Maybe that's what we need," he said. "Zold, I want you to arrange to have a piano brought in from the town, the baby grand from the school."

"Yes, sir," the sergeant replied.

"And you'll play for us," the colonel said to Bela.

"Yes, sir, I will."

"We'll make an evening of it." Bela smiled. "And what happened to your head, Beck?"

Bela didn't answer.

"I asked you a question."

But Bela stayed silent.

"I bashed him," the sergeant offered.

"With what?" the colonel said. "With your rifle?"

"Yes, sir."

"And what good are these men when we make a habit of knocking them out?"

"I'm not sure, sir."

"Hand me your rifle, Zold."

"Yes, sir."

The colonel sat up, signaled for the sergeant to bend down, then bashed him with an awful thud on the side of his head, as Zold had done to Bela. The sergeant fell to the floor, as Bela had done. He narrowly missed the bedpost.

"I've still got it," the colonel said, flexing his muscles.

The colonel had done Bela no favors. Now Zold watched him all day long, studied every move he made, waiting for him to slip up again. But Bela did not slip up again. So Zold took to smacking Bela's brother when he could, though not with the butt of his rifle—with the flat of his hand or with his fist. He did so with gusto.

Bela asked the sergeant not to anymore. "Please," he added. He said it was unnecessary to beat Zoli or anyone else. The sergeant couldn't believe what he was hearing. But Bela's status had changed. He had risen suddenly to the position of privileged inmate. The sergeant lowered his hands. They were trembling.

Bela waited for the men to get back to work. He didn't want to further embarrass the officer. But then he said, "Also"—the sergeant snorted like a bull—"might I trouble you for a little writing paper and a couple of pencils? I like to write down my thoughts now and again before I go to sleep."

Bela wasn't sure if he should have tested Zold, but that evening, while the men were having supper, a corporal found Bela and his brother and handed Bela some card paper and two small pencils.

Bela expertly fashioned the paper into a little notebook and even found some string to bind it together. That very night, he felt moved to write a poem in his new notebook, but to his surprise the muse did not visit him.

And the piano did arrive, as promised, from nearby Szifla. It had been the school's solitary remaining instrument since the war had broken out. The concert Bela was to give was timed to coincide with a visit from the town of Colonel Vad's wife and two daughters. The colonel wanted to show off how civilized he was being under the circumstances. He even arranged to have the men fed well, the first time they would have meat in over a month, juicy roasted mutton, also brought in from Szifla. He wanted them full and gleaming.

Cots were arranged in the largest tent—the barracks, they called it—each of the cots to seat three men, and all set in concentric semicircles around the piano. The colonel, his family and two officers were permitted proper chairs with upholstered seats borrowed from the colonel's office.

Bela was the last to enter the room, and to everyone's surprise he was not wearing his camp uniform but a neatly laundered white shirt with French cuffs, as well as black trousers and patent leather shoes, a pair found to fit him, clearly.

The sergeant was visibly grinding his teeth, ready to strangle the young man making himself comfortable on the straight-back chair set in front of the piano. There were no sheets or books of music. Bela would have to play what he remembered by heart. Luckily, he remembered a great deal. He opened, naturally, with a Hungarian rhapsody by Liszt and moved directly to a polonaise by Chopin, followed by a serene étude by the same composer. People clapped hesitantly at first until the colonel's wife clapped sharply, followed by the colonel. Then a couple of the men hooted and cheered and several more got to their feet. Bela played a piano adaptation of the most popular arias from Franz Lehar's *The Merry Widow*, and this caused the colonel to sing out loud, even stand during the popular "Vilja Song." When Bela got to the part when the chorus was to join in, the colonel waved all around for everyone to stand and join in, and everyone did stand, and some did sing.

When the Lehar was done, the colonel asked his eldest daughter what that piece was that she loved so well. "It's by Schumann," she said. She walked timidly to the piano, introduced herself as Zsofia, glanced back at her father, then described the piece to Bela. "It's the one for children," she told him.

He looked directly into her eyes. "Yes. Schumann. It's his *Kinderszenen*," he said.

Zsofia was wearing a formal forest-green dress and put a white hand flat on her heart. The hand was trembling. "Yes, that's it. His *Kinderszenen*." He could hardly hear her.

Bela waited until Zsofia had made the journey back to her seat before he began. The music made her blush. She was looking down at her feet as she listened. She was blushing a hot red, ready to bruise if she got any redder.

And the music—with a child's purity and desire—was not at all for children, or not for children alone. Rather, it seemed to be addressed to adults, the child still living inside them.

Bela dared glance once in the direction of Zsofia. She could have passed for Carmen, with her black hair, her white skin and the roses in her cheeks. And the black eyes—her "liquid eyes," as Bela would describe them later.

Bela took a breath before beginning Chopin's second nocturne, in E-flat major. Within a few seconds, Zsofia was sobbing, her head down, and her mother began crying too, the two of them raining down into their laps, the mother's shoulders and back heaving with the sound of the notes. The younger sister looked amused by the whole scene and clapped once loudly when she saw what had become of her mother and sister, then covered her mouth with her hand,

Colonel Vad got to his feet even before Bela had played the last notes. "Enough for now!" he said. "The party is over."

People weren't sure what to do. The colonel clapped his hands sharply. "Let's go," he said. "Everyone." It was really his daughters and wife he was shooing. Then he turned to the men. "Everyone, up! Get these cots back to where they belong." Zoli heard him say it: "Swine Jew. Swine Jews."

The sergeant was hustling everyone up. He turned to Bela. "Up, swine." He almost pulled the seat out from under him. The two men stared each other down, but Zoli grabbed his brother from behind, clamping Bela's arms to his sides.

For three days, Bela was allowed no provisions, no food, no conversation with anyone, not a word. The sergeant caught him taking a single sip of water in the factory building, something they needed to ask permission for even under normal circumstances, and he slapped the tin cup away from him and threatened him with the butt of his rifle.

When he could have his meals again, Bela was given only broth and potato peelings. His brother tried to sneak a small piece of hardened cheese to him, was caught, and was himself deprived of provisions for three days.

The new deprivation weakened Zoli considerably. He began to cough while working in the factory, a dry cough he could not control. And by night he seemed ready to combust as he heaved and barked.

7

On Thursday of the following week, as Lucy was getting dressed in a sharp dark blue jacket-and-skirt combination set off by a white blouse for her job as manager of HR at the insurance company, she suggested Ben let his father use his own car for the driving test. "He's most used to it."

Lucy and Ben had a modern marriage: no one did the housework. And they weren't sexist either: neither of them wanted to be the man or the woman. The bed was strewn with hair curlers, a rejected bra, the Life section of the paper, two hangers and a clear plastic bag from Absolute Dry Cleaners.

"Of course he'll drive his own car," Ben said. "If he smacks into something, it will be end-of-car, end-of-license, all in one go."

"And what about end of him?" she asked.

"And maybe the end of him."

"Don't say that."

"I didn't. You did."

Ben sighed. Poor old bastard. Sammy had taken him out for a practice drive the night before, and Frank the night before that, so their father should have been limbered up for the challenge ahead. But he was allowed a single challenge. If he failed, he would never drive again. Or at least not legally. Lucy didn't disagree with the ruling that his license be suspended; she just worried what that would do to him, how it would reduce him. But for Ben, expressing one's character behind the wheel was a little like expressing it behind a cannon. Some people should simply be prohibited from certain undertakings and pastimes: flying a plane, firing a cannon, skydiving, living inside a whale, standing in line at a restaurant and operating a motor vehicle.

"Velda called yesterday afternoon," Ben said. "She wanted to speak to you."

"I know," Lucy said. "She left a message last week too. Why didn't she just speak to you?"

"She thinks you're her best friend," he said. Lucy sighed. "I guess she can join the lineup," he said. She sighed again. "Are you going to call her back?"

"I will."

"Or possibly you won't."

"Yes, possibly I won't. You should go," she said. "Your father will be frantic."

Here they were again: a 10:30 appointment, and Ben got to his father's place at 9:15, but Zoltan was already sitting in his red Saturn in the driveway with the engine running. As soon as Zoltan saw his son, he pulled out, and Ben had to stop sharply to avoid a collision. Ben parked and joined his father in his car. Zoltan began rolling before Ben got both legs in. But when he did manage to pull the door closed, he was struck by the sweetness in the air. His father had bandages on the thumb and index finger of his right hand and two criss-crossed on the pinky of his left.

"Dad, what did you do to your fingers?"

He didn't answer.

"White gloves might have been better than all those bandages," Ben said.

Again, silence.

"Do you have an air freshener in here?" He glanced all around him. The air was cloyingly sweet. They were traveling about as fast as a stout walker. Someone behind them honked.

"No, I don't have an air freshener."

It began to rain, a downpour. Sheets of rain rolled down the windshield, but Zoltan didn't turn on the wipers. He didn't like the noise they made. And seeing other objects, whether clearly or blurrily, hardly made a difference.

Then it hit Ben: Chanel No. 5, except far too much of it. More like Chanel No. 500. "Dad, are you wearing perfume?"

As they turned the corner onto Bathurst Street, they bumped over the curb, violently, even at walking speed. Zoltan was sitting way back—almost lying back—so that his foot barely reached the pedals. If he hadn't been wearing his fedora, they'd have looked like a driverless car. Ben reached over to turn on the wipers, but his father turned them off after a single wipe.

Then it hit Ben, part two: the bandages on the fingers, the strong perfume, the evasiveness. "Dad, you broke the bottle of Chanel in the bathroom, didn't you?"

Zoltan turned on the wipers once, then off again. He was silent.

Ben gazed at his father, thought of the stalwart bottle of Chanel No. 5. It was still sealed, as he recalled, intact within its understated white box. No one had ever seen the naked bottle—until now, apparently. It had been his mother's, of course. It had come from his aunt Yvonne, of Elizabeth, New Jersey, when she visited eleven years ago. Aunt Yvonne, actually a first cousin of Hannah's, had never in her life purchased a bottle of Chanel No. 5. When Hannah opened the gift-wrapped box, Ben overheard his uncle Milt asking Aunt Yvonne, "Was that the perfume that Myrna gave you?"

A look of murder was her reply.

Myrna was Milt's cousin. She used to live in Pensacola, Florida, in a retirement residence. Ben didn't think anyone living in a retirement residence in the history of the state of Florida had ever actually purchased a bottle of Chanel No. 5, which meant that someone once gave it to Myrna. For the record, poor Myrna had been dead for seventeen years, Yvonne for eight years and Hannah for two.

So this morning, by sending the bottle of Chanel No. 5 back to its maker, the Lord of Flowers, Ben's father was fulfilling the destiny of all such bottles of Chanel No. 5. Who knew who the original purchaser might have been? It might have been Pyramus, who'd been bequeathed the gift by an all-seeing god so that the young man could present it to his Thisbe before their sad demise, or it might have been a Union officer, carrying the gift to his Confederate mistress, a gift his own mother might have received from a gentleman and lady, visiting from Paris.

Blowing rain spun and rolled down his father's windshield. "Dad, are you going to turn on the windshield wipers again?"

The figures of the cars and people in front of them refracted through the rainy glass.

"Dad, just out of curiosity, was there no cellophane on the Chanel box?"

"I don't have to tell you," he said, as he slowly ran a red light.

"Why would you, all of a sudden, take the cellophane off the box? That's all I'm asking."

Zoltan fixed Ben with his sharp eyes. It was disarming.

"Please turn on your wipers."

He did, on and off, giving the windshield a third single wipe. He kept an old pajama top beside him to wipe the inside of the windshield, because he didn't like to turn on the noisy defroster.

"Dad, I could have helped you clean it up. You should have called me."

"It was five in the morning."

"Still, you could have left it until I came to get you. I could have come a bit early."

"Let's not talk about it anymore."

"Okay, but I was really just asking why you would even touch it."

"Was I not allowed to touch it?"

"It's not your *right* to things that I'm asking about."

Ben felt the car braking. He thought his father was going to pull over or turn around, but he did neither.

"Are you here to help me today," Zoltan asked, "or to question me?"

"Sorry, Dad. Truly."

"Okay."

"Truly."

"*Okay*, I said."

They did their do-si-do down the road for a while. The merciful rain let up, and Zoltan cleared the windshield with another quick wipe.

"Should I take the 401?" he asked.

"I don't think the highway is a good idea today, Dad. We can go straight along Sheppard Avenue to Keele."

"The 401 has an exit at Keele."

"So does Sheppard. Just take Sheppard. You'll get there just as quickly. You drive the same speed whether you're on a highway or in your driveway."

Zoltan looked straight at his son again while crossing three lanes on Bathurst. Ben tried to smile, but his father was having none of it.

"Dad, please keep your eye on the road." Zoltan huffed at him. "Should we lower the window to air out the car?" Ben asked.

"No, the examiner might like it. It might sway him."

"I hope you're joking," Ben said. "What are you going to do—make like Mata Hari on your driving test?"

They made it to Sheppard remarkably uneventfully. Though he drove recklessly, Zoltan drove slowly and in a car not big enough to knock over a building or a telephone pole, though certainly big enough to hurt himself and others. He'd been pulled over several times and given a breathalyzer test, but he rarely drank, so he was a reckless snail, really.

Just as Ben was taking his first deep breath on Sheppard, his father veered into the passing lane, cutting off an impressive SUV. They heard the plaintive cry of rubber, followed by a blast from a horn worthy of that vehicle, and then a second blast. Ben shrank into his seat, so now they looked like a driverless, passengerless car. He scanned the dash and the side panel to see if there were sufficient airbags.

The road narrowed, they came to a red light, and the SUV arced in front of them and screeched to a halt, cutting them off—blocking them, in fact. And out jumped the driver.

It was a woman, at least eight months pregnant, possibly more. She scooted around to the front of the red Saturn and screamed at Ben's father. Zoltan locked the door and checked to see that his window was closed. Ben did the same. They were being terrorized by a woman who was about to give birth, and Ben considered with a note of shame and nausea: he was scared. The woman thumped the car and mouthed obscenities.

"Now, is that not an idiot?" Zoltan said. "And soon she will have an idiot child."

The woman slapped the hood of the Saturn with an open hand. They must really have given her a scare, but Zoltan was unperturbed. He viewed her as some kind of menacing over-sized insect trying to fly into the car. He checked to see what was on the radio, found a weather report and said, "Sunny day ahead. No more rain. Perfect day for a driving test."

Then she was gone. The woman got back into her car and scorched across the intersection on the amber light. Zoltan wisely decided to wait until the next green.

"Where shall we have lunch after the test?" he asked.

"Dad, we've just been assaulted by a pregnant woman."

"We can keep that to ourselves."

"I have no intention of spreading it around," Ben said.

At the green, Zoltan glided across two lanes without a care. "It's the perfect defense," he said. "You get yourself big with child and then you can yell your fool head off at who-ever you want, wherever you go. You can even hit people or dent their cars. Who's going to hit back? She's not as dumb as I thought."

They skidded over the curb and Ben's face slapped against the side window. He checked a tooth to see if his father had loosened it. He said, "Dad, how are you possibly going to pass the test today? You haven't so much as signaled since your forty-eighth birthday, and on that occasion the signal was on the whole day long."

Zoltan looked at his son full on again from his reclining position. "Trust me. They won't know what hit 'em."

"No, they won't."

"Don't be a smartass."

"A *smartass*? You chipped a tooth of mine here." Ben was still rubbing the side of his face.

"Look," Zoltan said, pointing to the Shell station, "they sell senna tea there. It's for regularity, as you probably know."

So here they were: his father could comment in glorious detail about the siege of Stalingrad; he could talk about what it was like to go into hiding while the invading army of Adolf Eichmann rolled through the streets of his beloved Budapest, followed by the tanks of Russia, which liberated Hungary but never left; he could add a long column of numbers in his head more quickly than anyone using a calculator; he could recite Latin poetry and did so often, too often (*"Militat omnis amans, et habet sua castra Cupido,"* Ovid tells us. *"Attice, crede mihi, militat omnis amans."* "Every lover wages a war, and Cupid has his own campaign. Believe me, Atticus, every lover wages a war"); he could appreciate that Canada's brand of fiscal conservatism and social liberalism was the best combination of a bad bunch; and yet it had all come down to one overarching question. How did one find the most convenient purveyor of the tea that loosened stools?

At the driving center, Zoltan parked the car on an extreme slant. It had begun to rain again, but lightly. "Dad, straighten out, because you'll be with the examiner next."

He straightened his hat.

"I meant the car."

"It doesn't matter."

"Dad, I'd say suit yourself, but we're talking about a driving examiner."

Zoltan sighed, pulled out again without looking and edged back in, still crooked but better, almost within the lines. Then he got out and strode into the building without waiting for his son.

Ben wished he'd inherited half his father's self-assurance. He guessed that his father's brand of confidence required a degree of blindness. Or conversely that too little confidence came of having too much vision, also of the blinding variety. He didn't know which was better. Ben's brand led to too little action; Zoltan's to too much.

The examiner hardly looked at them as he read the doctor's report in Zoltan's file. His mousy hair was tousled, as if he'd just come in from taking a drive in someone's convertible. The man looked twice at the name. "Zoltan Beck?" Zoltan nodded. "Is it your own car we'll be taking out, Mr. Beck?"

"Yes, it's the Saturn out front. Red."

"Okay." The man ticked a box. He looked up at Ben over his reading glasses. "Will you be joining us?"

His father said, "It's better if he doesn't. He makes re-marks." The man looked at Ben again. "He's a remark maker," his father said.

"Okay, it's up to you."

Ben felt relieved, actually. He wouldn't have made remarks, but he would have been biting back a few. He walked them out, watched them get into the car and waited for them to depart. The examiner was waving the air in front of his nose.

Ben took a seat in the crowded waiting room. He flipped through a brightly colored Chinese magazine and felt like a child, gazing at the pictures of hens and gnarled roots and a formidable dragon. He traced the lines of the letters, the dazzling Chinese characters, to see what sense he could make of them.

A real child sat down beside him, a little girl. He didn't know where she'd come from. He scanned the adults to determine which of them she belonged to.

She peeked over at Ben's magazine and even leaned toward him. But then she went back to her father. She pulled a gar-ment from her father's backpack, donned it and returned to Ben. It was a red silk cape with a dragon embroidered on the back. Quite a fierce one. The little girl modeled it for Ben, turning all around, prancing back and forth in front of him, pulling the soft hood over her head.

Ben and Lucy's daughter Anna had worn just such a cape when she was barely four. They'd received it as a gift from an old friend of Lucy's who'd moved to China for business.

The package arrived from Beijing for Anna's birthday, and its impact was sensational. Anna wore it all day. She wore it to bed and wore it outside. She wanted to bathe in it, and Ben was on the verge of letting her when Lucy intervened.

"How many times in life do you get to bathe in a red silk cape?" he asked.

"*Never*," Lucy said.

Anna was howling, not letting her parents remove the cape. Lucy and their six-year-old daughter, Leah, had to banish Ben with his sympathetic looks from the bathroom so they could peel it off her.

Soon Halloween arrived. Ben's brothers came over to his place with their children. Frank's son, Marvin, was dressed as Oscar the Grouch, complete with the garbage can he lived in, but something was off about the costume, so he looked more like a pencil sharpener, albeit a large and impressive one. Sammy's one-year-old daughter, Ruthie, was dressed as a baby but with cat whiskers. Leah was dressed as a very scary princess, one carrying a magic wand, like Glinda, the Good Witch of the North. The wand was made of a souvlaki stick with an origami paper star, which Leah had learned how to make at school, fastened perilously to the end.

And then there was Anna with her red cape, as Little Red Riding Hood. They went from house to house all the way down one side of their street, then crossed to double back on the other side. Everything was going perfectly Halloween-ingly until they hit one house. Leah and Marvin got to the doorbell first and rang it well and often. Eventually, a man with a bad goiter bulging like an udder from his neck opened the door holding his plastic pumpkin full of treats, and they were all taken aback. Poor guy. He was cheerful enough, but Anna, faced with someone whose Halloween costume was given to him by Nature or God or the Underworld, backed away, and Ben saw in the streetlight the glint of fear in her eyes. She wanted her father to pick her up. Her lower lip was quivering. He pulled her red hood over her head, and she buried her face in the crook of his neck.

To make matters worse, at the next house they caught up with three teenagers who were kicking the smiling jack-o'-lanterns that waited on the porch to greet them. The boys looked at the Becks over their shoulders with that awful look of power and venom and said, "Smashing pumpkins, baby!" One of the boys had pumpkin guts and seeds glistening on the steel toe of his black boot.

Anna was sobbing. Ben's neck and shoulder were soaked. He turned to cross the street and head home, but Frank put his hand on his other shoulder and pulled him back.

"You can't go," he said. "Your kid has to suck it up. *You've* got to suck it up." Frank had the look in his eye too, almost like the teenage boys—mighty, unforgiving.

Ben's heart was racing. He clutched his young daughter tightly, hesitated, but then dashed across to their house. Leah didn't have a care and continued with her cousins and uncles for another half hour before returning home. When the kids were done, Frank had driven off without stopping back in, and Sammy didn't have anything to say about it. He said that Frank had not said a thing other than goodbye.

When Ben's father returned with the driving examiner after what felt like an hour, the man was grinning tightly, as if at their practical joke. He looked at Ben and said he'd be right with them.

Zoltan stood by Ben's chair and stared at the office beyond the counter into which the man had disappeared. The little girl with the cape was sitting across the room from them, her cape by her side on the bench like a slain dragon.

"How did it go?" Ben asked his father.

"I think it went all right."

"Oh, good."

"Let's wait for the verdict. I've been driving for over six decades, don't forget."

"I know—you're very experienced. Why don't you take a seat?"

Zoltan stayed standing, shifting his weight from one foot to the other, then backward and forward, like a parallel parker. He squeezed his fedora down tightly onto his head. A group in the far corner erupted in laughter, followed by sporadic applause. Zoltan and Ben looked to see who they were congratulating, but no one was being singled out.

A man entered and approached the counter. He waited for the woman at the nearest desk to help him. He had long red hair tied in a loose ponytail and wore a muscle shirt—an unfortunate choice, because his muscles flitted around inside his loose skin like a cat in a sack. He'd filled out most of a form but was asking what number to put in a box he was pointing to. The woman said, "K."

"What number?" the man asked.

"K," she said.

"Oh." He pulled his hands back through his ponytail a couple of times, sharpening it, then marked the box.

A quarter of an hour passed before the examiner emerged and summoned Zoltan and Ben back up to the counter. He looked as if he needed to lie down. "Mr. Beck," he said, "I gave you sixteen out of a hundred. Let me see . . ." He was scanning his long sheet. "You pulled out without signaling, or looking, really. You didn't signal throughout the whole drive, in fact. You didn't turn on your windshield wipers in the rain. You didn't once look in your rearview mirror or your side mirror. You crossed lanes twice, inexplicably. You drove blessedly slowly, but you cut off another car and stayed in the passing lane, although he was honking at you consistently."

"He was an idiot."

"Possibly," the examiner said, "but he was trying to pass, and you blocked him. You were driving in the passing lane. You turned onto Wilmington without stopping at the stop sign. In fact, you maintained your standard cruising speed. Then, for the stretch of a whole block, you were staring out the side window through the rain until I asked you to look straight ahead. What were you looking for?"

"There was a store in that neighborhood that sold white gloves, but I didn't see it." The man peered over his reading glasses at Ben. "I wear white gloves," his father went on, "when I develop a rash between my thumb and forefinger." The man and Ben both looked at the bandages on Zoltan's hands as he indicated where the rashes tended to show up.

"So," the man said, and blew out his breath, "I gave you a score of sixteen percent."

"Is that a pass?" Zoltan asked.

The question that occurred to Ben was how his father had managed to get even sixteen points. Did one get points for knowing how to start the engine, knowing where the steering wheel was, knowing which was one's radio knob and which was one's own knob?

"No, I'm sorry. You didn't pass," the man said. "Your son will have to drive you home. Driving isn't for everyone."

"What about life?" Ben's father said. "Is that for everyone?"

"I'm sorry. I really am. You'll hear from the Ministry of Transportation within a few weeks, but you may not drive as of now."

"Oh," Zoltan said.

"It's for the best," said the examiner.

The sun had showed itself again. The rain was biding its time in the clouds, taking a short rest.

Zoltan handed Ben the car keys. "Don't give them back. Just drive off. Give the car to Leah and Anna. Don't even look back."

"Let's go for lunch, Dad. Lucy's asked her boss for a little extra time today. If we eat at Steve's Restaurant, she can meet us."

"Oh, Lucy," he replied faintly. "That's nice. Okay, Steve's. But no Velda today."

"No."

"Or any day."

"No Velda."

Ben got behind the wheel, slid the car seat forward at least three notches and turned on the engine. He was relieved he wouldn't have to switch on the wipers—or, to please his father, wouldn't have to *not* switch them on. The car still reeked, but Ben spared his father the agony of rolling down his window and watching the man shiver with the draft. Even in the early days, the boys were not allowed to open the windows when they drove anywhere as a family. Zoltan would smoke up a storm, but the windows had to remain sealed.

They drove along in silence. Ben didn't dare turn on the radio. He knew what his father was thinking. The sentiment permeated the sweet air. How could his son have forsaken him? Really, this failure had nothing to do with him but with Ben. If Ben were so concerned about his father's welfare and the welfare of the nation, why hadn't he acted twenty years before? No, it wasn't safety at issue here. It was power. Ben needed for once to prevail—he needed to add transportational power of attorney to his portfolio.

But was Ben not the one who turned off the TV or radio without kicking up a fuss when his father asked? Was he not the one who stayed to help raise Sammy when Zoltan was done doling out his bits of fatherly guidance? Was he not the one who took Sammy to hockey games and read to him when their mother was busy folding their underwear or ironing Zoltan's shirts or baking them all a cake? Was he not the one who listened to his father's long—albeit well told—tales of Stalingrad, Eichmann and Theodor Herzl? Was he not the one who looked in the library for the Latin poets—even if in translation? Was he not the one his father summoned in the night to lift the fridge as he stuffed muffling newspapers underneath it? Was he not the one who worried about turning on the windshield wipers now because his irritation was likely to be worse than the pattering of rain on a car?

When Ben left home, Sammy was quick to follow, leaving his parents for his studies soon after Ben was married, long after Frank was married, though Frank didn't count, because he was always out even when he was still officially living with them.

Finally, Zoltan said, "So now you have your Story of the Week."

"What's that?"

"The old man scored sixteen percent on his driving test."

"I won't tell anyone."

Zoltan sighed.

"Well, not *that* many people." His father was silent. "Dad, it's just driving. You can still walk. You can still ride a horse—lord, help us. You can call a cab, or call *us* and we'll take you places. You can still listen to music or go to the movies or play beach volleyball. You can still win the Nobel Prize for chemistry. There's nothing standing in your way that wasn't there before."

He didn't answer. He didn't even look at Ben.

"I'm not going to tell people."

"I really don't care," he said. "Tell whoever you want."

"Look," Ben said, pointing to a convenience store on Sheppard, "I think you can get senna tea there." But his father kept his head down.

As they drove along, Zoltan sitting beside Ben as if Ben were the father and he the child, his license suspended, his wife gone, Ben found it difficult to remember the formidable figure his father had been, though formidable he was: confident, commanding, absolutely convincing, even when he was talking nonsense, even when he was saying that Europe was a failed experiment and should be paved over and turned into a parking lot, a man never needing to impress, who met Lucy the very first time dressed only in his shorts, in winter, in his overly heated house. The man who was certain now, still, that it was the driving examiner who had it all wrong and the pregnant woman who was a fool, never giving too much of himself, only what was enough, wanting within the glorious glow of his confidence to teach his children when enough was enough, wanting Sammy to be satisfied prescribing glasses. Why would anyone need to restore sight to the blind? Why, if you lived in a place where you could get bananas in the dead of a white winter and heat your house the second you felt a nip—*overheat* it, if you felt like walking around in only your shorts—why would you need to climb every mountain and ford every stream, found new nations, build a twelve-hundred-condominium tower or a fifty-thousand-seat base-ball stadium, invent new codes for algebra or swim across Lake Ontario? Why, when you lived in a time and place when and where you could be in the middle class and still get absolutely anything you could ever need, including love and medicine, why all this restlessness? These very thoughts often sprang from the man who'd wanted to be at his colonoscopy appointment a half day early and who wanted to harass the receptionist until it began, and then wasted it all by not preparing for the appointment as he'd been told.

The world was not designed correctly for Ben's father. Roads were not made for him, straight lines weren't, directions weren't. He needed a vast, paved plain—Europe, say—except that he would get lost as he made his way out and would never be seen again. Rain was not made for him, nor fragile Chanel No. 5 bottles, nor fragile anything, nor windshield wipers that made a sound, nor refrigerators that made a sound, nor colonoscopies, nor sharp implements used in carpentry, nor humans—maybe except for Hannah and Lucy. Sometimes. And Ben's daughters too. He was very taken with Leah and Anna.

Lucy was at Steve's Restaurant before them; she'd internalized Zoltan as deeply as Ben had. She hugged only him, and before they'd sat down, he was saying, "It's all bad, Lucy. The driving instructor failed me—not just failed me, plunged a knife into my heart."

She glanced at Ben. "It's okay, Father." She'd begun to call him that, and it more than pleased him.

"There are no second runs at this, I guess."

"I'm afraid not. I'm sorry."

He took off his fedora and slid into the booth. The hat had carved a perfect line across his forehead.

"There are no second runs at anything," he said. "You'll see."

Usually by now he'd have finished reading the menu and been looking all around for the waiter, but not on this occasion.

Zoltan did pick up the plastic menu, but he let it flop around in his hands. "Do you know what your husband asked me last week?" he said.

"No, what?" She gave Ben a look.

"He asked me, à la Saint Augustine, 'Are you here on this earth just to use it or to leave something of value behind?'"

He was telling on Ben, trying to get him into trouble. Lucy glared at her husband. She had a tear in her eye. She had a big heart, especially for people who needed extra care. And her own parents were gone now.

"And what did you say to Ben?" she asked.

"I said I did some good, even if I did bring him into the world."

She reached across the table and took one of his hands, and he let her, a huge concession. "You did a lot of good," she said. "You were very good to your family. You raised three good sons with Mother. You brought your family to safety in the New World." Ben had told Lucy what his actual answer had been.

"Oh, it wasn't about being good," his father said. "I had to leave. *I* was the one. Hungary was not right for us. I would have left ten years before if my wife and mother had let us. If men have always been truly in charge, someone forgot to tell my wife and mother. Anyway, I did it for myself, and my boys got to tag along."

"But you *did* bring us," Ben said, trying to help. "You didn't just climb out your window in the night like Paul Gauguin and take off to Tahiti. You brought us out too."

Zoltan raised his eyebrows, considering whether Tahiti would have been a better move. He then looked at Ben through the cut of his eye. "Yes, I did," he said. "Yes, your mother and I brought you to a country with practically *no* issues. Imagine that. Never in the history of the world has there been a place like this, and such a time in such a place. All you think of here is what gym to sign up for and whether to have sweet potato fries rather than the regular ones. There is no question of survival here, except on the outer fringes, and even there people like us are driving around in vans and dropping off sleeping bags to the homeless—some of whom refuse to come in from the cold." He held up an emphatic finger. "There is never an issue here of who hates us this week, who's going to chop off our heads for the accident of our births. The issues are historical ones, mostly. They're nationalistic issues stoked by romantics in a nation that isn't one—doesn't want to be—is an *anti*-nation—come one, come all—show us your Ukrainian dances—pass the cabbage rolls—it's all good."

A few years after the Becks had arrived in Canada, Ben was invited to his friend Larry Wilson's house. He was all of eleven, and they were heading into the Christmas holidays. The Becks didn't have a Christmas tree, nor did they open presents, nor did they wait for Santa or sing carols. In fact, Santa passed by the Becks' house altogether. Yes, the Angel of Death passed by their house, but so did Santa.

Frank and Ben and even their brother Sammy, who'd started kindergarten that autumn, were, however, allowed to stay up late to watch *Miracle on 34th Street* or *The Wizard of Oz*. Sammy rarely made it through, but he seemed to like to sit with his brothers, as long as they also ran his trucks with him and built a Lego castle resembling the one in the Emerald City. Eugenia, their grandmother, sat with them to watch, and she sensed that things weren't quite right with her grandsons, especially Ben. There was a restlessness in the room but also something deeper. She gave each of the boys five dollars to buy themselves whatever they wanted, and Ben knew that she understood him and his brothers better than anyone. She then made a tradition of it, giving each of the boys money in a nice card she'd picked out with a special note of devotion she'd taken some trouble to compose. Ben treasured these notes and kept them in a shoebox with other memorabilia, including a matryoshka doll he'd brought all the way from Hungary.

But this one year, Ben was invited to Christmas Day lunch at his friend Larry Wilson's house. He felt like the refugee he was, about to be let in at last. His parents thought it best for him not to go, but his grandmother saw how dejected he was and pleaded his case for him. Even Frank saw that Ben could be an escapee this once, and he stepped up and made a powerful speech. "Look at the poor bastard," he said to them. "What a drag he'll be here if you lock him up—and lock *us* up in the same cell." Frank not only persuaded their parents to let Ben go, but he also gave him some money to go get a gift.

It was Christmas Eve and night was falling. Ben rushed out to get something, took a streetcar all the way down to Queen and Yonge to Simpsons and Eaton's department stores. The Christmas windows were ablaze with whirling elves, polar bears, reindeer, ballerinas twirling and snow falling inside and out.

But the doors were locked. The stores were closed. He went to Honest Ed's discount store at Bloor and Bathurst and found it closed too. He panicked. He ran up Bathurst until he saw that Jacob's Milk & Variety was still open, but the elderly Jacob was about to turn off the lights. He had his keys out. Ben asked him please to let him in, and Jacob did.

He dashed in and frantically searched up and down the three aisles. The wooden floor creaked. Steam rose from his neck from the snow, which had slid down his collar. He picked up chocolates and put them back, a pencil and eraser set, which he put back, a set of spurs, which he strongly considered, but no, the plaster busts of Elvis and several Lassies in various sizes, no. And then, eureka. He came to a plaster cast of the Last Supper. He stood in awe of it. There was Jesus, the man in the center, the one whom all this hoopla was about, and he was surrounded by his great and famous followers.

Ben didn't have quite enough money, but Jacob let him pay the two dollars he did have and even found a suitable box for his gift. Larry Wilson had told Ben that Jacob had his phone number tattooed on his arm, and there it was, on his forearm, as he carefully packed up Ben's purchase.

Lunch at Larry's was as big as a big dinner. They ate turkey and cranberry sauce, stuffing and sweet potatoes, followed by pudding and tarts and fruitcake with clumps of fruit like plastic. Larry's little sisters giggled all the way through the meal, and Mr. Wilson asked about Ben's favorite subjects at school, but nothing else.

After lunch, Larry and Ben opened their presents. When Ben opened his very first Christmas gift, wrapped in reindeer paper, his hands were freezing. They were white and speckled. Larry had bought Ben three Classics Illustrated comic books: *Treasure Island*, *The Last of the Mohicans* and *Oliver Twist*. Ben held them to his chest.

Larry opened the Last Supper, which Ben's mother had wrapped so nicely. When he saw what it was, he said, "Oh," and let it slide to the floor with a clump. He tried to smile at Ben. He said he got a hockey net from Santa and asked if he wanted to take shots on him, but Ben told him they'd do it another time.

Ben thanked Larry and his parents, got on his coat and boots and rushed out of there. Larry followed him out to the end of his walk to ask if he would come back the next day, and Ben said that he would.

He ran two blocks without looking back. Soft snow was falling, and when he turned the corner at Kendal Park, he could smell fires burning in chimneys.

Ben got to his house and up on his porch. He saw inside that his grandmother and parents and brothers were lighting the Hanukkah candles. He watched their yellow glow for a moment before going in.

That night, Ben's father dropped in on him before bed. They didn't exchange a word, but Zoltan gave Ben another five dollars.

"You did a lot," Ben told his father again.

"No, I didn't do a lot. I did what I could. I did *something*."

"Great," Ben said. "Now let's have lunch."

Ben handed Lucy a menu. His father said to her, "Do you see how impatient he is?"

"Yes, he is," Lucy said, and they all smiled.

—

Ben was alone again with Zoltan on the way back to his father's place. Zoltan was sitting in the passenger seat of his fragrant car. Ben told him he was teaching the *Odyssey* over the next several weeks.

His father loved Homer. He could quote him in the original ancient Greek. "Oh, Omeros," he now said, "with his Penelope and his Telemachus." He said something in Greek to Ben. Ben could feel the heat of his look. "And his wine-dark sea," he added.

"Mysterious," Ben said.

"What is?" his father asked.

"The sea. That it was wine-dark. What could he have been thinking? The sea in Greece is sixty-eight shades of blue: beautiful, brilliant blue, blue, blue."

"But Homer could not see blue," his father said.

"What?"

"There is no blue ever mentioned in the *Odyssey* or the *Iliad*, not once. Did you find any reference to it? There is no blue in any ancient Greek text, or Hebrew or Chinese or Icelandic."

"*What?*"

"Maybe they could not see blue," Zoltan said. "Maybe they were color-blind. Maybe blue was the last color to arrive in the palette of our eyes."

"Or maybe it wasn't," Ben said. "Maybe there are colors yet to arrive, ones we haven't got names for."

And then. And *then*. What would it have been like to be the first person to see blue? It would have been like "The

Emperor's New Clothes": That's not gray, or at least that's not the color we've been calling gray. It's something else. Everyone would look with you and then at you. Nobody would be able to say what it was. Possibly only you knew. But you wouldn't have a name for it. Maybe your name was Blue.

Ben's mother had the bluest of eyes, cornflower blue, wine-dark blue. But she had taken the physical blue of them down with her. And his father would be taking down the fact of them. As would Ben. As would anyone who knew her and saw them.

When they got back to his parents' house, miraculously, the sun was shining through the beveled glass in the front door, scattering light through the vestibule, the colors clanging for them like wind chimes.

8

One morning, Colonel Vad summoned Bela to his office. A corporal came to get him. The man kept his head down, so Bela and his brother believed it was bad news. It was almost always bad news.

Mrs. Vad was there with her husband, but it was the colonel who spoke first. He said, almost apologetically, that he wanted Bela to give piano lessons.

"You're the only one who can do it," Mrs. Vad added.

Bela didn't know what to say. "Where is the piano?" was all he could think to ask.

"I've had it moved to my house," the colonel said. "It's in our parlor. We'll start the day after tomorrow. You can have lunch here with the men as usual, and then my driver will take you to my house in Szifla."

"He can eat with us instead," Mrs. Vad said. "He can clean up here and then come directly to us to have lunch, followed by an afternoon lesson."

Bela was surprised to receive a package the next day containing the white shirt and black pants he'd worn at his concert. They'd been laundered and pressed and brought to him at the camp.

If he had not been a pariah before, he became one now. Before he'd given his first lesson, the men in the camp knew what the new detail was for Bela. It must have been the sergeant who'd told. An inmate named Tunisz came up to Bela and Zoli in the mess tent that very evening, and before anyone could react he slapped Bela resoundingly across the face. "That's for making yourself better than the rest of us," he said. "Are you going to turn the other cheek now?"

"He *is* better than the rest of us," Zoli told him, and Tunisz slapped him too, even harder, so that he fell back against Bela.

Zoli went wild and was ready to lunge, but Bela restrained him. "Leave it."

Tunisz was standing in front of them, still taunting them. Another man stood up beside Tunisz, looking just as fierce. He might have been new. Neither Bela nor Zoli recognized him.

"Would you rather give the music lessons?" Bela asked Tunisz calmly.

"I could," the man said. "You might not believe it, but I could. Well enough for them. But no, they want Ferenc Liszt himself. Why not? They have him, and he happens to have time in his busy schedule."

Sergeant Zold stepped into the tent. He was followed by the corporal, the messenger who'd come the day before to summon Bela to the colonel's office. Tunisz snorted, but he and his friend moved off.

The men were gone the following morning, both of them. Bela and Zoli looked for them and even asked someone if he'd seen them, but no one knew what had become of them. There were a few possibilities: they could have been transferred to another camp, deported to Auschwitz or shot and dumped somewhere. The third option was often the most expedient one, especially this deep into the war. And if the third, it might well have been the sergeant or even the corporal who carried out the deed.

Dressed in his fresh white shirt, black pants and a lined leather jacket, which had also been supplied to him, Bela was driven to the Vads' house early the following afternoon. The countryside between the camp and Szifla seemed too dumb to him—indifferent, unaware of what was going on to the left of it and to the right of it. The driver didn't say a word to his passenger until Bela was getting out of the car. "I'll pick you up later," was all he said, and Bela nodded. Was he to feel privileged? Grateful?

For some reason, Bela had expected to see a lavish, ostentatious house staring back at him. Instead, he stood before a stately but conservative house made of stone the color of Dijon mustard, with white-framed gabled dormer windows. Still, the house commanded the street.

The two Vad girls were as happy as could be to receive Bela. They helped him off with his jacket, and the younger sister, Enek, who was home from school for the mid-afternoon break, giggled all the way into the dining room. Enek looked like her sister around the eyes and mouth and shared the white skin, white as porcelain, but she had a rounder face than Zsofia. Both looked more like their mother than their father.

Enek took a seat at the dining room table a bit too close to Bela, and white though her skin was, her cheeks were inflamed.

Mrs. Vad had prepared casino eggs, and the dish made Bela smile. Naturally, they were not served such lovely treats in the camp, and when Bela tried the salad, he remarked that it tasted like home—the eggs were like the ones his mother often prepared. The remark saddened Mrs. Vad. "I'm sorry," she said. "This is a terrible time. I'm sorry we have to meet under such circumstances, and yet these circumstances brought you here."

"Yes," Bela replied.

"I've never heard anyone play music the way you do," Mrs. Vad said, "not even at the concert hall, not even in Budapest." She poured him a glass of chilled white wine.

"There are many good players," he said. "I assure you. There must be at least one good music teacher in town."

"Yes, many good players, and a couple of good music teachers. There is music everywhere in this country." Bela waited. "But you have something extra," she said. "A special gift."

Enek was grinning. She suppressed a giggle and went on blushing instead, infecting Zsofia with the blush. Bela saw that the girls' mother was embarrassing them and tried to act as if he hadn't noticed. Zsofia leaned forward to say something, but then Mrs. Vad went even further. "Your playing doesn't just please your listener," she said, and she let out a breath before saying, "It looks after your listener, takes care of your listener."

And now Bela felt the heat in his own face. He felt radiantly out of place.

Enek gobbled down her meal, and Bela did his best to concentrate on his food too, but he wanted to get to the lesson to see how skilled the girls were at the keyboard. It was only then that he realized he didn't even know which girl he was going to teach, or was it both, or Mrs. Vad herself, since she was doing so much of the talking? His face was on fire.

Enek stood up. "I have to go now," she said, and curtseyed. She swept out of the dining room and clumped up the stairs, taking with her the tingle of adolescence which had somehow insulated the others from one another and from themselves, so that now they felt exposed and vulnerable.

"Have you studied music long?" Bela asked Zsofia, looking at her properly for the first time that day. She wore an amber pendant with the petals of an ancient flower captured in it. The pendant hung from a mere filament of gold around her neck. He wondered whether Zsofia had taken music lessons at school, since the piano had come from there.

"Yes, actually," she said. "I thought I played well until I heard you the other night. Now I feel I have to start all over again. Can we start with Chopin's études?"

"*Start* with them?" Bela asked. "Of course."

They moved to the parlor, and there was the familiar piano. The book of Chopin's études already stood on the music rack. A single portrait in oils looked down from the wall above the instrument. It was of an old matriarch, certainly a grandmother or great-grandmother of Zsofia's. The eyes were the giveaway. They were black as holes in the canvas.

"Let me see how well you play," Bela said, and he took a seat on a soft chair beside the piano.

Zsofia made herself comfortable on the piano bench, waiting for instructions. Mrs. Vad brought in Bela's glass of wine as well as a plate of chestnut crescents, still warm and fragrant. She placed these on a small cherrywood table beside Bela and withdrew.

"Choose anything from the book. Your favorite piece," Bela said.

She chose the tender Opus 10, Number 3. What an exquisite thing it was too, this little piece, giving truth to the struggle between sadness and love. Pretty and correct though the interpretation was, Zsofia's playing was tentative. She gave the piece an apprehensive sound, an uncertain one, her fingers lacking the confidence to plunge into the music's moods. There was a delicacy to the playing, like the thin gold chain that held the amber. Yet despite the hesitancy, the music was good enough to pull him toward it, to entice him. His was, after all, just an interpretation too. And who was to say what the composer had intended exactly, or whose fingers understood his meaning most assuredly? Could it have been many possibilities? Could the music speak as clearly to an aging lover recalling his prime as to an eight-year-old girl? Or to a young labor camp inmate and his expectant protégé?

So here it was again, music's habit of turning aside language, showing itself to be superior to it, speaking out of both sides of its mouth. Bela felt shaken. Was this new doubt engendered by the music itself, this new experience of it?

Zsofia was asking him if he could play it for her. "Of course," he said, and he stood, waiting to swap places. But Zsofia slid down to the end of the bench instead, giving him plenty of room.

He took a seat beside her. His eyes were drawn to the amber pendant. If he didn't know better, he'd have sworn he could smell the sweet fumes rising from it. He could feel for the first time his own hesitancy as his virtuoso fingers loomed over the keys.

When he played the étude, he did so with Zsofia's fresh influence thrown over his playing. When he finished, he turned straight to the twelfth nocturne, Number 2, through which he searched for his former confidence.

Zsofia closed her eyes and swayed slightly, stirring the humid air between them.

Her mother entered and saw the two of them. She waited for Bela to finish the piece, seemed to be steadying herself with a hand on the corner of the piano.

When he did finish, Mrs. Vad said, "Maybe this wasn't such a good idea. Not maybe—this wasn't such a good idea. It was just that . . ." Her hand was still on the piano, but she took it away now and began to gather things.

It was suddenly apparent to all of them how much of themselves they had poured into that afternoon, even Enek.

"But he hasn't finished his wine," Zsofia said. "He hasn't had a bite of your biscuits."

"Yes, I know," said her mother. "He can take some with him. He can take all of them with him. Another time, possibly. Please."

Bela was on his feet.

"But we have only just started *this* time," Zsofia said. She was the last to stand.

They heard something falling on the floor in the room above them. "Please," said Mrs. Vad. "Both of you, please. I made a mistake. I don't know what I was thinking."

Mrs. Vad called the tavern where the driver was waiting, and she gave Bela his jacket and escorted him to the door, asking Zsofia to wait in the parlor.

They stood together in the vestibule. "It was our piano all along," Mrs. Vad said to Bela, "in case you were wondering."

"Oh," he said.

Snow had begun to fall. They could see it through the window and hear it brushing against the front door.

"We lent it to the school for a time, but they have no further use for it, so we had it brought home."

"I see."

"The two good teachers are gone from Szifla," she said. "They were deported."

9

The following Thursday, Zoltan called Ben to say that he'd misplaced his dentures. He knew Ben didn't teach on Thursdays.

"Are they not in your mouth?" Ben asked. One never knew. Zoltan had spent his life misplacing things, and Hannah and the boys had spent their lives hunting for them, everyone anxious, everyone relieved when they'd found them. But sometimes Zoltan's watch was on his wrist, his glasses on his head.

"No, they're not in my mouth." Ben could hear the extra wind coming out as he spoke.

"When was the last time you saw them, or rather used them?"

"I don't remember. I think at the Tim Hortons, but I went back there early this morning to ask if I'd left them there."

"You asked them?"

"Yes, I asked if they had a lost and found."

"And?"

"And they said no."

"Then what?"

"Then they gave me a free coffee."

"Was it good?"

"Quite nice."

Lucy was trying to listen in. Ben covered the receiver. "O Perfidy! Obloquy!" he said to her. (He was teaching composition to theater students.) He told her what was up, but she started asking too many questions. "Soft you now," he said.

"Can you take me to my denturist?" his father asked.

"Don't you have to call him first? Doesn't he have to get dentures ready for you?"

"I called him this morning."

"When? It's only eight twenty now."

"A few hours ago."

"And he answered his business line in the middle of the night?"

"I don't know if it was his business line. But he has the molds for my teeth."

"I'll be there in half an hour, Dad."

"I appreciate it."

"Dad," Ben said. "Shouldn't we be making another colonoscopy appointment?"

"That would solve the problem of that vile liquid, Expulsor."

"What would?"

"Not having any teeth."

"I'll be there soon," Ben said, and hung up.

Ben's father did not have teeth because he was fed up with teeth. He'd had a painful abscess one day, years before, and he told the dentist, "That's it. I'm done with teeth." So he asked the dentist to recommend a denturist, and he never had need of a dentist again. That was the way he was. If he'd had a bad arm and could have it replaced, he would have. That went for all his body parts and organs. If they faltered, get new ones. Like getting car parts replaced and then, ultimately, trading in the car. He would have traded in anything and everything if he believed the old ones were faltering. His wife, if he had to. His children. He had proudly traded the Old World for the New World. And if that didn't work out, he'd replace the New World with a Newer World, if there was one. So he was much more at home anyway with a denturist than with a dentist.

When Ben got to his father's place, Zoltan was standing at the door with his attaché case. "Are we going somewhere else?" Ben said. Zoltan ignored him. "Are you taking notes with you?"

"I don't have to tell you."

For years, Zoltan had left the house with an empty attaché case—or not entirely empty. Sometimes he put his sunglasses and reading glasses in it. They would clatter around inside. But he left the house wearing his fedora, a suit sometimes and an attaché case as if he were going to the office.

Except he wasn't. By the time Ben was in university, Zoltan owned some apartment buildings and didn't really have to hold down a day job. All he had to do was pick up the rent checks from the various superintendents who collected them for him. Sometimes there was trouble and he tended to it anxiously, but those times were rare. Most troubles—plumbing, electricity, noisy parties—could be handled by the supers. Zoltan hardly even wanted to hear about them unless he had to.

He'd gotten himself into this business after years of being a radio salesman. He found tool and die making too wearing, so he'd opened up a business as a distributor of German radios: Blaupunkt, Graetz, Telefunken and Südfunk, fine radios, the finest, he believed. He was not a retailer—he would not have been able to stand that end of things—so he was an agent for German manufacturers, a wholesaler who sold to radio stores.

Zoltan loaded up his car with sample radios and stereo consoles. He thought station wagons were too clattery and jangly, so he kept getting himself sedans. He would pile up the trunk and the back seat to the ceiling, and even the passenger seat beside him, and drive off with no view out the rear or on the right. Across Ontario and all the way out to Vancouver, he depended entirely and eternally on defensive drivers to honk at him or slam on their brakes if he cut them off.

The worry was always *that*: that he was driving. The arrangement he and Hannah came to was that he would phone home from wherever he was across the big land, just as a sign. Two rings and no more meant he was safe. More than two rings, something was up and Hannah had better answer. No rings, trouble. Death. Or at the very least a coma.

Amazingly, this job of his went on for years. Zoltan would show samples of radios, retailers would place orders and Hannah would ship however many were required. Zoltan called the outfit the Zoltan Beck Trading Company, and he had a little storage shop on St. Clair Avenue West near Bathurst, where he warehoused his stock. He had business cards printed up with the "Avenue" of the address spelled "Aveune." When Ben pointed it out to him, he said no one would notice.

"I noticed," Ben said.

His father looked at him contemptuously.

Hannah wanted him to get half his money back from the printer, but he said no, maybe when these cards ran out. All ten thousand of them.

Zoltan ran into trouble when the tax department told him they wanted to audit his business. Given his background, he did not trust authorities. They wanted to see receipts and invoices from the previous five years.

What they didn't know about him (nor would they have cared) was that he liked to throw things out—not just throw them out but tear them to pieces before he did so. He tore up everything: letters the family had received, a paycheck Ben once got for a summer job, holiday cards, an expired calendar, dumb photos, photos that were not as dumb, books and magazines he had finished, a drawing Sammy had done for him in kindergarten, memorabilia, anything, everything, including receipts. He was a human shredder.

So he came to Ben—who was all of thirteen—and told him he wanted his son to forge documents, accounts payable, receipts, invoices. "You're such a good artist," he told Ben. "An excellent copier."

Ben spent a whole weekend, at least twenty-four or -five hours of it, forging documents from the most recent copies, using carbon paper expertly, carefully tracing signatures, hundreds of them, and his father plied him with his favorite chocolate bars: Hershey's Almond Joy and Cadbury Crispy Crunch, as many as he wanted. Zoltan bought a box of each and a case of Coke, back in the days when Coke came in shapely bottles. Ben was wired by the end of each day, short of breath, his heart palpitating.

What surprised Ben most about the undertaking was not how well he adapted to his role as a fraudster but how comfortable he was with it. Just six months earlier, he'd had his bar mitzvah. Rabbi Zagon, who had given Ben his lessons and was to conduct the service, did so at a deep discount rate. In fact, the Becks were not entirely sure he was a rabbi.

He'd said he was when he got off the boat from Hungary with them, and who was to argue, or care?

Except for Frank. When Frank had his bar mitzvah, he went through his Orthodox Jewish phase, which was the way he did many things. If someone beat him at checkers, he was willing to play a thousand games until he could prove himself unbeatable. When someone beat him at Ping-Pong, he fashioned a Ping-Pong table out of an old door, propped it up on some legs against a wall and pinged and ponged all day long against that wall until he could not and would not miss a single rebound. And when he was about to have his bar mitzvah, he grew *peyot*, dressed in the garb, complete with the tallit and black fedora, and appeared each day at dinner as if he were fresh off the set of *The Addams Family*. But his bar mitzvah was the envy of the world: solemn, the prayers beautifully recited, the glow on Frank's face holy, the condescending smile radiant but serene—serene as a synagogue candle whose flame you discover, on closer inspection, is a light bulb made in the shape of a flame.

And then he became an atheist. Enough of that.

Sammy, meanwhile, had started grade school at Talmud Torah, so he was off to the races. He, in fact, ended up having his bar mitzvah in Israel.

But not Ben. He went to lessons with Rabbi Zagon, who had him open his prayer book and promptly went to sleep, complete with a roaring snore. He slept through every lesson, and Ben just stared at him, read the English translation on the left hand side of the page to himself, went out to the kitchen, sat and ate cookies with Mrs. Zagon and their daughter Suzie, who'd started life as Zsuzsi and who was not going to have a bat mitzvah. She couldn't be bothered. The rabbi's daughter.

When Ben's big day came, his family and their guests all went to the hockey rink near Dufferin and Eglinton. It was converted on Saturday mornings and high holidays into a synagogue for Rabbi Zagon and the most moderate of the Hungarian community. Ben read from a Torah with the Hebrew words transcribed with English lettering, their pages taped into the scrolls when they opened them. An elderly cousin visiting from Rochester came up to read too, but Rabbi Zagon quickly rolled up the Torah and packed it away, much to the cousin's chagrin.

As Ben was forging at the Zoltan Beck Trading Company, his father would come by and pet the back of his boy's head, holding up the forged papers and admiring them, saying how talented Ben was. His father was usually economical with the looks he gave people. Quite often his look was reproachful. Occasionally it was warm. But on this weekend, blessed rays poured forth from his face as he watched his son and heir forge and gorge. He had never been nicer to Ben, before or after—not ever—in the whole of Ben's life.

Since Zoltan was not a saver of memorabilia, let alone a hoarder—quite the opposite—Ben was surprised to discover a mysterious envelope tucked in among the receipts and invoices at his father's office. It was a card from Hungary but addressed to the Zoltan Beck Trading Company rather than the Becks' home. It was postmarked five years earlier. Why had his father kept it? Why this one thing? He kept almost nothing. He willfully destroyed or discarded all effects, including personal ones that the family had brought from Hungary. If they had value, like silverware or stamps, he sold them.

Ben pulled the card out of the envelope. It looked like a paper doily with a pattern of lilies at its center, and it contained a lock of blond hair. Ben's hands were trembling. There was a handwritten message in Hungarian, which Ben could make out:

Zolikam,

    I shall never forget your generosity. I enclose a lock of our girl's hair.

SV

Our girl's hair! There was a girl. Ben didn't know what to do, who to tell. He could tell no one, not even his mother. Especially not his mother.

He replaced the card in the small filing cabinet but could hardly continue.

A year after the tax incident, Zoltan got out of the business. He found the driving wearing too. Who else knew what occurred along the way? It was a big country. Zoltan would never say, and no one wanted to ask, though Ben viewed his father more suspiciously after his stint as a forger.

A family friend, Iris Danzinger, once suggested to Hannah that her husband might be having affairs on his month-long sojourns. Hannah said she didn't care—he always came back to her. "You love some people *because*," she said, "others *despite*." This is where Ben found comfort, in his mother's stoicism.

Between the radio business and the building business, Zoltan opened a bookstore. He always loved books. He read voraciously: history, Victorian fiction, crime fiction, plays even, especially classical ones.

So he announced one evening at dinner that he'd bought a bookstore. "It's called Book Garden."

"You didn't tell me we were doing this," said Hannah, as she served goulash from a tureen.

"As Polonius said to Laertes, his son, 'This above all: to thine own self be true.'"

"And?" Ben said.

"*And*, Mr. Literature, do you know what is inscribed on the Temple of Apollo at Delphi?"

"I do not."

"Γνῶθι σεαυτόν. Know thyself."

Sammy and Ben looked at each other, then down at their steaming plates.

"I'll sell all my favorites," their father said. "Plus textbooks. The place stocks textbooks. Plus greeting cards."

Zoltan was a worse store owner than he was a driver. He didn't like customers. They annoyed him. They would want to browse, and he would say, "What are you looking for?"

"Just looking," they would say.

"But I know what's here better than you do." And he would block their path, so they would leave.

Students would come in asking for obscure titles, and he would go downstairs to the stockroom for a quarter of an hour to look for them while upstairs they robbed him blind.

He had a helper, who was slightly better than he was. Her name was Ms. Smith, and she had the most striated skin, as if she had been supplied with double the skin she needed and it never fully adhered to her face. She could have been ninety for all anyone knew. She drank tall glasses of vinegar, usually white but sometimes cider, if she could get a certain brand. She found that it cleaned her out quite nicely. She basically ignored the customers but at least would wait for them at the cash and take payment.

Zoltan lasted only a few years in the Book Garden and sold it for a fraction of the price he'd paid for it. When he broke the news to Ms. Smith that he was leaving, she cried inconsolably. She took quite a swig of her vinegar. Zoltan made it a stipulation of the deal that the new owner keep her on.

The salient point was that his father didn't like working for anyone, nor for himself, for that matter. That was why he'd arranged to buy some buildings. He borrowed heavily, but he always paid everyone back. He was nothing if not honorable, like the gentlemen in suits he thought he modeled himself on.

When he went out daily, all dressed up and carrying his attaché case, it was all strange and suspicious, but Hannah didn't seem to care. There were sightings of him by various friends and relatives, mysteriously entering buildings, stopping at the bridge club and reading menus posted outside restaurants, but by dinner time he always came home, except in his traveling salesman days. And no one asked him anything.

Yet he was a man so ready to deceive, as with the tax people. Ben could only assume his father would readily deceive any of them. To his credit, though, Zoltan didn't lie when they asked about his whereabouts or deeds. He gave his usual refrain: "I don't have to tell you."

But as to leading a double life, Ben had his doubts. His father might have managed one and a quarter lives, one and a third at most.

Ben couldn't pretend to know how such a man as his father came into being. At best, he could assemble only a composite sketch.

Just as Ben and his father were about to head off to the denturist, Ben asked, "Dad, before we leave, can we retrace your steps, do a process of elimination?"

"No, we can't."

"Did you have your teeth with you in the bathroom?"

He didn't answer.

"Did you use them at breakfast? Did you lend them to someone?"

"We can't do a process of elimination," he said.

"Fair enough, but just give me a sec," Ben said. He scooted straight up to his father's bedroom, and there, grinning up at him from Zoltan's pillow, were his teeth.

10

The winter of 1944 brought its own icy forces to Hernyo, more relentless than those of the Germans. The winds seemed to rise up from the ground, sleet blew in, down the slope of the mountain, and slapped the camp, challenging the men, overwhelming some, when they stepped outside. One day and night, it snowed so heavily that the men had to trudge through waist-high snow, without boots and coats. The men who'd been laying rails were made to gather firewood and to compete in pointless exercises only to prove who could stay standing and who would collapse.

These men were also assigned to clear some trees, their

trunks turning to iron as they braced themselves against the wind and snow. Next they were to dig a large, shallow pit not far from the barracks, all in anticipation of the unfortunate demise of what turned out to be almost a fifth of their number. Twenty-nine men perished in just three weeks.

The factory men were treated slightly better, because the demand for howitzer shell casings had only increased, doubled in fact, since the German army had so badly depleted its munitions the previous year in Stalingrad.

But some of these men too had taken ill and were coughing through their work, some of them as badly as poor Denes Kis had, the small man who was the first casualty of Hernyo Camp. The Beck brothers were among the coughers. Their barracks at night sounded like a kennel full of barkers calling out to their owners.

Sergeant Zold had restrained himself with the factory workers, mostly because he also had begun to worry about filling the orders from Budapest, which was to say from Berlin. The pleasure he had taken in the first men's demise had turned to alarm as others fell or didn't wake up in their cots.

The coughing worsened. The barracks were cold and the bedclothes skimpy. People sometimes shivered themselves to sleep. Bela said that however they got to sleep, rest was the important thing. He said this to his brother, but loudly enough for others to hear.

A man named Oliver Biztos, who was at least a decade older than Bela and had a young daughter at home in Eger, told Bela to shut up. "You were the one who turned this camp on its head," Oliver said, "with your stupid piano playing and your privileges. Who the hell do you think you are?"

Bela didn't answer. He wrote something in his little notebook. From the back pages forward, Bela wrote notes irregularly as a kind of journal, while from the front he'd written his poems, or sometimes single lines of poetry, or mere images. The writing was tiny, microscopic. He wasn't sure he would ever have enough paper to hold his thoughts and memories.

Bela seemed to be getting a little better and stronger before many of the other men did, while his brother was plagued with an unending cough. Bela often shared his warm evening broth with his brother. Zoli said that it was good. It tasted like chicken soup.

"Chicken and horse," Bela said. "Half and half. One chicken, one horse."

Zoli laughed for the first time in weeks.

The winter hardened. Zoli got sicker, like so many of the other men. Bela still coughed, but the coughing had its own rhythm, like something coming from outside of himself, a signal to return to the waking memory of Zsofia, the amber scent of her appearing and fading, rising and falling.

He found the long hours of work a welcome distraction from all the illness, and the stove was warmer in that tent. Even when they were called for lunch, he wanted to stay on.

"You're lucky," Zoli whispered to his brother before bed one night. "You have that place to go to. Your Zsofia. Like an oasis, where it is warm and sunny. Even if it goes nowhere—where might it go?—you can at least visit her in your daydreams, or your nightdreams. Lucky bastard."

"Yes," was all Bela could answer.

"I hope I find such a girl, my own oasis."

"Of course you will," Bela said. "There will be life after this place."

And Bela was the first sick man to get well. Why wouldn't he be? thought Zoli. Bela had such a rich repository, he found it easy to reach inside himself for some hope. And ironically, the very act of doing so more than replenished the internal resources he used up. And he had his notebook. He was always making sense of things as no one else could. And his poetry, and his love, his sunny oasis. Bela even felt strong. He made an extra effort to pull his brother back into health and to shield him from despair. "Think about home. Home is still there waiting for us, the hearth blazing."

"Do you really believe it's exactly as we left it?" Zoli asked.

"If it isn't, we'll make it so again."

A couple of the men were taken to the infirmary. They were forest men who'd been working outside all day and were among many who begged to be transferred to the factory. Neither made it back to the barracks. Bela and Zoli kept checking their cots. Soon a third coughing man was taken, and they didn't see him again either.

Even for those who were well or better, the barracks were a dark icebox. It made the inmates forget themselves, forget who they were, sealing them off from whatever life they once had, and from whatever life that may or may not still lie ahead. Bela threw his arm around his brother one evening at dinner when Zoli refused to return to their barrack. Zoli didn't care. He was taking off. Let them shoot him. He said he couldn't stand another night of this life. Bela gave him all of his dinner, some kind of warm gruel with bits of egg in it, and he persuaded the cook to let him steal an extra bowl of broth. Then, when the sergeant stepped out of the mess tent, the cook brought over still another bowl of the soup and one more of the gruel and urged Bela to have some too. The cook was called Voros, meaning "Red," and no one knew if it was his first name or last. The men also didn't know if he was one of them or an employee of the camp. He wore the same khaki uniform they did, plus an apron, naturally. But Voros appeared to favor the Beck boys, especially Bela. He paused to chat with him whenever he could and seemed to want to commiserate with him. He was the one who managed to salvage the white shirt and black wool pants Bela had worn for his concert and to the Vads' home. Voros had been asked to dispose of them by the sergeant. Instead, he stashed them away for Bela.

So, with Voros's help and encouragement, Bela and Zoli trudged back to the barracks with the others, Bela with his arm still draped over his brother's shoulder.

The cacophony continued into the night, but Bela was used to it and was tired enough now to sleep through it. He brought over a lantern and wrote in his tiny notebook. After a while, he got up to check on his younger brother, who was sucking the tip of his thumb, and waited for him to cough, but he didn't. Zoli was asleep, and Bela sat with him, waiting to be sure the others were asleep too, or getting there.

When Bela was certain he was the only one left awake, he crept to the ramshackle cupboard in the back where the rags and other cleaning things were stored and where Voros had hidden his once-crisp white shirt and pants. He pulled out the shirt, crept back to Zoli's cot and threw the shirt over the flimsy blanket he had been issued. Then he climbed under his own thin covers and closed his eyes.

In the middle of that particularly frigid night, the wind pounding at the rickety walls, the barrack door creaked open for just a moment in the darkness, then closed again. The men burrowed themselves as deeply as they could into their pathetic covers. Despite the racket, they stayed asleep, most in a deep sleep, in which they could fly away or travel back to a bed they once loved.

A hand touched Bela's shoulder, perhaps a single gloved finger. He bolted up. Someone was quietly shushing him. Zsofia's face was suddenly near his. He was sure he was dreaming. But he could feel her warm breath and then, impossibly, her lips searching over his scruffy face for his own. They paused to listen for the men all around them. She had slipped in without disturbing them. Bela kissed Zsofia cautiously at first. He was clinging to the dream, for surely that's what it was. But Zsofia pressed harder, circling his lips with the tip of her tongue. She held his neck, clinched him to her, spread herself out on the narrow cot with him, opened her fur coat and folded him into the warmth of it. She seemed to have brought a whole weather system with her, another climate. She kissed his ear, traced a lobe with the tip of her tongue, and said to him that she had brought a coat for him. It was a trench coat but thickly lined with wool. He must hide it somewhere safe, she told him. And he must leave the camp. Escape. The Russians had breached the border. The Germans were on the run. Before long, the Russians would roll through the camp. The wind flapping against the barrack walls drubbed out her voice. She was speaking right into his ear. He could barely hear her, but he strained. She asked him, please, to save himself and, please, to find her. She didn't know if she could live for long without him. She would go anywhere with him, flee the country if she had to. She had never felt this way about anyone before and never would again, couldn't again, wouldn't try. She knew her own heart.

He asked her, please, to stop talking. They listened again for the men. They would be found out. But then he whispered, "Here we are. Look at us."

Zsofia stayed almost until dawn, the two of them enveloped in the heat of her coat. She was like the sun, like a late-summer harvest. The pricking of the wind made him tingle when she left him. He felt bereft. He hid the coat she'd brought him in the back of the cleaning cupboard and folded himself in the idiotic blanket.

When Zoli woke up in the morning, he removed the white shirt and quickly hid it under his blanket. Bela was scrawling furiously (and microscopically) into the back of his note-book. The wind had died down, and a thin chill sat on the plain between the mountain and the forest. Maybe the wind had changed direction. Maybe the mountain had turned its other shoulder against it.

At the latrine, Bela told his brother about what had happened, making sure first there was no one within earshot. Zoli was coughing and grinning at the same time, but he was not wheezing anymore. He'd been wheezing for weeks. How could he not have known about Zsofia's visit? How could he have slept through it? He was grinning about the Russians too, until Bela whispered, "Do you think they'll liberate us or just mow us all down? We're making munitions for the enemy. We're Hungarians. We're Jews. Beasts through and through, in their eyes. We have to get out of here. I have a coat—"

"You have a *coat?*" It wasn't until that moment that Zoli believed any of Bela's story. "How did she get into the barracks, the camp?"

"I've told you everything I know," Bela said. He had a shine that morning, like someone transformed.

But before the Russians arrived, another adversary entered the camp: typhoid. Oliver Biztos came down with the fever that very afternoon. Dr. Fischer identified the spots on his chest and let the colonel know. The camp commander, who had told no one about the Russians, wanted to know how many more men were likely to contract the infection. The doctor couldn't say.

Bela became especially concerned about his brother, whose coughing had deepened, heaving up from the well inside him. The wheezing was back, and Bela went to ask Dr. Fischer about it. Bela and the doctor had remained friendly since Bela's brief stay in the infirmary. Dr. Fischer had revealed that his daughter aspired to be a pianist and had wondered if Bela would consider giving her lessons, should this bad time pass. Bela said he'd make a deal with the doctor: he'd give his daughter lessons if Fischer could make Zoli well. That was how Bela found out about the typhoid. "I'm almost certain that's what it is, judging by the symptoms," Fischer told him, "and I don't have medicine for typhoid. I have asked for antibiotics but have had no response. Maybe you can get some," the doctor said.

A few days later, another man showed signs of serious illness. Bela became extra concerned that his brother was susceptible. He asked the sergeant if they might get some medicine into the camp, and the sergeant looked ready to hit him again. Zoli was still working alongside the others. Once, he asked to sit down, and surprisingly the sergeant let him. A couple of more days passed, and Zoli's cough worsened. That same afternoon, the sergeant was called out of the factory by an anxious corporal, and for the first time the factory was left unguarded. Bela urged his brother and other coughing men to take a break. A quarter of an hour later, they were still sitting when Bela knelt down in front of his brother. He told Zoli, "We have to leave now. Trust me. It must be now. We'll get the coat Zsofia left me. You'll wear it."

"I can't do it," Zoli said.

"You can't wear the coat?"

"No, I can't go with you. I'm too weak. I'm tired. I'll wait here."

"You're not waiting here. I will never see you again if you wait here. You can make it, I promise. I'll help you."

"I'm not an Olympian. I'm not anyone's darling. The Sirens don't sing to me. Go ahead. Come back later, Bela. Come back to get me once I've had a rest."

Bela felt his brother's forehead. He was hot, his forehead damp. They heard the camp's two cars roar to life, one of them after some chugging and coughing of its own in the cold. Bela peeked outside through the flap covering one of the two windows. The officers were leaving. The colonel was climbing into the back of his Mercedes. Bela summoned the other men to look. He told them about the Russians.

Bela got down on his knees in front of his younger brother again.

"Wait for me," he told Zoli. "I'm not leaving you here, but for now do not move. Rest." He patted his brother's cheeks and got to his feet. Zoli nodded off immediately.

Bela ran to get Fischer. The doctor said he would warn the forest men. Oliver Biztos was lying in the infirmary. Fischer couldn't wake him. He was breathing but burning up. The doctor hurried outside and Bela followed. One of the cars slowed, a window rolled down and Fischer was shot three times before the car sped on. Bela rushed to the doctor, but the man had been shot twice in the chest and once in the throat and was dead.

Bela thought he could hear music. Was it possible? Yes, it was faint but unmistakable. Rachmaninoff's second piano concerto.

The men from the forest had heard the gunfire and were staggering up to see what was happening. Bela told everyone the news and went himself to the infirmary to get Biztos. Zoli was out of the work tent by then and tried to stop his brother, but Bela pushed by him. Bela found that Biztos too had stopped breathing. His mouth was agape.

Bela went to their barrack to get the trench coat out of the closet. He came back to find his brother crouched over the dead doctor. He forced Zoli to put on the coat and began to lead him away. His brother was too weak to argue.

Now many of the men had emerged. They were madly scrambling away from the camp, some down the path where the cars had gone, a group the opposite way, but Bela urged whoever remained to go with him into the forest. He said it was their best chance. The Russians would surely come along the road. He looked especially hard for Voros, the cook, but couldn't find him anywhere. Only his brother followed him into the woods.

Before long, Bela saw beads of sweat on his brother's forehead. They hadn't traveled far, but far enough to hide. The afternoon light was fading. Zoli's lips were parched. Bela reached for a clump of snow and fed it to his brother. He spotted a lean-to not too far away where the railway men had stored tools and supplies they needed to keep dry. Supporting his brother under his arm, Bela led the way there. Zoli helped

Bela clear part of the shelter and gathered evergreen branches to soften the frozen ground and make the two of them more comfortable. Zoli was coughing like someone born to it. Bela helped his brother recline in the shelter and promised to be back soon. Zoli begged him not to go, but Bela said he had to try to get some supplies. He had heard nothing, not a sound, except for the occasional rustle of winter birds or small animals scampering away, so he decided it was worth taking the risk of returning to Hernyo.

There was no one in the camp, no Hungarians and no Russians. The doctor was still lying in the path. He looked blue from this distance. Bela entered their barrack, took two blankets and headed for the mess tent, where he found some tins of tomatoes and beans. He tiptoed toward the officers' barracks, still afraid someone might have been left behind, and found no one. But he heard something, a familiar sound. Was it static? It was coming from the colonel's office. He peered in. A record spun on the phonograph, the needle butting against the end. Bela entered. He rummaged around the desk and looked through its drawers, found a compass and a pocketknife in the middle drawer, a small package of chocolates, some cigars and some valuable wooden matches. In the bottom drawer he found three vials of penicillin and a syringe. The colonel intended to be the last man standing, if there was to be a last man.

Bela packed all these items in a small canvas bag he found in a cloakroom. There were no coats there, unfortunately, or even gloves or scarves.

And then he heard something else, something outside, the roar of an engine, so he picked up his bag, slipped out and stole along the edge of the forest before entering it. Now he heard another engine, vehicles approaching, and he ran as fast as he could toward his brother.

Zoli was asleep, but Bela roused him, told him they could rest but they would have to move on. There were people coming, Russians almost certainly, but maybe Hungarians, people from the town, possibly, from Szifla. Maybe they had seen the officers or a group of the men fleeing. He kept thinking of Zsofia. What would they do to her if they found her?

"It's not safe here," Bela said quietly. "Let's rest and decide what to do in the morning. Before dawn. We can't build a fire. It will attract attention. But we can have a cigar," he told his brother, "and some beans and tomatoes. I even stole a couple of spoons, and there's a knife here in the bag."

And for the sheer madness of it, the brothers each began with a cigar. They smoked them right down to the butt, Zoli coughing out every puff. Bela worried that someone would hear the sound of his brother's hacking, but Zoli soon drifted off to sleep.

Zoli awoke before the morning light had settled in. Bela was writing in his notebook. He was alarmed at how white Zoli looked, ghostly in fact, his pallor accentuated by dark circles under his eyes. Bela asked his brother how he was feeling. Zoli sat up, and Bela reached with the back of his hand for his forehead. He asked him to breathe deeply. There was no wheezing and for the first time no coughing. He opened his brother's uniform top, could feel the heat even in the buttons. They seemed to radiate heat. Zoli's chest and shoulders were covered in pink spots.

Zoli looked down at himself. "How decorous," he said. His normally shiny raven hair was dry and tangled.

Bela put his hand on his forehead again. "We could light another cigar off your forehead," he said. "You've looked better."

"No more movie star good looks, I guess," Zoli said.

"No, you have typhoid good looks," Bela said. "Labor camp good looks." The two of them started laughing. "We both do."

Zoli launched into a new round of deep coughing, then said, "I can still be a superhero. I can be Typhoid Boy."

"Please. Typhoid Man."

"Yes, of course. Typhoid Man." Zoli burst into tears and held his brother desperately, kissing him on both cheeks with his warm lips, the first time he remembered kissing him since they'd been very small. Bela was staring into the dark portholes of his younger brother's eyes. "Please stay with me," Zoli said. He was sobbing. "Please don't leave me."

Just then, two motorcycles roared by above them at the foot of the mountain, one after the other, following the route from the camp to the town. Bela and Zoli scrambled to their feet. Zoli said, "We have to get to the town. Maybe we can find some medicine there."

"I have medicine," Bela said.

Bela quickly prepared the first vial of penicillin, took off his brother's trench coat and rolled up his sleeve. Zoli began trembling in the cold air. Bela injected him with the penicillin.

"Put the coat back on. We'll go to the mountain," Bela said. "It's our best chance."

"The *mountain?*" Zoli said.

"Yes, but not over it. Around it. Let's try. Do you know where we are?"

Zoli thought it was a trick question and smiled.

"We're no more than twenty-four or twenty-five kilometers from Kiskunhalas, where Grandfather's summer house is. It is due southwest, and we have a compass." Bela took it out to show his brother.

"Oh, Hajnal," Zoli said. "But Grandfather's gone."

"Yes, of course he's gone, but the house is not gone. There might be someone there who knows us and can help us get home."

Hajnal had been confiscated by the authorities at the start of the war, and Ben and Zoli could only guess who it belonged to now. The Hungarians still? The Germans? The Russians?

The Beck boys spent all of that day and into the night following the base of the mountain until they came to a cave. It was large, deep, dark and empty. Zoli could hear the echo of his own cough magnified a great way in. Bela made a comfortable place for his brother and himself on the blankets they had brought.

"I'll gather some firewood," Bela said. "We have matches."

"And cigars," Zoli said. "Take this coat."

"Keep the coat on!" his brother said.

Zoli sat down, placed a rolled-up blanket behind him against the stone wall and a minute later was asleep. Bela gathered dry kindling and the driest remains of an old fallen tree. He took great care to build a lively fire, then opened a tin of beans and one of tomatoes. He was determined to make his brother a little stronger before they moved on. Zoli slept through it all. Bela felt his brother's forehead, brought in some snow and spread it over his cheeks and neck. Zoli woke with a start. He had to be reminded where he was. Zoli did not want a single mouthful of the food. Bela fed it to him until he spat out the fifth and sixth spoonfuls.

Bela asked his brother to get ready for the second injection.

"Already?" Zoli said.

"Yes, I think the first couple are the most critical."

Bela was smiling afterward. He tried with little success to feed his brother a little more and brought in some more snow, this time to melt, and made him drink it right down. They did not talk for a long time. They sat listening to the wind outside. Zoli was coughing a little less. Bela checked his forehead. He had cooled down a little.

Finally, Bela said, "I can fully understand why I might not be allowed to play music. It would arouse and possibly offend listeners. And I might put flavor into it, a mysterious cosmopolitan spice, a stink, which might cause harm. But archaeology. I was barred from continuing in archaeology. 'The Jew goes for a dig,' it would say in the newspaper. 'He finds something unsavory. But not just unsavory. *Damaging.* The real story of John the Baptist.'"

Bela tried to feed his brother another spoonful of beans, but Zoli shook his head no and covered his mouth with his hand.

"Do you remember that one time before the trouble began? I traveled with my archaeology class to the Greek island of Naxos. Do you remember?" Zoltan said he did. "On the promontory, we saw the lintel of Apollo's door," Bela said. "That was really all that was left of the great temple built in the sun god's honor. A lot of good it did the Greeks. Ironic, really, if you think about it. Enter this doorway— into what? Into the open air, into the world. The building is gone. The building was an illusion.

"But the thing that stands out for me about the great ancient island, now poor, very poor, was that there was a smooth, gentle slope leading down to one of the bays, and historians and archaeologists determined that it was used as some kind of ramp. Naxos is close enough to Athens that artists and artisans and sculptors and painters lived there— moved there for all we know—made the great artworks, the great and wondrous and shapely women in marble—perfect things, caryatids, who stood as pillars in the Acropolis, holding up the roof with their heads—made all these treasures, which were then expertly and gingerly coaxed down this slope to waiting ships, transported to Athens and—God knows how—moved up to the temple."

Bela's voice was trembling with excitement. His dark eyes had turned liquid in the firelight. His brother listened to his voice over the crackling of the fire. Bela begged him to take another spoonful of tomato at least, so Zoli tried, one spoonful only, screwing up his face as if it were bitter.

"Well, on this slope, which was being used as a ramp, lying on its back in three perfect pieces, was a dark green marble kouros, a massive marble soldier, a guard, taller than you and me put together and there it lay in three pieces, a thing of dark, sculpted beauty, ready to stand guard in the noblest palace in the world but then *dropped*—dropped off whatever ingenious contraption they were using to slide these works down the slope into the waiting ships. Dropped. Broken in three pieces and just lying there on the slope." Bela turned his eyes, radiant in the firelight, toward his younger brother. "And there it lay for twenty-five centuries. Untouched. Unmoved. And there it still lies on that same slope, looking up into the ancient sun over the Aegean. Washed by rain, smoothed by breezes and wind, walked over by insects and animals. What a sight to behold. What a companion across the ages. Not judging me. This whole but ephemeral piece of flesh that I am. Fragile. Locked in my own time, just as the broken statue was locked out of its own time, a recumbent, masculine sleeping beauty, never moving yet traveling to wherever the world saw fit to take him, lying in whatever country saw fit to draw a border around him, hoping for tolerance from the new landlords and the ones after that."

The boys stared at the flames for some time; they listened to their snap and crackle. Zoli had stopped coughing for the time being. After several minutes, Bela said, "I wonder about our relationship to goodness, whether we'll ever be able to strive for it again, or are we to leave the job of attaining to goodness—or evil for that matter—to those who hold the reins?"

"We shouldn't strive for anything. We shouldn't *over*-strive. We shouldn't overreach. Achievement is overrated," Zoli said. "Who needs it?" He chuckled weakly. "It leads to bad things."

Bela didn't respond. Instead, he said, "I sometimes have fantasies of returning to a cave, just like this one, where everything began. Or maybe things didn't begin here. Maybe this was the second thing. People were born out in the open and found shelter from the elements, from predators, in a cave. In many respects, life was so much simpler. You went out, got back to your cave to rest and eat, or you didn't. You survived, or you didn't."

"Just like now," said Zoli. "Just like us."

"Yes, just like us."

"Would you like to draw pictures on the walls of your cave?" Zoli asked.

"No, pictures are where the trouble begins," Bela said.

"Aren't you contradicting yourself? The kouros, the caryatids?"

"Yes, I guess I am. Survival. No survival. Extra bits complicate matters, but sometimes for the better."

"If you could live in a cave," Zoli said, "would you do it by yourself?" Bela didn't answer. "Would you take someone in with you?" Bela was staring straight at the hot fire. "Would you take Zsofia in with you?" But then Bela's eyes were closed, and Zoli decided not to disturb him. He draped one of the blankets over his brother's shoulders, then threw the trench coat over him too. Miraculously, Zoli was still not coughing.

When Zoli awoke, he found he wasn't trembling. He ran his hand up and down his throat in search of the cough. For a moment, he felt lightheaded; he felt almost hopeful, if not happy. He found the trench coat spread over him like a blanket. The fire had cooled. Bela was not there. At first he thought his brother might be outside rummaging for some firewood, but when he sat up a small scrap of paper fell to the stone floor of the cave. The writing was as tiny as could be.

My Dear Zoli,

I must go into Szifla to find Zsofia. I can't return home without seeing her. Please go ahead to Hajnal without me. I'll join you there in a couple of days, but if not I'll be home in Budapest in a week. I will be as careful as I can, and you should be too. Using the compass, you can find your way easily enough if you're strong. If you need to rest, I have left you all the supplies. Inject yourself with the last of the medicine first thing this morning. I felt your forehead before I left, and the fever seems to have lifted. You coughed only sporadically through the night. I cannot tell you how relieved I was. I dare say it might have been one of the best nights we've had in months. Freedom is its own medicine. Please do not think to follow me, I beg you. I will see you in a matter of days. Look after yourself.

Your loving brother—Bela

11

The happiest Ben had ever seen his father was the day he and his brothers surprised their parents with a fiftieth wedding anniversary party. They went all out. They booked a Hungarian restaurant downtown called Ye Olde Wooden Platter; they hired a Gypsy band, with its crying violins; and they invited their parents' oldest friends from the immigrant community, some forty people. The last part, inviting the friends, fell to Ben. He asked Lucy and their daughters to help, but they preferred to help with the other arrangements. They feared the old friends would need to break into Hungarian when they called, and that would be awkward. "In any case," Lucy said, "they want to speak to you. You're the one they watched growing up in the New World." Very lame, Ben thought.

The trickiest part in contacting his parents' friends was for Ben to get his hands on their address book. He would need it for a couple of days, so he waited until they took their week-long winter trip to Florida before going over to their place to borrow it. Ben was surprised by how hard it was to find, and he realized it was because his mother knew everyone's address and number by heart. His father didn't, but he rarely made any personal calls. If he had to, he just asked Hannah for the number. She had a gift. She remembered everything: people's numbers, people's birthdays, everyone's favorite meal, what size clothes and shoes they wore. If there was a book she'd borrowed or a spool of thread, she would bring it back without fail at the next visit. You'd never have to remind her. So Zoltan didn't have to remember anything, or chose not to.

Ben searched the most obvious hiding places for the address book, including the kitchen, where bills and recent letters were stored, the telephone table in the den, the filing cabinet in his father's study, and finally his parents' bedroom. There, in his mother's socks and stockings drawer, he came upon the old book with its familiar white cover featuring a geranium and a happy bee. But other documents and effects were hidden there too. Ben couldn't resist rummaging through them. He looked at expired passports, flipped through them to watch his parents age. He studied the date stamps from visits outside the country: mostly to Florida and New York, and two trips to Israel and one to Italy, but none to Hungary. His father had not wanted to return, though Hannah would have gone if he'd been game. There was an envelope of expired deposit slips, an odd place to keep them, since the financial files were kept downstairs in the filing cabinet. A couple of dozen of these slips had stamped and cancelled money orders attached to them. They were drawn on a Hungarian bank account and featured the signature of Szilvia Vukcsics. Ben could find no other notes, nothing to explain the deposit slips for certain, but all of them were for the same amount.

Ben had, of course, known that his parents were receiving reparation payments from Germany and Hungary for the people they had lost and for their own suffering. But why Szilvia Vukcsics? Who was Szilvia Vukcsics? What a name. He sat down on his parents' bed with the envelope. It was then he remembered the mysterious card at the Zoltan Beck Trading Company. He stood up again to search through the stockings drawer, but the card wasn't there. He hunted through his father's tallboy, every drawer, every corner. "SV," it had been signed. He remembered clearly. Szilvia Vukcsics. Plus a lock of golden hair belonging to a girl—"*our* girl."

Pieces were missing, and now Ben was intent on finding them. Surely his mother must have known something, but perhaps it was one of those things you knew but did not know—because if you didn't want to know something badly enough, you didn't.

Ben searched all the other drawers in his parents' dressers. He felt right to the back of each one, underneath bathing suits and underwear and pajamas. He went to the closet, where he knew his mother had stashed a box of old photos, and there was the familiar pale blue carton, paler even than he remembered. Inside were the photos of Frank and Ben as little boys on the streets of Budapest, with their grandmother, then with their grandmother and Great-Aunt Nora. A splendid family photo taken in the thirties at Hajnal included Ben's great-grandparents, their thirteen children, and their children's children, among them Ben's father and Bela. The two looked young and handsome—and confident, smug even—the whole world in front of them for the taking.

Ben set the box back where he'd found it. He rummaged through everything else, even feeling between the hanging garments, and was about to give up when he saw a solitary black shoe on the floor in the back. His mother was clean and neat, not obsessively so, but meticulous. She tidied things up daily, so how had an old shoe without its partner survived?

Ben had to get down on his knees to retrieve the shoe. He saw the contents immediately, though they had been folded and tucked well inside. There was the card addressed to the Zoltan Beck Trading Company with the lock of hair inside it. So his mother did know. She knew something.

But what? Had she asked her husband? How broad a sweep did her moral compass have? Broader than the planet probably. As vast as history, and history was vaster than the planet—darker, more glutinous, plumper—as big as Jupiter and with as many moons. At one point of this compass was the murder of your parents and six siblings merely because of the accident of their birth. On the other was the New World, where you sat in the comfort of your central heating and watched television and dropped off blankets and sleeping bags for the homeless. And somewhere in the middle, buried, but not deep, was Szilvia Vukcsics and the lock of hair. What did it matter? As always, Zoltan came back to Hannah.

But something else was in the shoe: a tiny notebook, small enough to hide in the palm of a child's hand, crudely bound, the pages browning. Ben sat down on the bed again to open the morsel. His hands were shaking. The handwriting inside was as tiny as it could be, and it was in Hungarian. On the first page was what looked like a poem. It was called "Zsofia."

Ben took the lock of hair from the card, placed it gingerly inside the little notebook, slipped these into his breast pocket, replaced the card in the shoe, replaced the shoe inside the closet, and made off with his treasures, along with his parents' address book.

Ben made the first call to Magda Nemet. "Vat do you know— Ben, Ben, Ben." Magda quickly informed Ben that she'd just had her hip replaced. She had taken a fall, and she now had nuts and bolts installed in her, like a car or a washing machine. She told Ben it was her third hip replacement. He made a mental note to check how many hips people had. Magda said she would be happy to attend the surprise party, but obviously she could not be expected to dance.

"How could I dance with all these nuts and bolts?" she said. Ben tried to imagine it. Certainly washing machines did a lot of churning with all their nuts and bolts, not to mention cars.

She then said, "Between Auschwitz and my hip replacement, I've done my share of dancing." What a statement. She was fourteen when, in 1944, she and her family had been taken from their home in Szeged, and she was the only one who'd made it back. She couldn't find a single relative left in Szeged. She visited the houses of her cousins, even distant cousins, and every one was occupied by a Hungarian family who acted as if nothing of consequence had happened. In her own home, her family's gardener and the housekeeper had settled in with their three kids. When he opened the door, Peter, the gardener, was wearing a burgundy cardigan that had belonged to Magda's father. It had been knitted by Magda's grandmother. Peter told Magda gently that she couldn't really live there anymore, but then his wife, Bea, invited her in for a meal. The young children stared at her while she sucked out the marrow of a beef bone then gnawed through a hard crust of bread. Magda stared back. What a sight she must have been. She must have looked crazed. She was wearing a clean khaki ensemble the Americans who had liberated the camp had given her. She had trouble filling it out. She had started her period early, Magda told Ben for some reason, but had not had a period in six months.

In the china cabinet, the familiar Zsolnay dishes were still arranged as Magda's mother had arranged them, but the great silver platter and menorah and tea set were gone. Had they sold these pieces, hidden them away, buried them in the garden? She didn't care, Magda wanted to tell them. "I'm a ghost," she wanted to say, "here today only to spook you." She looked again at the children, though, and decided simply to leave and leave quickly.

As she stepped outside her house for the last time and gazed up and down Alma Street, the street of her childhood, looked up at the elm in the front yard standing guard over it, she took a deep breath. She could feel the eyes behind her, watching from the window.

Where to? What now?

If she hadn't been asking herself those questions at that very moment, with her back to the house, which she had resolved never to look at again, she would not have seen the boy who would help determine her path for the rest of her life. He was standing outside *his* house in almost exactly the same way, except the tree standing guard over his house was a walnut tree. When Magda was to tell this story for decades to come, she always asked the listener—asked Ben—was it fate, was it chance, was it an accident that she spotted the only other returnee of that day, spotted Tibor, two years her senior, two years ahead of her in school, the same school she attended, and in her brother's class—her *late* brother's class. He was her *late* brother Andras's friend, in fact, who had come to break Sabbath bread with her family more than once. Tibor. Tibi. Tibi Deutsch. Though of course that last name had to go, had at the very least to be translated. Nemet. Hungarian for *Deutsch*.

"Oh, well," Ben said. He didn't know what else to say. He'd made this call from the kitchen and was staring out the back window at the garden, the red maple tree that stood guard over his daughters' childhood. "Too bad about the dancing," Ben said. "We're having Gypsy violins."

"Achh," she said. "Talk about bad luck. The Gypsies had nothing to return to, whichever ones made it back. No homes, just streets. Mean streets. No one tells that story."

"Well, they have their violins, I guess."

"Achh," she said again. "We have violins too, but we have more than violins. We also have our voices. And we have big mouths. We talk and talk until people fake deafness to shut us up."

Ben was still staring at the maple. "Oh, well."

He repeated the details of the party so Magda could write them down. It took a while. "Ye Olde—"

"What do you mean *Ye?*" It was bad enough she had to learn English. All Magda needed was *Ye.* "Vat do you mean *Ye?*"

"Y-e. It's an old-fashioned word."

"Y-e," she repeated.

Ben kept staring at the maple tree, imagining its cousins, the walnut tree and the elm. He imagined that they were not impressed by the abracadabra of it all. As long as the sky stayed up and the ground stayed down, they kept mostly to themselves. When the end of the world came, they'd go down with humanity but without flinching or singing dirges. They'd just turn into carbon like the rest of life, all flora and fauna lying still and equal, until the next goons came along to convert them into fuel.

When Magda finally got down the instructions, she said, "Do you know what else?" ("Vat else.") Ben waited. "My Tibi and I found a place in a barn that night with some good-looking dairy cows, and he said right then—I was all of fifteen; he was all of seventeen—he said we should stick together. You had to be there, Benny. There was a warmth there, among the cows. You could smell the milk—and you could smell the dung!" She laughed. "The smell of life, the cycle of life. Tibi took my hand in the darkness, and he said—I'll never forget it—he said, 'We can be angry at the families living in our houses. We have lost a lot of people, and we have a right to be angry at our tormentors. We can be angry at the people who died, the people who meant so much to us, for leaving us here to live. Or even worse: we can be angry at ourselves for not going down with them.' Ben, he was looking at me in the darkness. I could see a bit of moonlight in my Tibi's eyes. He said, 'Or we can put aside our anger.'" She paused here. "He said there was a time when being indoors, that was a concept." Magda chuckled. She said, "Benny, my grandmother's family never wanted to get sun, because it meant they worked outdoors. You should see the old pictures: all these pale women, all dressed up." Another chuckle. "Tibi said we can get out of this place with our things or we can get out with ourselves, probably not both." Now she laughed a throaty, smoky laugh. "So we never looked back. Not entirely, never absolutely, of course, but looking back never helped anything. Think of everything that was behind us. Think of everything that was ahead of us. Better to stay just where you were: in the moment."

Ben could see why his parents were so fond of Tibi and Magda. His father had come from an exalted position and knew there was nothing in particular to recommend it. A chauffeur drove him to school each morning with his brother, and a maid washed his back in the bathtub (until he was older than he ought to have been).

The Becks had left an empire behind in Hungary, and Ben's parents really didn't care, especially his father. What the Nazis didn't confiscate from their family, the Russians did. After the Iron Curtain lifted, Hungarians tried to go back and get things or sue for bigger things—buildings, factories, land—but there was no one to take the big things back from and no one to sue.

His father's paternal grandfather held property all over Hungary. Some ten thousand people worked for him. And he had Hajnal, the famous summer house where all the grandchildren, including his father, leapt and frolicked. The house was all white and grand. You could hide out in a hundred different nooks. The grandchildren fought over the privilege of lighting the famous long meerschaum pipe, which had to have a stand to hold up the bowl. He had a butler who held all the keys and spent the day locking and unlocking sugar boxes, liquor cabinets and inner and outer doors.

And then there was the table in that summer house with the round raspberry-marble top onto which the Norwegian painter Edvard Munch had painted a crow sitting on a cemetery gate and crowing into the blue darkness over the gravestones. He'd acquired the treasure when the bohemian Japan Café in Budapest finally had to close its doors before the First World War. Famous artists passed through there—Picasso, Manet, Rousseau, Schiele—and of course their Hungarian counterparts—Rippl-Ronai, Szekely and Ivanyi-Grunwald. The custom had begun when a couple of poor artists couldn't pay their bill and the owner asked them to paint a tabletop instead. The owner cleverly preserved each work beneath glass. After his death, the sons auctioned off these tables, which was how Ben's family came to own one.

There was one other remarkable object in that house, something Ben's father told him about only once. Mary was Zoltan's favorite cousin and his great-grandfather's favorite grandchild, and his great-grandfather surprised her on her tenth birthday by unveiling a grand dollhouse, an exact replica of the house they were standing in, down to the smallest detail, including in the sitting room a mini-meerschaum pipe on a tiny stand, waiting to be lit. It even had a sprinkling of tobacco in its bowl.

Upstairs in the dollhouse, there was a bedroom like Mary's, with the same plump bed and walnut headboard and the same bedspread crocheted with a pattern of sunflowers.

Mary gazed at this miracle of a—what, a toy?—hardly a toy—a building in its own right, a house within a house. Zoltan was the only boy willing to play with Mary and her magnificent dollhouse; she needed a male voice to speak the grandfather's lines and ask for the pipe to be lit. But it was not so much the replica house Zoli was interested in, the perfection of it, the security of it. It was Mary. Zoli asked his mother secretly if first cousins could marry, and she said they could—they had in the past; two of her own sisters had done so; *she* had done so—but they shouldn't in this case. Times were different.

But that was all gone now. They were just objects. Not Mary, of course. Mary was gone too, it so happened, shot in the street in Budapest by an Arrow Cross guard (one of the fascist police sanctioned by Hitler), on her way to a private music lesson. She was found lying in the street with her sheet music fanned out like wings.

Ben's father insisted he had no interest in any of those things—the objects, that is; they were just objects—nor did he have an interest in trying to get to that place again in the New World. He used to say, "There is so much in the world, it's hard to know what portion of it is yours. But when I look back at all that my grandfather and father had, I knew it was too much. I wanted a house, a yard and a tree, a place I could go about my life in peace." He was beaming when he said it. "In fact, I *preferred* it. Palaces are a headache, believe me."

Frank didn't believe Zoltan. He approached his father to say he knew that his grandfather Vilmos, Zoltan's father, had important dealings with the Dunhill family. When he wasn't being a doctor or a government official, Vilmos was an inventor and had met the Dunhills more than once in Geneva in the thirties. He offered them his drawings for the innards of a butane lighter, and the enthusiastic Dunhills put a deposit down on the drawings. The Becks then never heard any more about it, and Vilmos died two years after the war.

Frank had seen the drawings as a schoolboy when the family was still in Hungary and had asked his grandmother Eugenia about them. She told him the story of the meeting with the Dunhills. The drawings had resurfaced when Hannah was cleaning out a cubbyhole in the basement of their North Toronto home, and Frank had asked if he could have them. Now he wanted to go after the Dunhills to claim the fortune that was owed to the family, but Zoltan told him to leave it alone. Frank insisted he wanted to do what was right. "Be my guest," said his father. Frank pulled papers out of his briefcase already drawn up to give him the authority on behalf of the family to get it done. Zoltan shook his head, sighed and signed.

Frank hired a high-priced law firm in London, showed them Vilmos's drawings, then a lighter manufactured throughout the fifties, which still bore many of the features evident in the drawings. Expert engineers confirmed that the similarities were remarkable. They took the Dunhills to court, and the Dunhills argued that the English factory where the lighter was to be manufactured based on Vilmos's drawings had been bombed during the Battle of Britain and no longer stood. They had later hired another inventor to come up with a design. Frank's lawyers fought for an appeal but failed.

Frank returned from England and wouldn't say a word about what had happened. When Hannah pressed him, he stormed out of the house. Zoltan smiled, a smile like a knife.

Ben's father wanted his family to enjoy what they had. They had come to a fresh new place. There was no reason to look outside of it, except to pity those who were not here with them.

Ben was flipping through magazines at his dentist's office one day when he came upon an article about the provenance of stolen art. The painting featured was a modern Hungarian masterpiece by Jozsef Rippl-Ronai called *Christmas, 1903*. It had hung in their living room in Budapest, and now it was hanging in Montreal's Museum of Modern Art. The Hungarian National Gallery in Budapest was demanding that its national treasure be repatriated.

Ben excitedly called his parents from the dentist's office and told them what he had found. His father said, "Leave it alone. What do you want it for? Can you prove it was ours? Do you not have enough here? You have a roof over your head. You have a beautiful wife and beautiful daughters. You have a good job. Lord knows, you eat enough. Look at you. What do you want it for?"

It wasn't even the money that Ben had craved. Though he was very young when they fled Hungary, he remembered a few objects from his first home. They visited him in dreams, had marked him in some way. He had stared at *Christmas, 1903* too often, trying to understand its mood and contrasting colors. It featured a Christmas tree in the background, which had been richly decorated, and two darkly painted women, both with their backs to the festive tree, one writing a note and the other looking out grimly at the viewer, wanting simply to get on with things, possibly. But why the darkness? A good day was coming. Family. Friends. Christmas. What could be better?

Then here again were the women with their tree, in Canada. They had followed the Becks like lost relatives.

Ben's parents had made it all by themselves in Canada, without an inheritance, and his father couldn't have been more pleased with their lot. He was never one of those parents who said he did it all for his children. On the contrary. He did it for himself, and they got to tag along.

So he settled. All the time. He accepted what was coming to him and wanted not a thing more. This TV is good enough. This job is good enough. This townhouse is good enough. This life is good enough. In fact, it is perfect because it is good enough.

That was why Zoltan would have been happy to see Sammy prescribe glasses in a mall rather than become an eye surgeon. "Success is overrated," he used to tell his boys. "I've been there. I'm on the rebound. Trust me."

Ben's next call was to Kulcsar, and it was blessedly short, which was why Ben had moved him up the list. Everyone called the man by his last name only, even his wife had. Ben wondered if his parents had called him Kulcsar too. Did they not give him a first name? Couldn't they think of one? Maybe they thought it hearkened back to biblical days, when people had only one name: Abraham, Moses, Solomon, Jesus, Kulcsar. Even on the gravestone it said just "Kulcsar." Beside his alloted space lay "Aniko Kulcsar." *Kulcsar* meant "key man"—"the man with the keys"—like the one Ben's great-grandfather had on his household staff to open the sugar boxes and liquor cabinets.

Aniko had been the first to go, and since she had died, Kulcsar had all but stopped talking, not that he was ever much of a talker. He was one of Zoltan's favorites from their first years in Toronto, largely because they could sit quietly while the women chatted. Often, when the Kulcsars visited, Ben's father would even read the paper through while Kulcsar watched him, and all seemed to be well. Once, Ben sat with his father and Kulcsar as they played chess, and after his father had made his move, Kulcsar studied the board for half an hour before he nodded off.

When Kulcsar did speak, he seemed to be talking to his own hands, and he always surprised people with what he was thinking about. His wife might have said, "The grapes are on special this week at Metro. Ninety-nine cents a pound." And he'd say to his sleeve, "They've unearthed a pair of wool pants which are three thousand years old. It was in the Euphrates River valley." And now to the other sleeve, "Wool is like hair. It never disintegrates. That's a good pair of pants. Durable."

When Ben called Kulcsar on this occasion, the man answered the phone with "Hello," but then he just waited for Ben to say things. Ben told him about the party (tried to imagine Kulcsar shouting "Surprise!" to his hand) and gave him the time and location. Ben pictured him, an unmoving passport photo, until he heard the scratching of a pencil, and then, "Thank you," or rather "Tenk you," before he hung up.

Next came Iris Danzinger and her fourth husband, Albert Kratz, the radiologist. He was ten years her junior. They were one of the most popular couples in the Hungarian community. She was still a ravishing beauty in her seventies, not a strand of gray skulking in the rich black soufflé of hair whipped high on her head. Even as a ten-year-old—especially as a ten-year-old—Ben found himself staring at Iris. It seemed to him that some people were so radiant they were designed to be shared like a sculpture, like a Venus or David. The only difference was that Iris Danzinger must have known, must have felt the eyes roaming over her, must still have felt them. Iris was also the best bridge player in the city, possibly the country, so people—mostly men—mobbed around her to watch her game and watch the shiftings of her cleavage as she played a card. It was at the St. Clair Bridge Club that Iris Danzinger threw off her third husband, the real estate magnate Robert Brodie, in favor of the somewhat better player, Albert, with the shrewd smile, broad shoulders and extra-white teeth.

Iris liked Ben's parents, Hannah especially, because Hannah would sit holding Iris's hand during rough patches in Iris's marriages. But Iris never cried, his mother used to say, not a single tear. It seemed only his mother could detect the subtle ebbing and flowing of emotions at good times and bad, hardly discernible to groping eyes. Still, it seemed odd that she should have chosen his mother to listen. Hannah showed her emotions all the time, whereas Iris had a subdued radiance, like winter light.

Ben walked in on them once, speaking softly in their den, as his mother served Iris tea and a sumptuous walnut cake she often baked. Iris glanced at Ben but entirely without embarrassment. Still, there was a dark, unseen force in the room. Iris always looked that way: like someone walking around with a secret, though she was the person least likely to have one.

Iris had no children of her own, as if to assert that she was the end of the line, that it had culminated with her. But she did have a nephew, Reuben, her sister's son, with the same raven hair as his aunt. Iris used to pet him at social gatherings, fawn over him, as he grinned and purred. When they were teenagers, Frank and Ben, and even Sammy later, used to run into him at Hollywood Lodge, up at Lake Simcoe, where Hungarians from Bathurst and Bloor used to flock every summer weekend. One year, Reuben beat Frank in chess in a best of seven matchup, then a best of ten, then best of twenty, though in fact, in the best of twenty, Reuben beat Frank eleven times out of twelve, at which point Frank brought his fist down hard onto the board, sending the wooden pieces flying all over the grass and a rook and bishop into the lake. Nobody retrieved the pieces. Reuben and Frank eyed each other almost to the death and then marched off in opposite directions.

Reuben stopped his aunt just outside the lodge, and they all watched her caressing his neck and smoothing back his raven hair as he spoke. She glared over her shoulder at the boys, then into Reuben's eyes. She kissed him softly on the lips, then his naked shoulder, sending a shiver over the entire grounds.

Ben had only an office number for Albert, and his receptionist took the message. She told him the doctor would call back only if they were not attending the party. She then asked, "Might Ms. Danzinger's nephew be invited to attend as well?" And Ben answered no, foolishly adding "Adults only," though Reuben would have been as old as Ben was by then. (In fact, he was Canada's top bridge player, though not quite as many people crowded around him to watch him play.) If Ben had said yes, Frank would have murdered him and possibly even one or both of his children.

As for Hollywood Lodge, Ben now called Klari and Janos Weisz, the longtime owners of the lodge, now retired. Ben couldn't imagine what this couple had been thinking when they took over the old place two hours north of Toronto and renovated it. The Weiszes were no more suited to being innkeepers than they were to being circus acrobats. That wasn't quite right; they did know how to cook and clean and keep books. But they could not have disliked and discouraged their patrons any more than they did. The boys would slip into the kitchen where Janos was cooking and meekly ask for the Ping-Pong paddles and balls, and Janos would hold up his hand to throttle them. If they lingered, he'd chase them out wielding a meat cleaver. Then he'd return to cooking his tremendous wiener schnitzels, which the Hungarians called *becsi szelet*, and cabbage rolls. If you asked Klari or Janos to bring fresh towels, they'd tell you to go get them yourself.

When you walked by Klari or Janos, you said hello, hoping to please them, but they would never answer. The geniuses of the business world could have written books about them— *How NOT to Run a Business, NOT EVER.* Yet the Weiszes never lost a customer, not a one, in all those years the Beck boys were growing up.

They loved Hollywood Lodge. As children, they swam and frolicked and burned in the sun. They played pinball at the nearby general store in Island Grove, or bought ice cream cones there and flirted by flexing their arm muscles extra hard when they raised the cones to their mouths. The adults bathed rather than swam, smoked and played card games at tables set out all over the lawn in the summer breezes, the tablecloths held down by stones provided by Ben, the King of Stones (only the flattest and smoothest, whitest and blackest to be used for this purpose). They played bridge and rummy and the Austrian game skat, with its colorful playing cards depicting the seasons.

It was all clear and blue and fresh at Hollywood Lodge, far from the smoky wars of Europe. What glorious, endless days they had in that place, when they were new to this country and still immortal.

But now the Weiszes kept mostly to themselves. They were still invited to the momentous occasions in the community, though Janos had been suffering from dementia for a while. When Klari answered the phone, she was refreshingly rude as always. "What?" she said. Not hello. Not how are you. No niceties.

And in the background Ben could hear Janos squawking and cawing like a caged tropical bird. Somehow it seemed fitting, but still—what a thing.

Ben told Klari about the party as unenthusiastically as he could and then waited. "*Caw, caw, caw,*" sounded in the background with uncanny regularity.

Klari said they would accept the invitation, though probably only she would show up.

"Of course," Ben said.

"By the way," she added, "I have some nice stones from Hollywood Lodge which I've been saving for you all these years. Just a few, really, but nice."

Ben was so choked up he didn't know what to say. She might as well have said she was holding gold ingots for him.

"Thank you," was all he said.

"Bye," she said, and hung up.

Ben called the Freudenbergers, Erzsebet and Elemer. She told him straight off the top that they wanted to remove her foot. It was the diabetes. She told the doctors, "I came in with two feet; I'm going out with two feet." The doctors said she'd be going out in a hurry, then.

All Ben could think of was that she'd be taking that terrific name with her. Erzsebet Freudenberger.

"Erzsi" had been a successful hairdresser in a busy part of town, Wellesley and Jarvis. Elemer was a travel agent, specializing in Eastern Europe and the Middle East. Erzsi owned her own shop, badly named Added Beauty. Ben guessed, if you did the math, you were going in to Subtract Ugliness.

He took his mother there several times if he had to be downtown, then would stop in to pick her up on his way back.

The place never ceased to amaze him. A theme was to
encase movement in the hair, so that some ended up with
hairdos like black waves on a rippling lake. Some had back-
swept golden tresses, as if they were speeding along in a convertible. One looked as if a raven had landed on her head and
squatted there, its wings outstretched. One was holy; she had
a burning bush mounted on her skull with a fire that burned
but did not consume. One looked a bit like an antelope,
not that there was anything wrong with that. She sleeked in
anxiously, fidgetingly accepted an antelope cut, then, looking both ways, sleeked out again into the wide world. One
looked as if she had silver herring tidbits vacuum-packed
against her skull. One went in for the tiger effect but came
out looking more like a muskrat. One had her hair done like
a shiny black umbrella then stiffened and sprayed to repel
rain. One had macaronic hair, little yellowish noodles hud-
dling close to her scalp. One had writhing sideburns, like
Heckle and Jeckle. One had thick, rich theater curtains,
parted slightly in the front. Some looked like triangles—isos-
celes for those with thin faces, equilateral for those with wide
ones, scalene for those who wanted to add a jaunt to their
triangle—and for those who wanted a bit of everything there
were trapezoids.

Then there was Hannah, who went to Erzsi for a little
cut, wash and blow-dry but no styling to speak of. Her hair

was thick and wavy and seemed, for the most part, to look after itself. Ben didn't even know why his mother felt she had to go to Erzsi at all. Maybe it was just to support her.

Ben gave Erzsebet the instructions for the party, resulting in long pauses. "Goodness, fifty years," she said at one point. Then, "Oh, well, Elemer and I have been at it for fifty-two years."

Ben asked if she'd got the information down all right.

"What do you mean? Of course. Why wouldn't I?" He didn't know what to say. "I wouldn't always have," she said, and chuckled. "At the beginning, I did not speak English. When we all came here. Not a word. Elemer too. Your parents too. Not a word. It was the time between languages. I remember having this fear: What if I forgot Hungarian? I would be mute."

Ben called Zsigmund Orszag, who wanted to know if Ben's brother Sammy could check out his left eye. Ben told him he would ask, but if his brother couldn't, he would be glad to have a look. Zsigmund said that the last time he was in the clinic he told Sammy he saw fireflies in his eyes at night and it was like they lived there. Sammy gave the man some drops for dry eyes.

Ben called Jack and Mary Balaban. Jack's story had been featured in a *Toronto Star* article. Using cement nails and bits of rope he'd found and then hidden near the scrap metal yard in Dachau, Jack had fashioned a menorah, which had survived with him, and which his family still used every Hanukkah.

Ben called Cica, whose name meant "kitty" for no reason he could understand. She would be away that day, unfortunately. But that didn't stop her from asking Ben about everyone and then not letting him say a word after "Fine."

"I was fine too," she said, "as you can well imagine. Until the blood cancer took my Bert in three days. He had a fever on a Friday, took a Tylenol, then a second, extra strength, and when the fever got worse we went to the hospital. He never left. Poof, he was gone. Three days to go down, after seventy-four years. After surviving the Third Reich, after surviving Eichmann, after surviving a labor camp, walking home from Transylvania—try to take that walk now, when you're healthy, let alone in his state—after having his head knocked in by a liberating Russian. He danced around the tank which was liberating us from the Nazis, and the Russian kicked him in the head, knocking him out cold. It was lucky the tank didn't drive over him. He wouldn't have been the first. Then we escape, we come here, have a life, have a child, and poof, a fever, followed by death. You were there, you know. At the funeral. Your parents were there. Fifty years, goodness. Bert and I had forty-nine. Didn't make it to fifty. He couldn't sprint one last time over the finish line. A man who had trudged all the way back from Transylvania from a labor camp with a salt cracker in his stomach, nothing more. We went back to Transylvania—very nice, the Carpathian Mountains—just to see, Bert and I, and our son, George, you know, and his wife, Sally. She's a pharmacist, if you can call the place she works a pharmacy. Why not work at Shoppers Drug Mart or Rexall? Why try to do it all yourself? And then what? Then she dumps George—for what? For an old lawyer with a bad leg, coming in to get a prescription, some kind of cream for his leg—what do I know? For him, she dumps my George, my only son, but he got the last laugh—that's for sure—he got the young beauty Rebecca from City Hall, in the accounting office, where, you know, George is head accountant, and they had the two little beauties, Welland and Rideau, whatever kind of godforsaken names those are—just because her grandfather helped build the Welland and Rideau Canals—an engineer, one of the best, tall and handsome, the way she's tall and beautiful—I think you've met her—why he, the tall engineer, couldn't have helped build the Adam Beck Power Station rather than the Welland and Rideau Canals, and then they could have had decent names, like yours: Beck? And what's wrong with Adam?"

"Well, then," Ben said abruptly.

"Oh," she said.

Cica held the world and Olympic records for most words spoken in an hour. If she'd been married to Kulcsar, who said nothing, the two of them combined would still have made it to the Olympic podium, even if only with a silver.

Cica lowered her voice. "So there you have it." Ben could hardly hear her. "Now there's just me. All by myself. Boo hoo." She was mocking herself, and with her Hungarian accent "boo hoo" sounded like *buhu*, some kind of spa treatment. "That's just me," she said again. "I leave a little of my mind on the pillow each night."

And so the day wore on, the whole of a Sunday morning and into the afternoon. Ben's work was done. The maple stood in the backyard. The fluorescent bulb above the sink sputtered. Ben should have felt relieved, but a great sadness set in that he could not account for, as if he'd taken some sort of grim roll call. But why grim? These were survivors, and he was calling with news of a happy occasion. In the end, the calls loomed larger in his memory than the party that followed them, larger than the presence of these old friends. Even though Ben often asked himself later if it wouldn't have been simpler to send out invitation cards, he never tired of listening to his parents' friends as they tried on English sounds like ill-fitting clothing.

The evening of his parents' fiftieth anniversary party, the Gypsy band—or Romany band, as they were more rightly called—played all of Hannah and Zoltan's favorites, mostly Hungarian music with a Romany flair—crying violins, honeyed sadness, songs that seemed to come from a dark time no one would ever want to revisit. But actually, the tunes often felt like songs about what could have been rather than what was. Hannah and Zoltan both sang along loudly to "Jaj, cica eszem azt a csöpp kis szád" and "Jóska, Jóska, veled mennyi baj van," as did others in the room. The band threw in "Hava nagila" to indicate that they got it and had business cards available on top of the keyboard.

But when the violinist opened *Zigeunerweisen*, by Sarasate, Ben's father stood up and put his hand on his heart as if for an anthem or a hymn. How could he not be stirred? How could they not be stirred? But by what? By country? By Canada? By Hungary? By marriage? By survival? By the home that was lost and the home that was found? The lives that were lost and the lives found? Or was it the sound of anticipation? It was not their sound, yet it was. It was a Romany sound that they had adopted on account of its beauty? Beauty above all. Beauty as truth. *That is all ye know on earth and all ye need to know.*

Hannah was glowing. She was pleased at how pleased her husband was, as if she herself had put him in this state, which she spent her whole life trying to do, or at least fifty years of it.

But others were glowing too. Lucy was, as were Anna and Leah. Iris Danzinger was. She looked regal and radiant as ever, and she had showed up with Reuben after all, because Albert had been called away. Iris, the queen, sat with her nephew, the prince, who spread his long arms over the backs of the two chairs on either side of him, one of them Queen Iris's. Ben overheard Erzsebet tell people about her two happy feet, both of which she was taking to the grave. Magda, her unhappy hips. The Balabans, their famous menorah.

And they feasted on—what else?—Transylvanian wooden platters piled high with schnitzels, Debrecen sausages, cabbage rolls, grilled lamb chops (or "lamp chops," as they were described in the menu), breaded mushrooms, breaded liver, dumplings, slaws, cucumber salad and beets. All of this was followed by plum dumplings blizzarded with ground walnuts and icing sugar, with espresso coffee and pear and plum *palinka*.

There was much cause to rejoice for one another, not just the happy couple. Their photographer got them all in a group shot, the old gang and the new. Everyone in the room said they wanted a copy sent to them.

And then Zoltan rose to make a speech. He said he was very happy to be there. He reached to take his wife's hand. He said he'd had a good life. "It was a good place to come to. The best, actually. Wasn't it, Hannah?" He looked around the room and said, "It's nice to learn, after all these years, that people don't change that much. If anything, they are just more of what they already were." He chuckled. "Look at us," he said. "We spend the first half of our lives indulging ourselves, those of us who are lucky"—he patted himself on the stomach—"and then we spend the second half of our lives depriving ourselves, saving ourselves for just such occasions, these few landmarks." He smiled to the left and to the right. "I would go even further than that," he added. "Young people think they will live forever—why shouldn't they?" He looked at his grandchildren. "It takes some years to be disabused of this notion. We immigrants never had this idea, or not for long. We came from an unsafe place. You don't get to feel immortal for long if you are hiding out somewhere for fear of your life. And we are the *lucky* ones, the ones who escaped capture and deportation and death." Now the room was quiet.

"Anyway, this is not the time for such thoughts. They can wait to come around again tomorrow." Still silence. The violinist was looking at his feet. One foot moved from side to side. Ben wondered what tune was going through his head.

Then Zoltan added one last kicker. "Frank and Sammy," he said, almost too quietly, "what time you must have taken out of your professional lives to organize such a party and feast. Thank you. Thank you all." He took his seat. People seemed to want to clap, so they did, sporadically.

Lucy gave Ben a look. *What?* Their daughters were outraged. Anna was getting to her feet, but he pulled her down again.

It was an extraordinary thing. Ben had never met a person less interested in being loved or admired than his father. He discouraged even those who did love and admire him. Ben was certain he did love him, as well as he could.

His mother was the one who showed most of the affection, and there was enough there for a truckload of children and husbands. It was better to be third in her affections than first in his. And Ben was third. But it was more than enough. The gas station attendant his mother smiled at felt more affection than Ben's father was able to show.

His mother made her sons feel happy to be alive. She addressed each of them, her boys, not by their names but as Susser Tzadik, "Righteous One." There were only thirty-six Tzadiks on the planet, but their presence meant the world could not be destroyed. So the boys were three of thirty-six. Imagine the odds.

She sat now before this gathering beside her husband after having spent fifty years at his side. Her glow lightened the shadows cast by Zoltan. She didn't make a speech, but really no one expected her to.

Anna and Leah did have a word with their grandfather. They were whispering, but the whispers had audible barks in them. Zoltan was looking at Ben the whole time. And then he came over with Ben's daughters. He put a hand on his son's shoulder, a bold act of intimacy for him. He said, "That's the trouble. The trouble started when we took it upon ourselves to name things: Sammy, Ben, America. Bolivia. Fiftieth. Twentieth. First son. Nineteenth century. Citizens. Refugees. It's all bad. It's drawing a line around things. Here, the nineteenth century began. Here is where Bolivia ends. It leads to bad things. I humbly apologize, Benny. I do." And then he gently slapped the side of his son's neck.

As the dishes were being cleared, the music revved up again and the dancing began. Most people danced a little, some a lot. Ben was happy to see the Balabans and the Nemets up on their feet, showing off the benefits of some dance lessons they'd taken, as well as Magda with her hips and Erzsi with both her feet. Ben danced energetically with Lucy, and they both danced with their daughters, Anna initiating a mini-hora, which caught on around the room. Frank and Sammy danced too with their wives and children and Ben's wife and children, Frank dazzling everyone with his best moves, as if he were a disco star making an entrance.

And of course Hannah and Zoltan danced to "The Anniversary Song," and Zoltan sang along as they danced.

So that's how it went. If this had been the last evening in Pompeii, when the hot murk flowed over the party, the revelers would have been encased in glee—many of them—most of them.

12

Zoli was frantic that morning in that cave in Transylvania. He didn't know what to do. Using the compass Bela had left, he turned toward Kiskunhalas, then toward Szifla.

What was Bela thinking? Was he thinking that he'd show up at the colonel's house and be asked in for tea? If anyone on the planet was to be invited in for tea, it would be Bela, but he inspired as much hostility in people now as he did admiration. He was someone whose life some people wanted to snuff out.

Zoli gave himself an injection of penicillin and shuddered. He righted himself with his clothing and belongings and shuddered again.

As he began to walk toward Hajnal, he told himself again that it was no longer his grandfather's place. Was their house in Budapest his parents' home still? He and Bela had not had a letter from home for over two months, and even that one read as if an officer of some stripe were holding a gun to their parents' heads. It was newsy, of all things. The neighbor's dog barks all day. There is too little flour to be had. Stupid. Absurd.

Zoli felt certain now that history had dropped him off in the wrong place, that there was no right place for his feet to carry him, that history would be more content to dispense with him.

It had been so much better with his brother. Who better to believe in than Bela? And where was he now? On an errand only he could pull off. Maybe. Could he charm the invading hordes? Only one at a time. The simple fact of him, of who he was, was enough to dispense with him in an instant. But Bela had his way.

Every now and then, Zoli paused and leaned against a tree or sat on a rock to catch his breath. But rather than resting, he would cry instead, wail, in fact. He threw up what little breakfast of tomatoes he had consumed. He wanted his mother, wanted to tell her what they had been through, wanted more, anything but this, trudging through a nightmare to freedom. This was not freedom, running from trap to trap. Did Bela truly think they'd found freedom? What Zoli was doing was trudging from a nightmare to a daymare. And even if freedom were to be his destiny, what good was it going to be when you had to drag memory along with it, and into it?

But his cough was gone. He paused to take account of it. Mysteriously, it had lifted from him like a heavy soul fled to inhabit someone else's chest, weigh down someone else's heart, poor unwitting sap—someone who might have medicine nearby, or more likely not.

Zoli made it to a hardened dirt road and was relieved to be heading somewhere, heading in one direction. He paused to open the last of his tins of food and to eat it with the understanding that it was his last. He walked along this route for the rest of the day, then found a sheltered, half-hidden spot just off the road, where he made a nest for himself and could settle for the night. After warming himself with a little fire, warming some snow in the empty tomato tin and drinking it as if it were the finest of black teas, he fell asleep in that nest as deeply as he might have at home. In fact, he felt he was home, was surprised to find, when he woke up, that he wasn't, that he was cold and needed to get moving. He felt strong, or at least stronger than the day before, stronger than he'd felt in a couple of weeks. Using his compass, he turned to look toward Szifla, as if he were turning toward Jerusalem, to pray in that direction, to cast his hopes that way.

But then he looked the other way and moved on. It was a blessedly sunny day, a little warmer than the day before. He walked for several hours, until the sun was high above his head, a winter sun bright and warming.

In the afternoon, Zoli heard wheels on the road. He ducked into some bushes. It was a farmer in a wagon ricketing toward him. Zoli's head spun. Should he stay hidden, take a chance and reveal himself, overtake him, overwhelm him and take his horse and wagon, take his clothing and whatever he was hauling? What would Bela do?

The man saw him rustling in the bushes and called out to him. Zoli emerged and told the man the Russians were coming. The man told him to hop aboard. He was older, or maybe he wasn't; maybe the sun and outdoors had aged him beyond his years. The man didn't ask Zoli any questions. All he said was, "You look like you could use a bite. I have cheese in the back. I'm selling it at the market."

"The market? I have no money."

"I don't want your money."

He stopped the horse, reached into the back under some blankets and pulled out a good-sized yellow cheese, aromatic even in the winter air, and offered it to Zoli. "I also have a bit of walnut cake my wife baked," the man said. "Let's share it." He opened a tea cloth with a generous piece of cake in it. Still warm! What glorious, fragrant oven had it come from? "Go ahead," the man said. He broke off a piece of the cake and held it in front of Zoli in his gnarled brown hand.

All Zoli could think was, What if the man found out? What if he found out who Zoli was? But the man didn't ask a thing, didn't want to know a thing. Zoli ate the cake quickly, greedily, felt its warm goodness flowing through him. The man offered him a cup of lemon tea sweetened with honey, still hot, from a bottle stashed on the other side of him. He even had a tin cup with him which he hadn't yet used. Zoli gulped down the drink, so soothing on his throat. He wished he could tell this good man about Bela, about their ordeal, but he just said again, "The Russians are coming through here."

"They've been," the man said. "A week ago. The Germans were here, then the Russians were here. The Germans burned down a covered bridge just the other side of that gully there." He pointed to the place. Zoli looked, out of politeness mostly. "They stole a stock of my winter cheese, but these here I had hidden under the floor in the barn. I thought someone was going to burn down my house, a German or a Russian, but they didn't. I have a lame little girl, and when she looks at someone directly, they usually leave us alone. She has a clear-eyed look," the man said, and it was only then that Zoli saw how clear-eyed the man's look was too, a blazing blue he hadn't expected, lit from behind.

Zoli ate the entire cheese the man had given him and then drifted off to sleep, the lined trench coat pulled securely around him. He woke to find that it was evening. How many hours had he slept? He had a wool blanket covering him, and he was taking up most of the wagon's bench. Zoli told the man it would be better if he got off. He didn't want to go any further into town. The man didn't argue with him but said he could come back eventually to the farm and stay with his family. But Zoli was already dismounting. He thanked the man profusely, even asked if he could have his name and address to send him something if ever he made it home.

"That won't be necessary," the man said, and he wished Zoli luck before he drove off.

Zoli didn't know what to expect in the town. He felt it best to circle around it, give it a wide berth and try to rejoin the same road on the other side. He checked his compass again and felt confident about where he might have landed.

He made a clumsy trek through brittle scrubland and hard snow, and when full darkness fell, a sharp wind blew up. He was very cold and tired again. He breathed in the hard cubes of winter air, felt them rattling through his lungs. He could not get his strength back. He wanted to find somewhere to rest. He was wondering now if he'd even come the right way. In the darkness up ahead, he saw what looked like a distant single light burning in a large stone farmhouse and looming up behind it an even greater structure. Straight ahead he was relieved to see a barn. He was worried that his cough would return, so he got as far as the barn when he decided he'd rather take a chance with the animals than with the humans.

The barn was a good-sized one, and solid enough to keep the wind out. What a difference it made when he could pull the wooden door shut. He heard shuffling and a single moo. He groped around for some time, bumping into things, kicking over a water pail before lighting a match to discover he'd made his way into an empty stall with plenty of hay on the floor to nestle into. Crows cawed outside the window, their black selves cut out of the white winter but now blending with the darkness. Their defiance reassured him, made him feel secure, as if the birds were standing guard for him against the elements.

He laid out his two blankets and burrowed into the hay, covering himself finally with the trench coat lined with wool. He fell asleep in minutes and slept for hours. It was the sleep of death, as it had been the night before, and just as Bela floated up in front of him, hovering at the roof of the cave over him, Zoli felt a sharp kick, followed by cackling. He thought it might be the crows, grown preternaturally powerful. Then came another kick. He opened his eyes and shot to his feet. Two children, a boy and a girl, neither more than eight or nine years old, laughed uncontrollably. The girl was holding a shovel, and Zoli thought she would strike him with it.

"You're a vagrant," she said. "A vagabond. I'm calling my daddy."

"Don't call your daddy, please," Zoli said. He moved toward the door.

But she had begun. She screamed for her father as Zoli opened the latch. "Please," he said. "Shush."

But the boy howled this time, and the girl cackled. What a pair they were, with a single-mindedness that made them scarier than adults.

"What's going on?" It was a man's voice. He pulled open the door. "Who are you?"

Zoli stepped outside, and there, over the man's shoulder, gleaming in the winter sun, was Hajnal, his grandfather's summer house! Was he en route to heaven? "Where am I?" he asked. He thought he might still be asleep.

"Kiskunhalas," the man said, a little taken aback. "Outside Kiskunhalas."

"Yes, of course I am," Zoli said. Fate was indifferent, it seemed, a joker at best, with Hernyo at one end and Hajnal at the other. Bela had steered him exactly right. Zoli had returned to a place that had been destined to exist in memory alone. The children were tittering. Zoli turned to them. "I was your age when I summered here. I played in this very barn with my cousins and brother."

"Master Beck," the man said. Zoli recognized him too just then. Istvan. A lead hand at the house. Only a dozen or so years older than Zoli. The father of these children. And still here. He lived in the farmhouse by the gate, the guardhouse.

"Please call me Zoli."

"How is everyone?" the man asked, as he looked Zoli up and down. "Your family?" He said it almost too quietly, hesitantly.

It was only then that the months of what Zoli and Bela had endured rose up in his mind. He began to sob in front of Istvan and the children, and now the children were quiet. The girl put her hand to her mouth. The boy watched his smoky breath but then held it in.

"Please come inside, Master Zoltan." He took the liberty of putting his arm around his guest's shoulders but only to urge him toward the big house.

"This is not our house any longer," Zoli said. "It was taken—"

"Please," said Istvan. "My wife, Ildi, is inside. She'll be happy and honored to see you."

Istvan and the children escorted their visitor to the house. They steered him toward the front door, but he wanted to enter at the side instead, through the kitchen. Ildi recognized him immediately and gasped, though the last time she'd seen him was almost a decade before, when Zoli was twelve. She'd been rolling out dough with a younger girl, and the two stopped what they were doing and curtseyed in their cloud of flour.

Zoli greeted them and smiled and sniffled. The stone oven was very warm.

Ildi and Istvan escorted Zoli into the parlor, where a fire was blazing. Another young man scampered into the room and offered to take Zoli's trench coat from him. "Please," he said.

Ildi said they would clean it for him and find him fresh clothes. They were gazing at his soiled camp uniform, at the state of his grooming, the dirt under his nails and in dark creases in his neck.

Istvan and the young man took Zoli upstairs, not to his old childhood bedroom but to his grandfather and grandmother's room. The boy set to building a fire in the hearth right away. The portrait in oils of his grandmother Juliana that had hung above the bed was gone.

Zoli asked Istvan if the Germans had used the bed. Istvan shook his head. "No one has. Since the lady and gentleman. Since your grandparents."

"How strange," he replied.

Istvan shrugged his shoulders. He didn't offer a further opinion. He reminded Zoli where the bath was, gave him fresh white towels and led him to the great wardrobe, still redolent of sandalwood, a fragrance that was once thick as ink in this room. The scent, the house itself, this deciduous house, softened everything.

Even so, a piece of Zoli's brother had broken off in him. He could feel its jagged edges each time he took a deep breath.

"Please help yourself to some clean clothes," Istvan said. "Anything, of course. The ladies will prepare a nice meal for you. I have just the thing in the farmyard."

"Can you put your hands on some penicillin? I've been unwell. I'm much better, but I need a couple of more shots of medicine."

"I will try," Istvan said. "There's a professor of medicine from the University of Szeged who lives in town. I'll try. I'm sorry about your illness. Can I ask him to come by?"

"No, please. I'm better," Zoli said. "I'm almost well. Especially now. I just need a syringe and the medicine."

He slept again in the plump bed until the winter sun went down. The penicillin was waiting for him on a white dish in the bathroom. He injected himself, took a bath, rubbed cream in the red spots on his chest, dressed in a warm brown gabardine suit, plus a red silk tie with a pattern of pale fish flying across it, one he remembered his grandfather wearing. He even searched for the pocket watch to go with the suit but couldn't find it.

He crept down to the dining room. A fire, almost too hot, had been lit there too. The Bouguereau painting *The Nymphs*, those naked beauties who had languished above the hearth for the whole of Zoli's fiery adolescence, was missing. Only its rectangular ghost remained in the golden wallpaper. He wondered about the table with the painting by Edvard Munch on its surface. He decided not to look. He did not need to know if it was still here.

Nor the dollhouse. He didn't want to see if Mary's dollhouse was still here either. In fact, he thought he'd rather not know.

A single dinner setting had been laid, with silver and with the Rosenthal dishes he knew so well, the Helena dishes. They were still here—and how had the silver survived? His linen serviette was monogrammed "JB," for Juliana Beck, his grandmother—his grandmother's trousseau—as were the dishes, the silverware, the platter and tureen, which two ladies, Ildi and a younger woman Zoli didn't recognize, now brought in.

They had roasted a goose for him and him alone, with a thick brown mushroom-based sauce and citrus marmalade and walnut chutney on the side, had prepared fat dumplings, a relish made of beets and greens, and root vegetables—parsnips, yams, carrots and sweet onions—which they had stored in the larder.

They poured him apricot *palinka* to warm the juices inside him. Where had they managed to hide *palinka* from the Germans? From the Russians? Had the Russians been here? Were they yet to come?

Istvan guessed what Zoli was thinking. "We have our hiding places," he said. "You can imagine, sir, in a property like this, what good hiding places there are. And I know them all." Zoli also knew that if the Germans had found any of these treasures in their hiding places, everyone here would have been shot, including the children. People were shot for much less, just to tidy up.

"My brother, Bela, will be joining us," Zoli said. "In a day or two. He wasn't far behind me. I just want to wait for him."

"Of course, sir," Istvan said. "We'll have a fresh bed made up opposite you, in his favorite room, as I recall, overlooking the stream." Zoli smiled, and Istvan withdrew.

And so here he sat, eating and sipping, alone in the grand dining room of his grandfather's house, in his grandfather's chair, trying to superimpose a new logic onto the old one, the two not lining up, like the time between languages.

When he was finished the main course, Ildi brought in a freshly baked *arany galuska*, a braided cake with walnut, honey and apricot veins. Her younger assistant brought espresso coffee and poured it into a small bone china cup he had known and admired much of his life.

Ildi said she'd heard that Bela would be joining them. "It will be lovely to see him," she said, then added, "to have the two of you together, I mean." She bowed a little and withdrew.

Zoli ate and drank and ate until his mouth lost all sensation. His stomach was throbbing. He could see his heart pumping over the surface of his abdomen. Then he pushed himself away from the table, hung his head back, tried to breathe. He had traveled from starvation to gluttony. He didn't know which was the deadlier sin, such was the state of his mind.

Istvan poured him more *palinka* and told him that he could stay as long as he wanted, days or weeks, if he wished—he and Bela both could, naturally—and when they were ready, Istvan would drive them back to Budapest. His grandfather's Bentley had been taken, but they had managed to hide the Austin 18 Norfolk beyond the ridge, covered in brush, where no one could spot it. Istvan's young son, whom Zoli had met in the barn, tittered in the shadows at the doorway. Zoli wanted to smile at the boy but instead looked at him heavily—with a heavy heart, heavy as stone. What paths were laid out for the boy and his sister? What might the future hold for them? Istvan shooed the boy away.

Ildi entered with the freshly cleaned trench coat draped over her arm. She said she'd found something in the pocket before she'd begun and thought Zoli would like to have it. It was Bela's notebook.

13

Lucy was worried about some of the heavy things Ben's father was saying lately, so she asked him if she could book an appointment with a psychiatrist. He agreed, but only if she would accompany him. His family doctor had ordered a CT scan of his head because of a little "fuzzy thinking" he had reported, though Ben believed that what his father was experiencing was "fuzzy listening." The scan was forwarded to the psychiatrist before the appointment, and it so happened Ben was free and could join Lucy and his father.

Before Dr. Ellis had even sat down opposite them, Zoltan said, "Why do people have to speak?"

The doctor looked at Lucy and Ben. He took his seat and clasped his hands in front of him on the desk. "I'd like to try to help you," he said.

"Do you see what I mean?" Zoltan said.

"You were the first one to speak," Dr. Ellis said.

Zoltan waited before answering. "If there were a land of deaf mutes, I would move to it," he said.

"And would you also be a deaf mute in that land?" the doctor asked.

If only the doctor knew. Zoltan had a muscular voice. A voice that could project to the back of the room, even when there was no one there. A voice that could sing. A voice that could bellow. A voice that could command a schooner in a storm, as long as he didn't have to steer the vessel.

"Well, I guess I would have to be," Zoltan said. "There'd be no one to speak to or listen to."

Dr. Ellis sighed. The psychiatrist could have taken lessons from Lucy. No one broke people open as well as she did. "How can I determine what's wrong if I don't ask you questions?" Dr. Ellis said.

"Even if you do, you won't be able to determine what's wrong."

Lucy sat forward. "Do you think his magnesium levels are high enough?" she asked.

"Let me see." The doctor opened a file and looked over the results. He had an extra-close look at the CT scan results. A good long minute passed before he said, "Have you ever taken blows to the head?"

"Yes, often," Zoltan said.

"In the war?" Dr. Ellis asked.

"Yes, as well as after the war."

"How do you mean?"

"I had some blows during the war at a labor camp." The doctor looked down at his hands in sympathy. "I then had some at work. Someone hit me with a wrench on the back of my head and a year later with a hammer. The same person. At the bridge club a few years ago, my partner sent me flying with a punch."

"Why would he do that?"

"Because I told him he was an idiot. He bid three spades."

"And?"

"And he was an idiot."

"My concern here today is how those blows might have affected your mental capacity now that you're somewhat older. I'm talking about the fogginess." The doctor took out a sheet of paper with a picture of a clock on the left side. The clock's hands indicated it was five twenty. Beside it on the right was a bare clock face. Dr. Ellis said, "Can you draw the time on this clock on the right side?"

"Yes, I can."

He handed Zoltan the sheet and a pencil. "Take your time."

In the center of the clock face, Zoltan printed the digits 5:20 and handed back the sheet.

The doctor looked at the sheet, glanced at Lucy and Ben and sat back in his chair. He didn't say another thing, but he did look Ben's father in the eye. Zoltan was as calm as could be. He watched the doctor breathing deeply and rubbing his hands together.

Finally, Dr. Ellis asked, "How can I help you?"

Now it was Zoltan who started fidgeting and glancing at the others. He looked like a student who didn't know how to answer the teacher's question. "I thought I was supposed to live six more months after my wife died, and it's been more than that. It's been years."

"That's not a hard and fast rule," the doctor said. "Some people live for years after the passing of their spouse. Some for a day. Some remarry, have a whole new life."

Zoltan looked amused. He checked to see if Lucy and Ben were too. They weren't.

"The point is to try to be happy," the doctor said. "To try to stay happy, if that's possible. Look how lucky you are. You are surrounded by love." He indicated Lucy and Ben.

"I'll tell you what I'm going to do," Zoltan said. "When I die, I'll leave my luck to you."

He had spent his life fleeing from misery. He hated misery. He could not stand to be in a room with a miserable person. If he and Hannah had visitors over and one went off on a miserable tangent—how her kidney was failing, how her son had swallowed the head of an electric toothbrush and choked, how his foot was coming off sometime soon, how he was always dizzy and saw animated flowers with his left eye—without excusing himself Zoltan would go upstairs to his bedroom, close the door and go to sleep. If misery was going to rain down on people, let it be as localized as possible. Let it rain on that side of the street only, on that person alone. He didn't want to have to open his umbrella. He could not watch the clips of the liberation of Auschwitz and the shoveling onto carts of bodies. He could not look at a news clip in which a body was recovered from a dumpster. He caught Ben watching *Who's Afraid of Virginia Woolf?* on TV, switched it off and said, "How could you watch such a monstrosity? Do you want to be unhappy? I can think of lots of ways. I know people who can give you lessons."

Lucy's eyes had welled up, and she looked away from Zoltan and the doctor. The Becks were her family, her only family. Her parents had died young, in their fifties. They were in a car crash. Her father might have taken his eye off the road or nodded off, but they drove into the guardrail on the highway and were hit from behind and sent sideways into the guardrail a second time. The car burst into flames. It would have been better for them if they had died instantly, but a truck driver who'd pulled over had braved the flames and got them out. Lucy's mother had ended up in a burn unit at York Hospital, and her father, who'd broken his back and was in a coma, was taken to St. Cecilia's. Lucy and Ben had been married for eight months, and Ben was just getting to know her doting parents, who wanted him to call them by their first names, Alice and Lester.

Lucy took a leave from work, and they shuttled between the two hospitals on a daily basis, especially Lucy, naturally. Her parents were in critical condition, and her once pretty mother, whose face was scarred beyond recognition and who could see out of only one eye, kept saying each day, out of the ruins of her mouth, that she wanted to see Lester. She could not be moved because of the risk of infection, and Lester had not woken up. He was on life support.

Lucy investigated. *Of course Lucy investigated.* Ben had never met anyone as determined, about certain things. She reminded him in this way of his mother. When Alice's condition stabilized, Lucy was able to arrange for a kind of astronaut suit for her to wear to keep her safe, and in this she was transported by a special vehicle to St. Cecilia's.

What an undertaking it was, almost miraculous, really. But they did it, or Lucy did it. On the day, the stars were in alignment. The weather was calm, as if it were trying to be as sensitive as could be, as if Lucy were the Goddess of the Elements, and Ben saw what could only be described as a glimmer in poor Alice's one remaining blue eye.

Everyone stopped to watch outside St. Cecilia's as they unloaded Spacewoman Alice and transported her with a half dozen helpers upstairs to the ninth floor, where Lester lay. A reporter with a camera tried to get in but was barred, though she asked nicely and repeatedly, asked Ben as well, saying it was the good news story of the month. "Not the year?" he said, and shrugged. "I wish I could help." Then a nurse escorted her to the elevator.

Alice was wheeled to her husband's bedside. Lucy and Ben were allowed to stand on the other side of the bed, and a nurse stood by to attend to Alice if she needed it. They listened to the two of them breathe through their devices. Alice reached with her space hand for her husband's hand, gingerly, because he had tubes behind bandages running into it. They watched Alice bob gently. Ben couldn't look at her through the window of her helmet. He stared down at his feet and Lucy's feet.

The whole visit lasted a quarter of an hour, but it helped Alice, and to a degree helped Lucy. Lester died less than a week later, and though she seemed to be getting better, Alice died of a stroke a couple of weeks after that. Lucy hadn't even told her mother about her father, but something in Lucy's look made her mother stop asking about him.

Lucy was the Beauregards' only child. She'd had a younger brother, Paul, but he had died of leukemia at two, when Lucy was four. Lucy had felt for years that she had not looked after Paul well enough, had kept him too long out back playing, even when his lips turned blue and he was shivering. She grieved over him into her adolescence and grieved for her parents well into her marriage. When she and Ben had their two girls, Lucy lamented the fact that her parents never got to meet them. How unfair it was, both ways.

So Ben's parents had become Lucy's parents. Zoltan, in particular, loved having this daughter, possibly more than his own sons, and she loved having him, even if he didn't always admit how much she meant to him. They always had a thing going. She wasn't just the daughter he never had; he might also have been the father she didn't have, or wasn't finished having.

—

Dr. Ellis had an exasperated look on his face rather than a sympathetic one. He said to Zoltan, "I just want to know what is in your heart."

"Blood, valves, flesh—plaque, I suspect," he replied. "Sometimes a heart is just a heart. It does not love golf. It does not love chocolate pudding. It does not heart New York. It is just doing the job it was designed to do."

Dr. Ellis made a steeple of his fingers and blew over the top. If there had been a flag there, it would have flapped.

"The beating heart and the ticking clock. It's no surprise that one must have inspired the other. They're just mechanisms. I just want to have an ordinary life," Zoltan offered. "I want to be invisible."

"So you want to be a deaf mute, and you want to be invisible. Anything else?"

"Yes. Thinking. It would be wonderful not to have to think. Cicero said, '*Amicitiae nostrae memoriam spero sempiternam fore.*' 'I hope that the memory of our friendship will be everlasting.' I *don't* want the memory of anything to be everlasting. Do you understand?"

"Are you running from some painful memories?"

"Do I have to be running from something not to want to think, not to have the thoughts flow again and again the way the blood does in and out of the heart? I just want simple thoughts: Is this a hole in my sock or just a spot of sunlight? Earlier, I ate this. Later, I will eat that. In between, I'll go to the bathroom. I will switch on this lamp. Is that liver pâté?"

What Zoltan didn't tell the good doctor was that, coupled with loving simple thoughts and simplicity, he despised complications and complexities. I will drive straight through this parking lot even if a man has dropped all his groceries and I have to drive over them. I will enjoy this seafood pasta even if I have to douse myself with the sauce and shower my next of kin with it. I will have quiet in the house even if I have to wake my son in the middle of the night to help me lift a corner of the fridge so that I can stuff a wad of newspapers under it.

What Zoltan couldn't see about himself was that, almost invariably, *he* was the one complicating matters. Some years before, Ben and his brothers had taken their father swimming in a newly opened Olympic-sized swimming pool in a local community center. The impressive pool was as clean and turquoise as could be. It was divided into three lanes: one on the right for beginners, one in the middle for experienced swimmers, and one on the left for serious, competitive swimmers. Ben swam in the right lane—among the children—flailing and trouncing around, gulping too much water, coughing. Sammy swam in the middle lane and did so with determination, getting himself ready for the day he could compete. He wanted to try out for a triathlon coming up in a year. Frank swam in the championship lane, blasting along like someone bound for the Olympics. There was an actual champ swimming in that lane with him, a woman, to his chagrin. She was passing Frank, infuriating him as she glided effortlessly by, as though he were a log in the lake she had to bypass with a little care. Then Zoltan stepped up. He'd been watching from the sidelines for just a minute, casing out the lanes. He was wearing a tiny, tight-yellow Speedo pulled up too high so that his testicles protruded on either side like earmuffs. And then he plunged into the championship lane, nearly on top of the woman, flipping her over. She adjusted herself and continued her campaign, now contending with a floating log and a grizzly bear.

"What is it you don't want to remember?" Dr. Ellis asked.

"If I tell you, I'd be remembering."

"Tell me anyway."

"I like to count things," Zoltan said out of the blue. "I like to count steps sometimes. From my car to the store. Up and down a staircase. The number of beats of my heart in a year, give or take. My days on earth. The number of last words spoken by someone. The number of last words heard."

"Spoken by whom?" the doctor said.

Zoltan looked away.

"Heard by whom?"

Zoltan was looking out the window. "I don't know," he said to the window, and then very quietly, "By my wife. By my brother."

"What did they say?" Dr. Ellis asked. "What did your brother say?"

"I don't know about my brother. I lost my brother—we did, my family did. He never came home." Zoltan avoided looking at Ben.

"I'm sorry," Dr. Ellis said.

Zoltan was shaking his head. He wasn't going to say anything more.

"What about your wife?"

He didn't answer.

"Did your wife say something?"

"I'm not sure," he said. He gripped the arms of his chair.
Ben thought that he was going to get up and leave, but he
stayed put.

The doctor looked at Ben. Lucy took his hand.

"Stay," Ben said. "That was all she said. *Stay.*"

"I told her I would go get myself a coffee and be right
back," Zoltan said. "Ben had just arrived. I'd been there all
day. I'd come and gone the whole day. I went for breakfast
and came back. I went for lunch and came back. I just thought
I'd get myself a coffee."

"That was all right," the doctor said.

Zoltan wanted it to be true. He was waiting for absolution.

Hannah had spent her life letting him do whatever he
needed to do or felt like doing: heading out each day with the
nearly empty attaché case, traveling the country with sample
radios for a month at a time, going to the bridge club night
after night, making mysterious appearances in odd neighbor-
hoods of the city. As her reward, she was permitted to calm
his nerves as the Becks stood in line at restaurants, Zoltan
ready to defend his family against the wait, ready to punch
the wall if need be.

But then came a seismic shift. The going down of Hannah
was the saddest chapter of their lives. Ben's father was not up

to watching her decline and becoming her nursemaid as she had been his for all the decades of their marriage whenever he needed her. Once Ben learned some of the story of Bela, he was convinced that that one death was all the death his father could take, the one that did in his spirit and resolve. So when Zoltan's own parents went down, one at a time, Hannah told Ben that his father was there in body only, looking away, making his best jokes when they occurred to him.

And then came his wife, after all those years of marriage, an ocean of marriage. She was declining precipitously in the hospital. She had stopped eating and drinking, not a morsel, not a sip. She was a determined woman. She did not want to be in decline. She wanted to be alive or gone, no in between. And she hadn't said a word in days. All of them had sat with her, filed by her, the sons, the wives, the grandchildren, the friends, so many friends, bringing flowers and plants, the last of the Hungarian community and others, turning the room into a garden, and she had tried to smile her trademark smile but hadn't the energy even for that.

Iris Danzinger, still statuesque at eighty-three, arrived like an empress in Hannah's room. She was wearing a black dress with a wide white Elizabethan shell collar. She had brought an elegantly ribboned box of French pastries. She nodded at each of Hannah's sons and smiled crisply. Reuben lurked at the door. She made her way to Hannah's side. She stared into her friend's milky eyes, cupped her face in her palm. Iris looked alarmed by the change in Hannah, the pallor, the indignity of her state, the place, the room, the foolish gifts all around them, including the frilly box she herself had brought, the vanity of it, seemed to be conferring grace upon Hannah, seemed to want to elevate her to a lofty place for which only she could conjure the wings. It was a moment of high drama, though not a word passed between them. Iris glanced back at Reuben, ghouling outside the door, dressed all in black like his aunt, and like her with a white collar sprouting out of the top, a love bite gleaming on his neck in the fluorescent glare of the corridor.

It took a moment before Lucy realized, as only Lucy could, that Iris needed assistance to leave the room. Lucy gently took her elbow and led her out toward Reuben. And then they were gone, like two figures who'd stepped out of a silent film classic in a grand theater and then stepped back up into it.

And then came Hannah's last day. Ben arrived after a short teaching day and found his father with her. Zoltan told Ben that Sammy had just left and Frank had been in earlier, in the morning. Frank had brought a cherry cheesecake, her favorite. His father asked Ben if he wanted a slice. He said no. Zoltan then went back to checking off her meal request form, though she hadn't consumed a thing in days. She hadn't spoken in days either. When Zoltan was done, he handed the little form to Ben. He'd checked off tea, with sugar and lemon, white toast with butter and jam, and Jell-O.

"Frank wants her to be force fed," Zoltan said.

"What? Cheesecake? Will he be coming back to do that?"

"No, intravenously."

"What do you think?" Ben asked.

"She doesn't want it. She wants to go, I think."

He stood up to look at her. He stroked her cheek and said quietly, "I'm just going to stretch my legs and get myself a coffee. I'll be back soon."

She opened her eyes, and Ben took her hand. She was looking over his shoulder at Zoltan. "Stay," she said to him.

He said he'd be right back and slipped away.

She wanted to say something more, seemed to want to blow out a word, but instead she closed her eyes again.

Stay. It was the saddest word in the world. Once, when Ben's daughter Leah was just two years old, maybe not even, he was heading out to work. Lucy had already left, and their nanny, Amelia, had arrived. Leah was eating grapes, which Amelia had washed and cut into small pieces for her. Leah was about to put one in her mouth when she turned toward the door, saw Ben putting on his coat, and was overcome with something—loss, loneliness, despair—a tide of it, the totality of it, as only a two-year-old can feel it and can infect someone with it.

"Stay," she said to him. She was sobbing, the grape hanging wetly and perilously just behind her lower lip.

Ben could not take the force of it, the wrenching in his soul. He was not leaving Leah in any danger. He was not leaving her alone. He was not placing her on the *Kindertransport.* He was leaving her in the hands of someone whose job it was to look after her, to see that her needs were met, even if it wasn't someone who loved her as he and Lucy did.

But what sense did it all make? Ben was on the verge of breaking down too. He was standing at the door in his coat. He couldn't *not* go to work, despite his daughter's desperation, despite his own. What sense did it all make? No sense. He stormed out of the house, drove all the way to the college wailing like a moose, howling like the giant baby he was, giving himself double vision, thinking that if he didn't stop he might run off the road like Lucy's parents. He couldn't imagine what he must have looked like when he arrived in class and asked his students to turn to the story "A Rose for Emily."

And when Ben got home that evening, he burst into the house to find Lucy there already and Amelia gone. Leah was eating supper. It was the end of supper, actually, and grapes again for dessert, Leah's favorite food. Ben had wanted to gather up his daughter in his arms as if he were returning from war, but she was content now, relishing the grape she had just swallowed.

It happened one other time with his brother Sammy. Ben was eighteen and going away to college, and Sammy was twelve. It had all been talked about and arranged. They knew for months that he was leaving. Frank had already moved out. Ben was Sammy's guardian, his champion with their parents, the one who'd read to him, played cards with him— his favorite games—war, fish—introduced him to music, taken him to his hockey games. And now he was going. Ben knew and Sammy knew. Yet as they finished packing the car, when Sammy came out with their mother to hug his brother, he looked into Ben's eyes and whispered, "Please." His face was reddening. He put his lips to his brother's ear and said, "Stay," the word rustling through the hairs in Ben's ear, causing him to shudder.

That was another time, and here was the third time. The saddest word in the world. It was the last word his mother said, and when his father came back to the room, she was gone. The nurse was there, and she told him. Her name tag said "Delia Rathburn, RN," and she was as prim and correct as could be, like someone ready to correct your grammar. She tightened her grammatical lips and said she was waiting for the doctor to make it official, sign the death certificate.

Ben stood over his mother, touched a stiff sprig of hair on her forehead. "Hannah?" he said. He wasn't sure what he was doing. The nurse stepped back. He'd taken to calling his mother by her first name in recent years, and it made her smile, so it stuck, even if so many other things made her smile. "Hannah?" As if a little affectation could rouse her from the dead. "Mom?" His scalp was tingling, as were his fingertips.

The color had lifted from the room, as if she had taken it with her, draining the actual flowers all around them.

His mother loved to be in charge of her life, her people, her home. She loved to be awake. It seemed to Ben, when he was young, that she was always awake, always waiting for everyone else to join her. So it must have been a glorious place she had surrendered to just now, a place where she could loosen her grip, where the grip no longer mattered, where she would not need or want to be awake and in charge.

Ben strained to gaze into the soul of this lifeless figure in front of him. Surely, in loosening her grip, she must have crossed over to something even more enticing, fantastically enticing, moving from the ruins of light into a palace of light—blinding, regardless of what side you were on, but blinding in entirely different ways, opposite ways. He tried to reach across the thin filament, the divide, like a figure in a sci-fi movie—with all his might he tried to imagine for a second the majesty of that light but felt singed by it and retreated.

His father came around to Ben's side of the bed, shook his hand and thanked him for being there.

Zoltan could not look at his wife. He turned away and headed back for the window to look out. "Hey, even the sky feels blue," he said. So there it was: the color that had eluded Homer and the ancients.

Ben thought he was meant to chuckle or at least smile at his father's remark. He wasn't sure what to do. He stared at his mother's lifeless face, a ghastly sight. He found himself *remembering* her now before the milk had ebbed up into her eyes. Had an alarm sounded? Were all the pieces of her scrambling for the exits? Where did triumph go? Surely it had wings. Where did the fierceness go? The cheer? Had they all taken up residence in his mother and were now departing? Had his mother herself borrowed this form, this body? Ben could not take the measure of what it meant to sit there, watching her pass through him as he had her. It was a sensation like lightning being sucked back up into the clouds as they rumbled by.

Ben was afraid to touch her, afraid of the jolt he might feel. He thought he should go around to the window to stand by his father, possibly even hug him, but he wasn't sure how to manage it. It was best to stay put, let a little time pass.

This last part they did not share with Dr. Ellis. He didn't need to know. They stopped the story at "Stay."

"It's all right," Dr. Ellis said again. Zoltan didn't seem to be listening. "There isn't a thing to feel sorry about." After another moment, the doctor asked, "Do you think you'd like to come back to see me again? Will it help you?"

To Ben and Lucy's surprise, Zoltan said yes.

"He needs a colonoscopy," Lucy said. "The last test was unsuccessful. Should we go to his family doctor?"

"No," Dr. Ellis said. "I can arrange that."

"Can we book it at my brother's hospital?" Ben asked. "At St. Cecilia's?"

"Of course," the doctor said. "If you think it's best. I have a colleague there in the GI ward."

"I also need a prescription for a fungicide cream," Zoltan said. He held up his hand. "I get bad rashes." His look was sad, helpless, as if he were asking for suicide cream.

The doctor came around the desk to look at his hand. He couldn't see anything. "All right," the doctor said, "but maybe for that you should go back to your family doctor. Meanwhile, I'll make an appointment at St. Cecilia's." And he smiled. Everyone smiled.

14

Though Bela was wearing his white shirt and black wool pants over his khaki camp uniform, by the time he reached the outskirts of Szifla, he was shivering with cold. A dusty dry snow was falling.

Just beyond a small wooden bridge over a creek stood a trio of pine trees with thick, dense foliage spread out over the ground like Victorian ball gowns. Bela thought he would seek shelter under one of them for a short time, just to warm up a little and to stave off the gusts now blowing.

He selected the tree farthest from the road and was surprised at how welcoming it was. He was certain he was the first ever to violate it in this way, and he felt grateful for the pine's embrace. He could feel a tingle returning quickly to his toes and fingertips and felt doubly grateful, as he steadied himself deep within the tree's chest, for its willingness to convert the mincing snow and slicing wind into its warm green breathing.

Bela nodded off, he didn't know for how long, maybe just minutes, or maybe longer, but he was awakened by the sound of stampeding feet and panting voices belonging to several men at least, several for certain, and then a single gunshot, followed by a hard thud nearby.

He wanted to peer out. He knew he shouldn't, was sure he shouldn't, but he'd acquired a strange confidence from the friendly tree, thought he could part its thick assembly of needles just to have a peek. Still he waited.

The men circled nearby, and a single man barked as another gunshot rang out. Bela inched toward the outer edge of the foliage, parted the branches and saw a Russian soldier standing quite close, looking down at his handiwork, a dead man, wearing the unmistakable uniform of the labor camp. It was Herman, a young man who'd arrived in the camp just a month before. In the distance, galloping away, Bela could see three other men in khaki uniform, and one of them was Voros, the cook.

A second Russian soldier joined this one, and the two lowered their rifles, raised a flask and laughed wetly into the dry falling snow, and then they moved on past the fallen Herman. The dead young man was looking straight at Bela, his light blue eyes open and seeming alert, even as the powdery snow brushed up against them, his baby face pale and puffy, pink, unshaven—he had not yet begun to shave.

Bela felt somewhat responsible for the boy, though what could he have done? He had told them to stay off the road. Why had they come this way? He was entirely responsible for his brother. Where would Zoli be now? Might he have come out of hiding somewhere too, unaware that marauding troops might shoot him for sport? Was he freezing somewhere? Had his fever returned? Had he found another cave? A hole? Some shelter? How could he have let Zoli wander without a guide and a proper nursemaid? What was Bela doing here? Did he think he was an actor in an old myth, Tristan come to claim his Isolde, blinded by some love potion just as surely as Herman was blinded by a fatal bullet? Would he drag his Isolde, who could never belong to him, who would surely be promised to anyone but him, drag her into a dark, dead wood, the two of them feeling alive just once and just for seconds before history came to collect them? But didn't Isolde have healing powers? Wasn't that why he was here? Did she not make them both invincible, invulnerable to the dark forces blowing over their ruined kingdom? Could she not lift them above the winds, smile down and brighten the empire, polish the stars, weaken the forces of history? Could she not bring him back with her soothing hands if she had to? Could he not bring her back with his beating heart if he had to?

Herman was a boy, with a boy's face. He was a stillbirth. The quiet now was terrible, a ripe quiet which settled in the place between quiet and sound, like the place between happiness and sadness, between excitement and resignation. Quiet was akin to peace, but it was also akin to solitude.

Bela ducked back in under the tree just as wheels squeaked toward him. He could still see with one eye, but just barely. It was a wooden flatbed cart. Herman was loaded onto it. Four other dead men lay on it, their arms and feet flopping as the cart moved. Three of them wore the khaki uniforms of the camp. Bela's eye searched frantically for the cook among the dead but didn't see him. A Russian told some other Hungarian men, locals, likely, to move along, and they and the cart departed.

Bela had to leave his hiding place, his body refreshed, his imagination in ruins. The tree had some kind of reach to it. Bela could feel its tingle even as he drew away. It was dark now, and the snow had slowed, as had the wind.

The lights of the town were coming on just over the ridge. He could picture Zsofia up there, so close now. Some one hundred paces in front of him there was a tavern with its lights on and beyond it a farmhouse, a barn and a large shed. A woman wearing an apron came out onto the porch of the house to shake out a tablecloth. Bela paused. When she returned to the house, Bela loped past it toward the barn and the shed. He could hear animal sounds, cows and horses certainly, and geese.

How would it be if he simply presented himself to these people? Would they invite him in to warm himself and enjoy a meal? Would they shoot him? Would they call the authorities? Call the Russians? Call the colonel? Who was the colonel in Szifla, what was his standing, with his distinguished yellow house? With those daughters inside? The daughter.

He crept to the shed and listened at the wooden door. Something shifted inside then was quiet. He was holding his breath. So were they, or he, or she.

The door burst open. Someone slapped a hand on Bela's mouth and hauled him by the neck into the shed. It was Voros. Behind him, a younger man was holding up an impressive spade and was poised to bring it down on Bela's head. The young man was Herman's age, a recent recruit too. Tears were streaming down his face. He was trembling.

Voros let go of Bela. "Come in, come in," he said. "This is Robert. He's Herman's brother."

"Oh, Herman," Bela said. Robert had the same eyes as his brother. He could tell even in the dark and through the tears.

"Robert's not yet eighteen," the cook said. "They weren't exactly insisting on papers when they took them. Herman was not yet nineteen."

"I'm sorry," Bela said. "He was your brother. I'm so sorry." Of course, Bela thought again of Zoli. He would never forgive himself if something happened to Zoli.

A shot rang out somewhere, but a good distance away, so it sounded like a toy. Robert flinched. The gunfire touched off a whole new round of sobbing. Robert crumpled into himself and slid to the floor. Voros reached under the boy's arm and lifted him up.

"We can't stay here," Voros said. "Not even for the night. We have to find somewhere safe."

"Yes," Bela said lamely.

"You're not coming, are you?" the cook said. "It's not safe here. It's especially not safe anywhere near the colonel. Bela, don't be a fool. Especially not you. What a waste. Come with us. We'll be safe in Budapest. We'll be safe back home. If not, you'll stay with me. I'm not a Jew, but I'm here now in this uniform, looking like one. I promise you safety, and Robert, and your brother too, if he needs it, if your parents are gone— if they're away."

"Away," Bela repeated blankly. "You go. I will follow you. I won't be far behind."

"You'll be very far behind," Voros said. "I would take my chances with anyone, and I mean anyone, even the Russians, before I'd take a chance with the colonel."

They stared at one another for a long moment, even the boy, who had a pleading look on his face, a desperate one. But Bela let the two men trudge out into the night. He watched them for a time, then he turned toward the ridge above them and the town.

Bela crept toward the colonel's house, ducking into the shadows at the slightest sound. He was warm now and pushing through the cold, the coals in him aflame. The lights were on in the kitchen and in the parlor, where he had played the piano. He could see the portrait of the matriarch.

A light came on in a bedroom upstairs. Was he to be Romeo now, not Tristan? Bela looked up to the stars to read his fate, but they were obscured by winter clouds. When he was very young, Bela believed that the stars poked holes in the darkness to let in air, and when he didn't see them for too long, he would feel himself choke. Even now, he felt a twinge of it, had to pause to take a deep breath.

They came upon Bela from behind, quietly and quickly, no doubt thinking him a prowler, and brought a rock down hard on the back of his head.

15

The second colonoscopy was a success in that it worked. The cleansing process emptied Zoltan out, largely because the pouring and drinking of Expulsor was overseen by Lucy the day before the Monday morning test. She stood over him as he drank every drop of the solution, waited for him outside the bathroom a dozen times. They watched TV together, some news shows and figure skating. He often used to watch figure skating with Hannah. Lucy continued the tradition. Zoltan put up with a lot when it came to Lucy.

A week later, they got the verdict from Sammy, who had looked up the results on the network at St. Cecilia's and checked with his colleague. He phoned to say he was driving over to Ben's house with his wife, Maureen, to share the news in person, so Ben and Lucy knew at once it wasn't good. Anna and Leah happened to be home for the holidays, and they were already sobbing when Sammy and Maureen walked in. It was advanced colon cancer. They called Frank and told him to join them, and he came right away. (His wife was gone, or at least no longer his wife. He had been living half-time with another woman before his wife figured out that he was away too much, even for him.)

Sammy made the announcement again so Frank would not think he was the last to hear. But he too already knew something was up. Lucy, Leah and Anna were clearly holding back tears. Ben found he could not say a word for fear of breaking down. Sammy stood up in front of Frank, who had thrown himself into an armchair, but he was like Ben. So it was Maureen who ended up telling Frank that their father wasn't well.

"How sick is he?" Frank asked.

"He doesn't *look* sick. He hasn't even lost weight," Sammy finally said. "That's the tricky thing about this kind of cancer. By the time there are signs, it's too late, or almost too late."

"Does he know?" Lucy asked.

"No. I asked my colleague to wait a few weeks before letting him know. It's highly irregular these days, but she agreed."

"Should we tell Dad?" Frank asked.

"I vote no," Ben said. "Not yet. We should all hang out with him more, a lot more."

"We need to find out what kind of treatment is available—if treatment is even worthwhile," Sammy said. "Dad is not going to go in for heavy treatment, if I know him."

"Let's not do anything right away," Lucy said. She looked very composed now but had her arms around her daughters. "You guys should take a trip to Hungary with him, the one we've been talking about, Ben. Your dad hasn't been back since you fled. Go, all of you. The three boys and their father."

"Without telling him about the cancer?" Frank said.

"Yes, without telling him. We'll just tell him the results were inconclusive. They need to run more tests in a few weeks."

"When are you thinking?" Frank asked. "About taking the trip, I mean?" Ben's older brother looked alarmed.

"Now," Lucy said. "You should go right away. While your father is still feeling well, or well enough. Ben is free. It's the end of semester. He just has to get his grades in."

"I can't go now," Sammy said. "I'm on city-wide call for three days over the Christmas holidays."

"I can't go now either," Frank said, but he didn't say why. "We'll split the costs. In fact, we'll cover the whole cost, right, Sammy?"

"Right."

"You don't have to cover the whole cost," Ben said. "We'll split it, as you said."

"He doesn't want to go back to Hungary," Maureen said. "We wanted to take your mother and him a few years ago. They had no interest. That was another time, another world, he told us."

"He always talks as if it were someone else's world, not his," Ben said.

"He likes to forget," Leah said. She was studying psychology. "He's a forgetter." And for whatever reason, this comment touched off a whole new round of sobbing. Ben cried too.

Finally, Ben said, "Isn't he going to get sicker on the trip?"

"Not necessarily," Sammy said. "It could be a little while before he has symptoms, at least bad ones, noticeable ones. At his age, the cancer might not progress as quickly."

"Still," Ben said, "I'm not sure."

"You have to go," said Anna. "You have to take him."

"You could leave in less than a week," Lucy said.

Ben said he would, if Lucy talked him into it. "There is something I have to investigate in Budapest."

"You have to *investigate* something?" said Leah. Frank laughed.

"I might."

"In *Hungary?*" Frank said. He looked at his brother as if he were talking about Saturn.

"Yes, in Hungary."

"What the hell are you talking about?" Frank said.

"If you're planning to come with us, I'll tell you," said Ben. "If not, you'll have to wait to find out."

Zoltan looked resigned to his fate as he and Ben stowed their carry-on bags and settled into their seats. Ben asked him why he'd been so resistant to returning to his homeland. Was it that it would stir up dark memories? Zoltan said, "I don't have to tell you."

Ben had pledged to Lucy and to himself that he would not fight with his father or upset him, so he left it alone. He found himself staring at his father, thinking about what lay ahead for him, for them. The light on the plane was like film, manufactured, like the air. For the first time, in this light, Ben saw weariness etched in his father's face.

Coupled with his father's pathological need to renew everything was the need to leave the past behind. Returning to the motherland was reversing the process of renewal, like rummaging through the garbage to retrieve whatever it was that was discarded, the half-eaten piece of cake, the cigar butts, the paid and torn water bill. It was more than a reversing of the process. It was an undoing of it. Following William the Conqueror, Richard the Lionheart, Pez the Dispenser, Catherine the Great and Vlad the Impaler came Ben's father: Zoltan the Discarder, or "Zoli" to his Hungarian friends— Zoli the Discarder.

They were served coffee and cookies. Luckily, Zoltan was sitting in the seat by the window. Ben had the aisle seat. Zoltan opened a sugar packet with such violence its contents showered both of them and even one of the people in the seats in front of them. The man reached his hand up to his scalp and glanced back at them through the break in the seats. Some granules had made their way behind Ben's shirt collar and down his neck. He seized the next packet away from his father, opened it and poured it into his cup, then repeated the procedure with one of his own packets. Then the cream, then the stir stick. If Air Canada had known about Zoltan, for safety's sake they would not have issued him a stir stick. He glared at Ben through the whole operation. What he wanted from Ben, most likely, was simply for his son to allow him to sprinkle and spray him all the way across the Atlantic. Just leave it for once, Ben told himself. Let it happen. But he couldn't.

"Dad, why didn't you want to go to Hungary?"

He didn't answer. He took a sip of his coffee. Finally, he said, "I was so glad to get out of that godforsaken place, that bitch of a continent." He looked hard at his son. "War!" he said. "War!" He was punching the air and speaking too loudly, like a lunatic. "Many of us were brutalized overnight. The most civilized people turned into warriors. Maybe it was always in us somewhere, but this brought it out—*spewing* out. And once converted, it takes a great deal to go back. A warrior can't sit around having a peaceful breakfast with his family, admiring the fresh flowers standing in the Waterford vase and enjoying the notes of music drifting over the room from the gramophone. You're seething, ready for anything, ready to smash the flowers, roar against the music, even blow up the children. So the country, the continent, blew itself up at last, and I was only too glad to get away. War is an event and peace is not. We are a species that needs events to rejoice about or grieve about or write histories about. No matter what, in too quiet times, even in the best of us, something erupts in us to bring about events. Let's hope I am wrong.

Let's hope it doesn't happen in Canada. But look at me. Look at us. Now I'm going back to the scene of the crime. You see?"

"You're going back just to visit."

"Sure, just to visit." He looked Ben in the eye again. "But you like to go to places to suffer. You willingly watch *Who's Afraid of Virginia Woolf?* You seek out sources of suffering, which is why we're on this trip, I suspect."

"I don't like to suffer, and I don't want you to suffer. Quite the contrary. But let me say that you seem to think I'm impervious to insults."

"I don't think that," he said. "I know you're pervious."

For Ben, the most remarkable thing about being with Zoltan was that his father's feelings prevailed. There was little room for Ben to feel things himself, so busy were they both with tending to his father's feelings. It took two pairs of hands, sometimes more, to accommodate feelings so large and so deep. But it must be said that Ben was also returning to a land he'd left when he was all of three. He had no more than a fleeting sense of what it was like in the "Old Country," but a conversely enormous sense of what it was like to be *from* there. He remembered that, in the days before the Becks escaped, he would wake to the sounds of bombs falling, like bad thunder and lightning, the lightning always striking nearby, darkening the dove-blue cloud of his new mind. How long could a storm go on?

The Becks escaped by foot at night across the border into Austria. Ben rode on the back of a soldier they had hired, clinging to the brass button at the neck of his jacket, the button cutting his hand. It was nothing in the grand scheme of things, having a button cut into his hand, but he still remembered it a half century later, so it was something to him, something momentous that night, the dividing line between what was behind them and what lay ahead.

And then there was Nadinka. How could he forget Nadinka? She was his father's first cousin, and she lived with them in Budapest. Her fiancé, Albert, who was a Freemason, had been taken to Buchenwald a month before the end of the war, and Nadinka had waited for him to return, just as Ben's grandmother Eugenia had waited for Bela to return, the three of them—his grandmother, then his mother with his grandmother, then Nadinka—heading to the train stations to check, looking over lists every day, like looking for your own name on a list of lottery winners. But Albert didn't return.

And when Ben came along, three years after Frank did, eight years after the end of the Second World War, he and Nadinka took to each other like best friends, apparently from the very first days of his life. She came to get him each morning when he woke up, and she played every game with him, but with real conviction. She was the ambulance to his fire engine as they rushed to the scene of an emergency, sirens wailing, all across the rug that ran down their corridor, and into their front room, up the leg of the round-topped table and around its lip until they reached the scene of the trouble: the flaming bowl of fruit with its dying plum and its bruised and outcast apple and its stuck-up grapefruit, bitter and patronizing. Here, they came to a halt to put out the fire and heal the sick and then paused to eat some fruit.

Ben was madly in love with Nadinka. He faintly remembered her chewing the ends of her black hair, and he remembered her smiling green eyes with brown spokes in them. He cried inconsolably when she left to go to the train station, left him in the care of their housekeeper. All of them left him, his three favorite women: Nadinka, his grandmother and his mother, in that order.

And then one day, Nadinka did not come back with his grandmother and mother. They told Ben she would soon, and of course he was very young and believed them. He waited, but she didn't return that day. She was not there the next day, though he waited with the ambulance and fire engine and, thinking she'd grown tired of them, waited all the following day with his tin general and tin sergeant and their tin horses and would not leave his room. If she had returned, he would even have let her take a turn as general.

Ben was eighteen and had finished high school in Canada before his mother told him that Nadinka had taken her own life. She was found in a small hotel room near the railway station. She'd swallowed a whole bottle of tranquilizers, all but one. She left a note to say she could not live any longer without her Albert, and please forgive her for what she was doing. The last line of the note was "—*for the person who finds me, to help you sleep*": that one last tablet in the bottle. Hannah told Ben this story only to remind her son of who

Nadinka had been and to say what a big consolation Ben was to her in those years after the war, her only consolation.

And now, on their return to Budapest, something of Nadinka stirred in Ben, a faint filament of her, like an ancient petal in amber from which to reconstruct the whole flower.

Ben reached into the seat pocket in front of him for his book. He could feel his father's eyes still on him. His gaze was palpable, like a heartbeat.

Finally, Zoltan said, "What are you reading?"

"*The Catcher in the Rye.*"

"Ah, *The Catcher in the Rye.* I love that book. I read it first in Hungarian, then in English. Haven't you read it yet?"

"Of course I've read it, but I'm giving a paper on it at a conference in Milwaukee."

"You've always been good at papers," he said. He wasn't being sarcastic.

"Thank you."

"What aspect?"

"Excuse me?"

"What are you saying about it?"

"I'm talking about the mysterious ending. The cryptic last pages. After saying how phony and hypocritical almost everyone is—after exposing Ackley and Mr. Antolini, his beloved teacher, and almost everyone else, and after wanting to save his little sister, Phoebe, before she falls into the abyss of adulthood, the corruption of it, the misery, the hypocrisy—Holden says he *misses* everyone he has told us about. He misses people *equally*, the phonies and Phoebe both. It's as if memory is the great leveler, the equalizer. It scrubs clean the sin and duplicity, so that once experience is locked safely in the past it cannot progress and therefore corrupt itself more than it already has. It's a stunning moment, that moment in the novel, in literature—how history, memory, can remake everything so ineffably. I ache for Holden," Ben said, and gulped.

His father was staring at him. "Yes, you ache."

And there it was again. That tone. Yet there was a tear in his father's eye. It was unmistakable. Ben let him collect himself and said nothing.

After a long moment, his father said, "Yes, ache for him, Ben, but don't try to make anything more of it. If you do, you're just trying to rationalize your feelings. Believe me, you can't make sense of aching. It just is—it has its own impervious essence." He was smirking. He then said, "Don't be too ambitious."

"What does that have to do with anything?" Ben said.

"I haven't emphasized that enough in your lives, you boys. Ambition is overrated."

"You have emphasized it enough."

What was his father divining in Ben, or was this just another precautionary note? Or was he seeing something in himself he needed to suppress or quell?

"You try too hard," Zoltan said. "You're too self-aware."

"Is that possible?" Ben asked.

"Yes. You and Lucy both. Self-awareness is overrated too. It's a killer of joy. People who are enjoying themselves who stop to say, 'Look, I'm enjoying myself,' have right away lost half their enjoyment. Just leave it alone. Leave things alone.

"Here we are, zooming our way to Hungary. It would be better if we had no names, no identifying marks," he said. "It's better to be a sheep, better to stand and eat grass, have an occasional cooling haircut, listen for the shepherd, say back to him, 'baaa,' nothing more. Better to be invisible— better to be invisible than to be the Prince of Peace. Everyone is exalting you—every *thing*, including the valleys, the heavens and the oceans. How good can that be, after a while? And even if people execute you, you poor bugger, you can't even stay dead. You have to come back and save people, get executed again, get exalted, then rise again. Or conversely, you can wake up one day and be Joseph Stalin. What part of the world do I conquer today? Do I conquer Europe, start with Europe? How long before I take over the whole planet? Oh, look, my barber of twenty-five years is being a little too familiar. He's asking me if I like a little gray hair coming in now. Time to slaughter his family in front of him before slicing his throat too. Trust me—it's all bad. I feel sorry for you if you have to wake up to that each morning—if you have to wake up to your own nature and mission. It's just a matter of degree. I would not want to be the Prince of Peace, or the Prince of War. It's too heavy a burden. I wouldn't want to be the Prince of Parking Lots, if I have a say in the matter."

His father's lack of ambition or opposition to ambition puzzled Ben, if only because he wanted to be the driver, the leader, always, the prevailing voice, in fact the only voice in the room. Yet if he were to pilot this plane, he would take his foot off the gas pedal, or whatever pedal they had, and they would plunge toward the ocean before he thought to correct their course, two seconds before certain death.

Ben tucked his book back into the seat pocket. Enough of Holden. "Dad, I want to ask you about someone." His father looked ready to pounce, but Ben persisted. "Can you please tell me about Szilvia Vukcsics?"

To Ben's surprise, his father said, "What do you need to know?" But Zoltan's finger was still on the trigger. Ben could feel it.

"How is she connected to us?"

"Did your mother tell you about her?"

"Some." Hannah had told Ben very little about Szilvia Vukcsics. So if his response wasn't the truth, it leaned toward the truth—it was truthy. And Lucy knew something too, though not all of what Ben knew. She did not know the bigger secret. Even Ben did not entirely know the bigger secret. He knew only that there might have been one.

Lucy had found Szilvia Vukcsics, who had contacted Ben's parents some years before to convince them to apply for war reparations. Mrs. Vukcsics had said she had a disabled daughter and badly needed the help, so Zoltan agreed.

When Hannah died, Zoltan let Mrs. Vukcsics know. He wrote to her and then called her. She did not respond, but the payments, which had funneled through her account (and three-quarters of which she would send to the Becks), stopped coming, so Zoltan was glad to be done with the whole business.

Lucy tracked Mrs. Vukcsics down again by searching through the vast financial networks accessible to the insurance company she worked for. The Becks knew that Mrs. Vukcsics must still have been receiving payments on their behalf. Lucy contacted Mrs. Vukcsics with what looked like an official warning that funds were about to be cut off. Szilvia called Lucy from Hungary right away to say she could tell the Becks something they didn't know and might want to know. She wouldn't say what. Lucy told her that her husband was visiting Budapest and could drop by.

But what Szilvia's information was and how much it was really worth, Ben couldn't tell. All he knew was he needed to take some cash with him to find out, as if he were visiting a fortune teller.

"Why does Mrs. Vukcsics live at our old address in Budapest?" Ben asked his father.

"They moved in there during the war and never left. We moved back in with them and displaced a couple of families who were squatting, but Vera Vukcsics and her daughter stayed. It's a long story. Even I don't know the whole of it."

As with Nadinka, Ben had a vague memory of a housekeeper who lived in another part of their apartment and who sat often with Ben's grandmother. Ben said, "But the daughter, Szilvia, had a child too."

"So your mother told you plenty."

"So yes, she had a child?"

"Yes, that's it!" he barked. "Now, let's close the subject, if you would be so kind."

"So I *know* Vera Vukcsics. We were there together."

"'Know' is a stretch. You were a baby, really."

A woman stood in the aisle by Ben's elbow. He hadn't noticed her. She was just a little twig of a human being. Ben found himself fearing for her, for her life. He shuddered and turned away. "Dad, you should also know that this trip was Lucy's idea." Zoltan didn't comment. "So can I ask you again— I mean, setting aside labels—aren't you at all curious about the place where you were born and raised? Why didn't you want to go back after all these years? Is it the anti-Semitism?"

"It isn't," he said. "I don't care much for Jews myself."

"What about Christians?"

"I don't care much for them either."

"What about Lucy? Do you care about her?" His father looked at him through all that weariness. "How about Leah? How about Anna?"

"Don't be an imbecile," he said.

Zoltan took a sip of his coffee. Ben took one too. "I might have a surprise for you in Hungary," he told him.

"A big one?" Zoltan asked. "Bigger than anti-Semitism?"

"No, not that big."

"Lucy is joining us. Is that it?"

"No, she's not. It's smaller than anti-Semitism and bigger than Lucy joining us."

"What is it?"

"I don't have to tell you."

Zoltan huffed and then glared at the back of the seat in front of him. He mouthed words to it. He was a mouther of words. He mouthed words to his books as he read. He wasn't reading with his mouth. He was answering it or someone. Smoking cigars, he mouthed words to the couch he sat on. For years, when he still drove, he would sit (almost lie down) in his car and mouth words to the steering wheel, confide secrets to the steering wheel, even though Ben was sitting with him, or his mother was, usually. Someone had upset him, and now he was answering silently to the steering wheel. Occasionally, you could actually hear him. He broke into a whisper, and he made all the appropriate gestures, pounding the steering wheel, slapping the dashboard. If you asked him what was wrong, he didn't hear you. You didn't exist. You were interrupting the rebuke he was giving someone, his bridge partner, or Frank (he argued a lot with Frank about business), or other drivers—"bad" drivers.

The truth was Ben didn't know if he had a surprise for his father, or wasn't sure. The last thing he wanted to do was disappoint him after taking him back against his will.

His father decided he had to go to the bathroom but did not excuse himself. Instead, he climbed over his son as if Ben were an immovable tree stump. Much as he tried, Ben could not get out from under him. Zoltan was all elbows and knees and bum, crushing Ben, bruising out into the aisle.

And then he was in line, a longish line. He turned briefly to Ben with a murderous look, as if this were one of the most trying moments of his life. Here they were: another line. But going to the bathroom was a must, and they were in a confined place. For hours and hours. Short of peeing in a sick bag or on the back of the seat he'd been confiding in, Zoltan had to go to the toilet in the usual way. He had frequently crossed the line from civilized to not, but he still drew the line with toilets, thank the blessed lord.

In these moments, his father's purpose overtook his look. When he had to go to the toilet, he got an intense toilety look, the whole of him needing to unbutton, unfasten and unload. His family all wanted him to complete the necessary three steps, but in order, so that unload would not move higher up the list. When he needed to eat, he had a slop kitchen look, everything around him getting set to rocket toward his mouth, face, neck and neighbors. When he needed to ask a question on the phone of, say, a bank person or a government clerk or a plumber, the whole of him was bent into the question, as if he were trying to turn himself into a question mark. He was so intense about every matter that he made everyone else intense too. Ben became anxious, even afraid, lest Zoltan punch the airplane wall, or still worse another passenger or a smiling flight attendant.

And then his father was in. Woe to the last occupant of the toilet before him, the person trying to open the door to get out as he was trying to get in. Unbeknownst to her, she was little more than a human outcropping to Zoltan, and he blasted by her, this great pink woman with macaronic hair, the blond noodles boinging with the grinding force of it, the face bruising deep red and darker, to purple.

Then he was in there far too long. Ben had begun to think that this was the end. The cancer had blown up in him. Blood was pouring out. They'd have to go straight to the hospital by ambulance when they landed, or worse.

Ben got up out of his seat and lined up as his father had, people ahead of him puzzling over the long delay, a couple trying the door, the flight attendant trying the door. Ben was about to wend his way to the front to see if he could talk to him through the door. But then finally, miraculously, he could hear his father fumbling with the latch, pushing and fumbling, pulling, bodychecking the door, until it sprang open.

He looked fine, happy even.

"How was that?" Ben asked him.

"It was spectacular. It was like passing a small farm animal."

Ben hoped nobody heard, but of course several people heard, so he kept his head down.

They got back into their seats. The shoulder of his father's jacket was torn. "What happened?" Ben asked.

"Oh, it's nothing," he said, brushing the shoulder as if it had a bit of lint on it. "It's just the seam." He sat happily back in his seat, smiling, ever the gentleman, thanking Ben for making way, nodding to the person across the aisle from them. "It's the one thing in life you never regret," he said.

"What is?"

"Taking a crap."

He was quiet for a time as they roared through the skies, but then he said, "I wonder how many of my brother Bela's fiancées are still around in Budapest."

"How many did he have?"

"Not any officially, really, but a few girls he dated found him so charming, so appealing, that they were sure he was the one. He must have set world records for how soon the girls wanted to introduce him to their parents."

"What about you?"

"They didn't think of me in that way."

"Why not? You were quite a looker too."

"Yes, but being good-looking was not enough. I was lucky your beautiful mother took pity on me, but she was the only one. You had to be there. My brother and I were both handsome in our day, I guess, but they thronged to Bela, whereas I must have frightened them somehow. They must have seen something in me that scared them. And those two things aren't compatible: being attracted and being scared. You can't cause a young woman's heart to quicken with affection and then quicken still more with fear." Zoltan paused here. He looked over at his son warmly. "I wish Bela could have met you. He might even have liked you—I mean, not much, but a little."

Zoltan closed his eyes and Ben thought he was snoozing, so he closed his too. He tried to imagine what lay ahead for the poor bugger—for all of them—but mostly for Zoltan.

He'd often done this, but especially since his mother died; he'd wondered and even dreamed in graphic detail about the various ways of going down. The latest was to imagine being eaten by something fierce, a lion or an alligator or a whale— what it must feel like to be crunched in a pair of mighty jaws, bits of you still sensate as they separated from the rest on their journey to the bottom of a dark, wet gullet. He wondered down to the finest detail. For instance, might your face remain intact? Might you say a last "Oh," a surprised "Oh," a distracted one?

But to be eaten from within. The lion inside, clawing its way out. The whale inside Jonah. He couldn't fathom it.

He glanced over at his father, and Zoltan was wide awake. He was wearing his fish-eating glasses. He owned at least a half dozen pairs. The fish-eating glasses, as their name suggested, were the ones he wore while eating fish, in order to ferret out the small bones. Another pair was his normal reading glasses. Another was his driving glasses. Another was his TV-watching glasses, ones that allowed him to watch a show and look down at the remote as required. Another, now defunct, was his tooth-brushing glasses. And here were his fish-eating glasses. They were big ones, like a windshield.

Zoltan knew what Ben was thinking. He said, "Lucy wouldn't let me bring all my pairs. She reasoned that my fish-eating glasses were the most subtle ones, ones I could read with too."

"Smart," Ben said.

"Very smart." And then, just barely audible over the din of the plane, he said, "Your poor, dear mother. It should have been your mother who got to take this trip. She had no hard feelings about Hungary. She never had hard feelings about anyone. She was stronger than I was, always was. *Tougher* is the word. She was tough. In fact, she was superior to me in every category, though I never let her know it or believe it. It was a different time. I was from a superior social class, and I was a man. It was the sort of thinking that prevailed. We didn't ask too many questions. In a land of freedom and equality and democracy—but *real* freedom, *real* equality, *real* democracy, if there is such a thing—everyone asks questions in the belief that there is an answer to every question. Not in my day. Not in those days. I never let on that I knew your mother was better than I was in every category. Or maybe she did know, and *she* was the one who never let on—she was the one who'd played along. In any case, everybody knew it. No one needed to make declarations. But it was not the way your mother thought about anything. People were not superior or inferior. She was humble. That was all, humble as could be." After a moment, he added, "We're not in that era anymore, nor are we in the era when someone else routinely polishes your shoes or sets out your clothing for you, let alone dresses you. Good riddance to it. Believe me, it's not good, even if you're the one whose shoes are being shined. Arguably, it's worse."

"I'm assuming Mom never got to meet Bela," Ben said.

"No. I met your mom at the end of the war, when I came back. But thank goodness she was there. She kept vigil with my mother. It was what won her over with my mother. After all, I was the only son my mother had left."

Suddenly, the fullness of Hannah's fortitude rose up in Ben, the fullness of her generosity, her ability—willingness— to forgive. What went through her mind when Zoltan finally told her?

Ben looked his father dead in the eye. Did he intuit what Ben knew? Would he have told him such a thing if he had? Ben glanced at his father's jacket, torn at the shoulder.

"I'm weak," Zoltan said. "I told you."

16

Bela lay unconscious on Zsofia's bed. The colonel was down at the police station being questioned by the Russians. He'd been gone for twelve hours. But it was not Colonel Vad that his family was fretting about.

"How could you have thought him a robber?" Zsofia demanded to know. "Look at him."

"He was outside our house on a winter night peering in," her mother said. "How would you have interpreted that behavior?"

Enek was sobbing. She was the one who'd selected the large rock from the flower bed. She had wanted to do the deed herself, but her mother had taken the rock from her.

Bela's head was wrapped in several linen towels, but the back of his head was still oozing.

"We have to call Dr. Braun to come examine him," Zsofia said.

"If your father finds Bela here, we'll all need Dr. Braun," said Mrs. Vad.

"Please, Mother," Enek said. "If we don't do something, he'll—"

"I'll call him," Zsofia said.

Her mother didn't try to stop her.

The doctor wasn't much help. He examined Bela by looking into his eyes with a small flashlight and by listening to his chest, but all he could say was that he could come out of it, or not. They would just have to see.

"He's from the labor camp," the doctor added. He'd noticed the familiar uniform beneath the white shirt.

"Yes, he is," Zsofia said.

"His comrades are not faring well."

"Why are they his comrades?" Zsofia said. "They are Hungarians, and now they're liberated, are they not? They are Hungarians like us."

She looked ready to pounce again, but the doctor backed down. He told them to call him if Bela stirred or they noticed any change in him and that he might come in any case the following day to have a look.

"It's best that you don't," Mrs. Vad said. "Not if there's nothing you can do for him. There will be trouble here either way."

The doctor nodded to show he understood and departed.

Colonel Vad came home at midnight. His wife and younger daughter were waiting for him in the parlor.

"Ah, you were worried about me," he said.

"Yes," they said in unison.

"We might have to get out of here," the colonel said. "They weren't satisfied with my role in the war effort. I'm surprised they didn't lock me up. But their commanding officer will be here tomorrow. I have to go back to the station first thing tomorrow or they'll make quick work of all of us. This is not going to turn out well. We'll have to leave here, if I come back at all."

Then Zsofia came down the stairs. "Ah, you too," the colonel said. "My three darlings."

"Bela is upstairs," she said.

"Bela who?" The colonel got to his feet.

"Bela Beck. He's lying unconscious on my bed."

"On your bed," the colonel repeated. He held his fists at his sides. He was set to storm upstairs.

The women told him what had happened. "The nerve of him to come here," he said. "Well, let me take another rock to his head to finish him off."

Zsofia stood in his face. "You'll have to take a rock to my head first," she said.

"Don't, please," Mrs. Vad said. She was on her feet too. "I was the one who invited him here for the music lesson."

"How dare you?" the colonel said to the three of them. "Do you know who that man is?"

"Yes," Zsofia said, "and I know who you are too."

The colonel slapped his daughter. "This is what you have for me now. I have spent a day being cross-examined by the Russians, and I'll have to do it again tomorrow. If I make it back here, we'll have to escape ourselves—*if* we can. Do you understand?"

"I won't be going with you," his daughter said.

He was about to strike her again, this time with his fist, but his wife jumped between them and took the blow herself.

She dropped to the floor, and without looking down at her, the colonel marched to the front of the house, pulled his wet coat on and flung open the door. When he did, two Russian soldiers grabbed him and spirited him away in their car.

A whole week passed before Zoli told Istvan he thought he'd better go home. He was completely recovered, certainly well enough to travel. Perhaps Bela would be at home to meet him. Istvan wanted to drive him to Budapest, but Zoli insisted it would not be safe. "I would not want you to drive me even to the train station, but if you would lend me the fare, I feel strong enough to get myself there. You've done so much for me already." Istvan reluctantly agreed, and Ildi packed Zoli four boiled eggs, some cheese and half a loaf of bread.

When Zoli's train pulled into the station in Budapest, he saw Russian soldiers and army vehicles everywhere and not a single German. People were walking about freely, and he was happy to join them.

He rushed home and banged too hard on the door when he got there. Vera, the housekeeper, answered. "Master Zoltan," she said to him, surprised.

"Is my brother here?" he asked, as he stepped in. He was peering over her shoulder. But she hardly gave him room to pass.

"No," she replied. "Your parents have been frantic about both of you. They'll be so glad to see you."

Zoli shouted past her. "Mother! Father!"

Vera stopped him. "They're not here."

"Have they gone out?"

"They moved out. They had to. The Germans moved them to another building. To the ghetto."

"And where might that be?"

"Behind the big temple near Dohany Street—only, the temple has been bombed. They're on Dob Street." Vera had begun to cry, and a teenage girl stepped into the vestibule to join them. She was taller than her mother. Vera took hold of her and the two of them cried together. "This is my daughter, Szilvia," Vera said.

Zoli had not met Szilvia. Vera didn't live with the Becks but came every day to work in their home. "We live here now," Vera said, as she looked down at the floor.

"And where is Mr. Vukcsics?" Zoli asked.

The question touched off a fresh round of sobbing. "I don't know what became of him," she said, sniffling. "He left one night in March in 1942 but never came back."

"But the war didn't come to Hungary until two years later." And then Zoli realized what he'd said. The man hadn't left for the battlefield. "You've had no word from him?" he asked gently. Vera shook her head. Szilvia was looking at him, wondering what was to come next. She had startling blue eyes and sunny hair.

"So you're here now," he began again, "and—"

"We're here with three other families, while we sort out all of what is to happen."

"Sort it out?"

A buxom woman in a bright orange blouse crept up behind them but hesitated and smiled. She had a mouth full of gold teeth.

"Of course there will be room for you here, as well as for Dr. and Mrs. Beck."

"Room?" he repeated.

Now Szilvia looked down too and began fidgeting.

"Your mother will be anxious to see you," Vera said, "both your parents. They're very anxious about you."

Zoli took down his parents' address and left with a warm goodbye. As he made his way toward Dob Street, for the first time in his life he felt like a stranger in his own city. The Szoke, the familiar club where his mother played her weekly game of canasta or gin rummy, had been blown open, its innards scattered into the street, chunks of brick and marble flooring, the legs of chairs, shreds of green felt from the card tables, shards of shattered crystal from the great chandelier, even burned and muddied cards. In the adjoining building, the Ellenor Bakery was open and bustling, but half the roof was missing and the bakery's awning torn. The business had spilled out into an improvised corner stand. Next to it, the French lace shop, miraculously, stood unscathed, as if it had put out a signal: We are too delicate to be harmed: think of the pretty bride-to-be under your roof; think of your little girls. The Chain Bridge had collapsed into the Danube and the library had been burned, its books turned to ash, all of it shoveled into a mountain in the middle of the street, an ash mountain. The little shoe repair shop, Bence and Hilda's shop, which the Becks had patronized since before Zoli was born, could barely be identified in the rubble, reduced to bits of shoes, buckles, a high heel, a trail of cleats like misshapen coins leading to a sewer grate, the detached finger of a tan glove, lost, pointing somewhere up the street toward the river. And what of Bence and Hilda? Had they been blown up with their shop? Were there bits of their flesh and bones scattered among the bits of leather? Or had they been dragged away somewhere? Was that what the finger of the glove was saying?

In its strange, unwholesome way, the setting made more sense to Zoli than Hajnal had. His family had been moved, his brother was missing, the buildings were down or listing, the order of things ruptured. After the experience he'd just survived, little else would have made sense.

Only Zoli's mother was home in the new place. His father had found his government office occupied by his "successor" but was back at work in the clinic. With the people streaming back from the camps and the battlefields, there was plenty to keep Dr. Beck occupied, even if his patients were not quite sure how to pay him.

Eugenia was delirious to see her son. She cried with such abandon that it took a couple of minutes for her to ask about Bela. Zoli told her he was safe, they'd both made it safely out of the labor camp, but that Bela was detained in Szifla.

"Detained?" Eugenia said.

"Yes, not by anyone. There was just someone he needed to see."

"But what's the delay? Your father and I can travel to Szifla tomorrow. Dr. Bauer can take his patients, or they can wait an extra day. It doesn't matter—"

Zoli took his mother's face in his hands. "No," he told her. "Szifla is crawling with Russians, and they're not as friendly as the ones here. And Bela is likely not there anymore. He would have fled from there by now."

"*Fled?*"

"Please, Mother. It's complicated. Please, let's give it a few more days and worry after that." Zoli couldn't bring himself to tell his mother that it had been over a week already since he and his brother had split up, even if he believed Bela was in hiding somewhere, likely with Zsofia, likely away from the Russians, and away from her father.

But when another day passed and his parents could not be consoled, Zoli walked out to a nearby café and paid to use their phone. He called the Vads in Szifla.

The conversation was simple and straightforward. Mrs. Vad answered. He told her who he was.

"Oh," was all she said.

Zoli began to say, "Your daughter—"

"My daughter is not here."

"My brother, Bela—"

"Bela is gone," she said. "Forever. Please do not call here again."

Zoli asked, "What do you mean forever? Did the Russians—"

"Yes," she replied. "The Russians. The Russians were here too. There is nothing more for you here, I promise you. I'm sorry we had to bring you here and keep you here. It turned out badly. For all of us. Please," she said. "Goodbye." And she hung up.

Eugenia and Vilmos searched everywhere. Zoli never found a way to tell them about Zsofia. They went to their grave not knowing. What good would it have done if they had known?

Hannah came on the scene one day. Her parents, four brothers and two sisters, including her baby sister Ruthie, had been killed in Tolgy, a small border town, yet here Hannah was, the last of her tribe left standing. She wandered into Budapest, a pretty blond, blue-eyed girl of sixteen, took a job in a small coffee shop that had withstood the invaders and soon met Zoli's aunt Hildy, Eugenia's sister, a regular at the coffee shop.

Hildy was very taken with her and begged her to come stay with her. Hildy's own daughter and husband had not made it back from Bergen-Belsen with her. It would do both of them good. It had been six months since Zoli had returned from the camp. When he and his mother visited Hildy one day, there was Hannah. Hildy quickly became a favorite relative of Zoli's. He visited every day, sometimes twice, and remarkably often straight after Hannah's hours at the Madar Café. Within a year, the two were married. Hildy was delighted and bereft, but Hannah never forgot her kindness.

Hannah joined her mother-in-law in the search for Bela. She went out with Eugenia every day to check for returnees at the railway stations. Maybe Bela had been injured and was finally well enough to come home. People were coming back from Auschwitz and from Dachau, from Buchenwald. From German hospitals. From British hospitals. Bela might have been badly injured. He might have been taken away to Russia with Raoul Wallenberg. Nobody could tell the Becks anything. Not even in Szifla. Zoli's parents hired an agency to check police records, anything. They found out nothing. And Zoli followed up with the same agency to search for the Vads. All they could turn up was a death certificate for Colonel Vad, signed by a Judge Lengyel and date-stamped February 12, 1945, just four weeks after Zoli and Bela had fled the labor camp.

17

When Ben and his father landed at Ferenc Liszt Airport in Budapest, Zoltan instantly became fidgety in the passport line. "They'll see that we were born here."

"They will," Ben said.

They stood a moment later in front of the official, and even before the man had opened their passports, Zoltan blurted out in Hungarian that they were born here but fled to safety and security in Canada and were here only to visit and only for a week, after which time they'd be going straight back home. Zoltan was visibly trembling. The man looked at the tear in the shoulder of his jacket and stamped their passports without a word, not even "Welcome."

Whenever they drove to the United States, Zoltan was invariably the one in a hundred who was pulled over at the border. They did everything but strip-search him. If Hannah were with him, they would smile in answer to her smile and commiserate with her before finally waving them through.

Ben and Zoltan collected their luggage, and Ben led his father straight to a car rental counter. He lit up at once. "So this was the surprise!" he said. "It is almost as big as anti-Semitism. You're going to let me drive again."

Ben had reserved the car for one driver, but the man at the counter now asked if he should add a second name. Ben asked what the insurance implications would be. The man glanced at the shoulder of Zoltan's jacket. Zoltan took out his wallet and flashed fifty Canadian dollars at the man. He took it and told them not to worry. "*Occasional* driver," he stressed.

"Occasional to never," Ben said.

The man didn't even ask to see Zoltan's driver's license. He seemed to be suggesting they'd "handle" it if they had to.

The car was brought up by a younger man, who helped load the Becks' luggage into it. Zoltan tipped him too and told him in Hungarian that he would be driving.

"Great," the young man said, though he clearly couldn't care less.

"Are you sure about this?" Ben asked his father.

"Yes," he said, as he threw back the seat so it was almost out of reach of the steering wheel and pedals. "You direct me."

His hands were shaking as he took the wheel by his fingertips. Then off they went.

"It's all the way into town. I booked us a two-bedroom suite on Erzsebet Street."

"Ah, Erzsebet," Zoltan said with relish. "The New York Café is on that street."

"Yes, the New York Café. I saw pictures of it online. It's spectacular."

His father slammed on the brakes and put a hand on his heart. "It's the most beautiful café in the city, for my money, and it has quite a history. Another surprise!" Someone honked and Zoltan took his foot off the brake.

Ben traced his father's sightline and was surprised he could see above the dashboard, but they lurched forward, then lurched again. Ben's heart was thudding mightily, but he looked across at his father. This was his last stand, his last thrill. He'd loved driving, strangely, because driving meant he was in charge. It was all about leading. He loved leading his people, founding a new family, taking them out to a new land, and now those days were behind him. It was a small price Ben was paying to let him drive for a short time. All he had to do was risk dying in a fiery crash.

There was a van parked at the curb and a woman getting in on the driver's side. Her door was still open and her bag still sat on the roadway, jutting out slightly into Zoltan's path.

"Dad."

"What?" he said, as he drove straight at her.

Ben was reaching over when his father swung the car far to the left toward a parked bus. Luckily, it was all in such slow motion that Ben could call out to him well in advance.

Ben knew that this was among his father's last wishes, as it were, so what could he say? At this speed, they would not die in a fiery crash after all, just injure themselves, possibly badly, along with someone else most likely. They had their seat belts on, and Ben noted that the car was equipped with airbags.

Someone honked from behind and his father veered the other way. Ben still hadn't even checked the GPS to aim them in the right direction, but going in the right direction was the least of their problems. Going at all was the bigger concern.

A blast came from a tractor trailer trying to overtake them, and which Zoltan seemed to want to sideswipe to express his excitement.

And then, once the tractor trailer did pass, Zoltan braked suddenly, tires screeching—incredible that they had any screech in them at this speed—and rather than pull over, he simply sat there, trying to grip the wheel with trembling fingers. "Maybe you'd better drive," he said. He still hadn't shifted to Park.

"Are you all right?" Ben asked.

His father looked pale. "I'm all right, but you should drive." He mouthed something to the steering wheel. Ben saw that he was about to open his door, whispering something, quite resigned to it. They were blocking the road. People were honking. Ben quickly shifted to Park before jumping out. Zoltan really was a dasher—he was over on Ben's side of the car even before Ben had a chance to catch his breath.

As Ben drove on, his father slumped in his seat. Ben pulled over to check the GPS, then continued.

"Driving was not the surprise," his father said dejectedly.

"No, it was not driving."

"It wasn't Velda Kerbel, was it?"

"*Velda?* Why would it be Velda?"

"I don't know. Velda was the surprise at home. I thought she might stop by to see us on her way to Milan to touch up *The Last Supper.*"

Ben wanted to unpack and have a little rest in their hotel suite, but despite his original reluctance his father was raring to go. Lucy had neatly packed their clothes—as neatly and pristinely as a boutique might have arranged them for sale—and Ben helped his father hang up the important outerwear and transferred their innerwear to drawers.

His father changed right away and came out of his bedroom to find Ben. He was wearing a navy suit and burgundy tie and looked neat and handsome, primly dressed as if to conceal the agents of death at work inside him. But unknowingly, of course. He didn't know. How could he know?

Nevertheless, Ben was happy for him. *Carpe diem.* He looked happy. An elegant suit was such a nice corrective. Lucy must have picked it out for him. It made his father look like a younger man, a better driver, a neater eater, someone still engaged in life, on his way to something.

Zoltan put on his long wool coat. He wanted to head out to the New York Café. He was greeting people they passed on the street. He was bursting to tell his son things. He was speaking only Hungarian to him now. Let Ben be the foreigner for once. Ben could smell snow in the air—he could sense flecks of it tinged with the Danube.

The New York Café was what New York aspired to be. It was like a mini–Sistine Chapel, but rather than featuring Creation, it featured its spoils. Its ceilings and walls were filled with bacchanalian figures, enjoying love and drink and life, held up by barley-twist pillars, some spindly, some writhing, giving the effect of movement and dance, as if a Nijinsky ballet could erupt from behind one of them, as if youth and music resided here and were sent out into the world from here. It was as if Michelangelo's *David* had impregnated a Fabergé egg (while the *Mona Lisa* looked on) and this room was their love child. It was where the Sun King's mistress might have taken her afternoon tea and biscuits—and not any mistress—his favorite, or at the very least his second favorite.

Ben could see why his father had put on a formal suit and felt underdressed himself in jeans and a black turtleneck.

A middle-aged British couple was ushered to a table just two over from the Beck boys. The woman was all abubble about some embroidered place mats she had bought. She was wearing a turquoise cardigan alive with flowers. The man had snakes and other reptile tattoos writhing down the length of both arms all the way to his knuckles.

Ben felt that the New York should institute a dress code, a restriction that would affect him too. Just what order of mistress of Louis XIV did they think they were having cake with?

It would be hard to be invisible in this place, which was why Ben's father had known to put on his suit. It was the best you could do. You could not blend with the New York— you could only try your best to aspire in the way that it seemed to aspire. Otherwise, it accentuated or augmented your look. If you came in wearing lime green, it made you look amphibious. It turned yellow into solar, and sultry into the mistress of Louis XIV.

A waiter approached the British couple, and the man said he'd like some Bakewell tarts. The waiter blushed and shook his head. "I'm sorry, sir. I don't know this tart." The man huffed. "*Bakevell?*" the waiter repeated.

The woman told her husband to leave the waiter alone and chuckled.

"No," the man said. "Why does everything all over the planet have to be Frenched up like this? Is that the only country of powdered poofters? Doesn't anyone else have nice sweets?"

"I will get the pastry chef," the waiter said.

"Never mind," the man said, and he got to his feet and stomped out. His wife buttoned herself entirely into her tight floral cardigan, looked meekly over at Zoltan and Ben, then down into her bag of embroidered mats before following her husband out.

The same waiter approached the Becks. He looked rattled. Zoltan, speaking in Hungarian, insisted they order the café's world-famous chestnut purée, and the waiter smiled and looked relieved. The dessert turned out to be an astonishing creation, as rich and creamy as the room itself.

Zoltan told Ben that the New York Café was the favorite of the literary set at the turn of the last century and that some of the country's greatest writers spent many an afternoon here and were treated like royalty, as befitted the splendor of the place. Whenever one of the greats came in—Ferenc Molnar, or the aging Mor Jokai, or Endre Ady, with his fresh take on the new century—his favorite table would be set and waiting for him. The great artists were promptly served their favorite *palinka*, favorite coffee, favorite sweets, and were handed paper and pen to record their thoughts.

"This was also a favorite haunt of Bela," Zoltan said. He leaned forward. His eyes were glistening. "The editors of the country's greatest literary journal, *Nyugat*—or *West, The West*—held their editorial meetings here up in those galleries," said Zoltan. "They received the verse or prose of the country's aspiring writers. Since we're in the New York Café, imagine the editors of *The New Yorker* waiting to receive your work and read it—or not—as they saw fit."

A Gypsy violinist appeared from around a corner and began playing over them. He had an expression of sweetness fixed on his face to go with the sweetness of his violin. Zoltan shooed the man away as if he were a giant insect, but the violinist didn't budge. Zoltan smiled up at him with a fakeness to match the man's. Still he played on. Zoltan pulled a ten-dollar bill out of his wallet, pushed it at the player and shooed him away again. This time the man turned, still smiling, and moved on.

A great gilded Cupid clock was smiling down at the Beck boys from beneath an archway. It rivaled the musician in size and sweetness. It had a white clock embedded in Cupid's belly with a single black hand pointing at the "I." Ben surveyed this fantastic room some more. He couldn't quite decide if it was the most splendid room in the world or a Las Vegas knock-off of the most splendid room in the world. Could it be both? Either way, it felt good to be there with his father. And he was right: you should sometimes just leave things alone.

Zoltan seemed to be feeling the same way. Ben sensed in his bones that he was the right one to have brought his father here. He sometimes wondered what purpose he served where his father was concerned, but Ben was his best listener. And Zoltan needed someone to believe in him. He sensed that his middle son believed in him. Lucy too, of course. Lucy and Ben were his last best advocates.

Of the three sons, Ben looked most like his father, but he often wondered how much of his nature he'd inherited compared to his brothers. Zoltan had to have passed on some part of himself, but if Ben wasn't fooling himself, he had to believe the larger part came from his mother. She would be on this trip and listening to him, if she were called upon, if she could have.

But who could take the measure of these things? Ben was part him, part her and part tree after all the chestnut purée he was imbibing.

He wondered what parts of him he would take, if he had a say in the matter, what parts he did take, what parts he didn't. And if his father had a say in the matter, what parts of himself would he have given Ben? And how had Zoltan been remade by his history and how had Ben? It was all too much to contemplate. It made people spiritual or even religious, reaching outside of themselves for answers, sending up questions into the heavens just to calm them down. Complexity was not calming, not compared to simplicity.

"Bela once brought a poem here, one that he'd been working on all summer," Zoltan said. "He folded it neatly in a light blue vellum envelope of our father's and brought it one evening to the New York. I came with him. I'd never seen him so anxious. In fact, I'd never seen him be anxious about anything. He was forever calm—and *calming*. In his presence, everybody felt better, all the girls—and me, his kid brother. Elderly aunts turned girlish in his presence. Our parents seemed to liven up when he was home.

"Yet here he was, at the New York Café, a supplicant awaiting judgment by the editors of *Nyugat*. He was barely sixteen. I was fourteen. He asked a pretty assistant standing by one of the pillars"—Zoltan turned around to point to it—"if he could take the envelope up to the gallery, and she yielded immediately. I was not allowed to go with him, so I sat down and ordered cocoa and chestnut purée. He was back within a few minutes. He said, 'Let's go.' I'd only just begun to eat my dessert, but he insisted. It was the first rejection of his life, the first rebuke. He never showed anyone another poem again, though he kept writing them, and though he'd already been published, and not just in student publications, in anthologies of contemporary poetry."

Zoltan stirred what was left of his coffee. He said again, "Bela's first rejection—he'd poured his heart out—poured it into this poem and eagerly awaited the great men of *Nyugat* to tell him no—to tell him to go reread his Wordsworth, in the original if he could—that poetry is 'emotion recollected in tranquility.' Bela had never been turned away by anyone, as I said, not as an intellectual, not as a musician, a swimmer, a lover, a poet. On the way home, he muttered something about Mendelssohn's Octet in E-flat major, a piece that the great man—great *boy*—had composed when he was sixteen and was a masterpiece that still rivaled every chamber piece written. 'Emotion recollected in tranquility?' Bela said. 'Where was Mendelssohn's tranquility? He didn't live long enough for tranquility. He couldn't wait for it to settle down over him.'"

Zoltan gave a mighty sigh. "It's been a big job just being me," he said. "I can't imagine what it would have been like to be my brother.

"After Bela disappeared, some years later, I sent the journal another poem of his, without explanation, without saying who I was or he was, or that he was gone—just a straight submission by Bela Beck. They accepted it surprisingly quickly, and praised it glowingly. I kept the letter from them for years and, of course, the issue the poem was published in. How thrilled Bela would have been. How proud we all were. It was as if some of him had carried on. And it all began here, in this wondrous place."

Ben felt for the first time that they were figures in the jewel box that was this room, figures in one of its paintings, who'd earned their place by once having offered it their people's art, whatever its shortcomings.

"Where is the poem, and the issue it was published in?" Ben asked.

"Who knows? I left it here. We left everything."

"Wow, Dad, I'm so sorry."

And there it was again: the one tear in the corner of his father's eye. Ben thought he had only the one.

"I wrote poetry too," Zoltan said.

"You did?"

"Yes, but my poems scanned and rhymed. They were very old-fashioned."

"Do you have any of them stashed away? Can I see them?"

"No, of course not."

How was it possible that this man—who murdered his way through a toilet line, who ate dinner with the delicacy of a combine, who drove a car not as if he were the only one on the road but as if there were no road, who went for a coffee when his wife asked him from her deathbed to stay—that this man wrote poetry?

After the New York, they took a walk down to the Chain Bridge, with its necklace of lights strung across the Danube. Zoltan said that he and his brother had swum the river many times before the war.

They came across a bronze sculpture, called *The Little Princess*, sitting on a railing with her back to the river. She had quite a crown on her. Snow began to fall, but in a celebratory way, as if to mark the season. It felt like confetti. How pretty it was. Snow made everything cold and pretty. It was like consolation for the cold, Ben thought. Surely it was designed for that effect. Imagine if it had been designed to fall in summer—warm white bits—it would have been redundant, bordering on kitsch.

Zoltan was shivering. He pulled his coat tightly around himself. Ben suggested they get a cab back to the hotel, and his father agreed right away.

The following morning, Zoltan was waiting for Ben in their sitting room. He was wearing his blue suit again, and even the tie. "After breakfast, I have some sights I want to show you," he said. "I hope we can take the car."

"Sure we can. I think, though—"

"You will drive," he said.

"Yes, I will drive."

They had a buffet breakfast in their hotel, the two of them loading up as if it were the end of days. "This is new here," Zoltan said, as he crunched through a croissant. He had a good-sized dinner napkin tucked into the top of his shirt, a prudent move. "When we first got to Toronto, we found an all-you-can-eat buffet, and we couldn't believe the concept. I don't know if you remember. You were very young. It was down on Mutual Street. The Town and Country, it was called. You could sit there and eat four whole barbecue chickens. No one would say a word. We'd eat and eat and eat, then go staggering out of there. It was the following Thursday before I was hungry again. What a concept. And look: now it's here."

Afterward, they drove across the Erzsebet Bridge to Buda, and Zoltan pointed to an immense building his grandfather had owned, the grandfather with the famous summer house. Ben asked him who owned it now. His father said, "Who knows? Who cares?"

Zoltan prattled all day like a tour guide. For someone who wanted to live in a world of mutes, he talked up a storm in Hungary, as if Hungary had unlocked something in him. He was showing his son places he remembered with the exuberance of a child. They went to St. Stephen's Basilica and gazed into a glass case at the right hand of St. Stephen. Zoltan remembered to remove his fedora. Could it really have been the hand of the saint? What if it was? They went to Matthias Church, to Margaret Island, in the middle of the river, named after the thirteenth-century princess who resided in a convent there, then to the spectacular parliament buildings, which showed up in all the postcards and clips of river cruises, the Dohany Street Temple, the cemetery where Ben's great-grandparents lay, their headstones pockmarked by bullet holes because a revolutionary battle had raged right there, in what Zoltan insisted on calling a "boneyard."

Ben tried to feel the history. Even the sky looked historic here. Generations of his family had been born here and flourished here. *He* had been born here. The history was his, yet he could feel it only faintly, so well had the New World infiltrated him—so well had his father done his job to convert him. But if converting was so simple, what did it really mean, these deluded individualities lining up behind a tribe—the player on the team, the fan in the stands, the citizen of a realm? How silly was a realm, and how ridiculous people were to pretend they could belong to one with any certainty.

Finally, they visited their old house at 4 Izabella Street, near Andrassy Avenue, or rather drove by their house. Ben was not allowed to stop in front of it, merely slow down, then move on.

"Why can't we look in?" Ben asked.

"Because we would then have to speak to whoever is there," his father said.

"Do you mean Mrs. Vukcsics?" Zoltan didn't answer. "Dad, isn't that who's living there now?" No answer, not even a shrug. "Are we in touch with the people in that house?"

He crossed his arms and looked straight ahead. "I don't have to tell you."

Ben pulled over at the curb not far up the street. "Does that mean Mom reconnected with them?"

"How did you guess?"

"Because she was a connector, and she knew the address."

"She sent them a card some years ago, and they answered right away, a week later."

"And?"

"And it turns out it was our housekeeper, Mrs. Vukcsics, Vera Vukcsics, who stayed in the house after we fled. The one we talked about."

"That really was her name?"

"Yes, Vukcsics." He loved saying it. Who wouldn't? Vukcsics, *Vookcheech*. "Mrs. Vukcsics took over the place, or a portion of it, a quarter of it. There are—or *were*—four families in there. Your mom and Mrs. Vukcsics kept in touch, off and on, and then . . ." His voice trailed off. Ben waited, turned the engine off. "And Mrs. Vukcsics had a daughter, Szilvia Vukcsics. A nice girl," he said, almost inaudibly.

"I take it Szilvia never married," Ben said.

"How do you know that?" Zoltan said in an accusatory tone.

"Because you called her Szilvia Vukcsics."

Zoltan let out a breath before saying, "Szilvia—her mother, Vera, had died—and Szilvia . . . Szilvia wrote to say that she could apply for war reparations and that she had a disabled daughter, and that her 'partner' had left. She asked if she could apply on our behalf, please—we wouldn't have to do a thing—and she would keep some of the money. And so she did. We signed papers so that the money could be deposited directly in Szilvia Vukcsics's account. We got a tidy sum to add to our pension, and Szilvia Vukcsics got a tidy sum to help with her living expenses and her daughter. I told you."

"What about now?" Ben asked. "Are you still getting the reparations?"

"Not anymore. Why do we keep having to go over this?"

"Dad, why don't we go in and have a chat with Ms. Vukcsics?"

"She calls herself Mrs. She has a daughter. Some things never change."

Zoltan sat back hard, pulling the brim of his fedora down further in front, casting a deeper shadow over his eyes.

"Dad, don't you think we should chat with her?"

"No, it's exactly what I don't want to do. It's too complicated. Life is complicated. When I'm gone, which can't be long from now, you and your brothers can give her a little extra from the inheritance just to see her through—but for now, please leave me out of it." He looked up at Ben with his deeply shaded hazel eyes, dark green in this winter light. "I'm weak," he said again.

That night, after his father retired, Ben called Lucy to tell her he had failed in his mission to visit Mrs. Vukcsics, at least with his father.

"Then you have to visit her on your own," she said. "She's expecting you. You at least have to get to the bottom of what happened there. Have you forgotten?"

"Of course I haven't forgotten."

"Call her now. It's only 9 P.M., your time. You can go over now."

"Of course I'm not going over now."

"Then call her and set something up."

Ben did as directed. Mrs. Vukcsics spoke reasonable English though with a heavy accent. Ben assumed it was from communicating with all the Americans and Canadians she had solicited reparations for. "I have been waiting to hear from you. When will you come over?"

"In the next couple of days. I have to slip away from my father."

"Why?"

"It's a long story."

Ben heard Mrs. Vukcsics light a cigarette and take a deep drag. "So you come. It has to be tomorrow. You will see why."

"All right, but can it be late?"

"Yes, late. Any time. I don't sleep."

The tour continued the whole of the following day. Zoltan and Ben visited the temple on Rumbach Street, where his parents had been married after the war. They stood in the street and looked at it through a fence. Its eastern wall had been blown up by the Germans and not a hand had been laid on the building since, so it stood as a ruin, with the image of Joseph and his many-colored coat still visible in the one remaining stained-glass window. "We were married under that window," Zoltan told Ben. "We were standing in the fallen stones and bricks and glass. Your mother and grandmother had swept up bits of glass and dirt from one little spot. We set up the makeshift bimah there, and we hung a clean white chuppah over it." Ben was taking pictures, but there was little he could make out through the fence, except for the impressive Joseph. What a stalwart window it was.

White holiday lights blinked from the buildings to the left and right of them.

As they strolled back to the car, Zoltan said, "This heritage of ours is a bit much for me. I'm the wrong candidate for it. I'm not sure how fate or God or karma could have gotten it so wrong. I should have been an Englishman from the Midlands who takes an afternoon drive, who enjoys syllables and imagines how they join other syllables to make words, who eats steak and kidney pie, who watches *My Fair Lady* maybe once too often."

And then what? Ben wanted to ask him. What would happen on your afternoon drive when you run down a shepherd and eleven of his sheep? What would happen when you have to line up in the drizzle outside your local pub wearing white gloves? He was not sure that Midlanders went in for white gloves, unless they were butlers or doormen.

Ben called Lucy again from the hotel that evening. She kept assuring him it was a great "mitzvah" he was doing. Ben was impressed that she knew that word, along with so many other Hebrew ones. She sounded very far away. She asked about Szilvia Vukcsics, and Ben told him he was going over there just as soon as he was sure his dad had settled.

She sighed and said, "Can you feel you're with a man near the end? Does what's coming depress you?"

"I'm trying not to think about it."

"How can you not?"

"I cannot because I'm trying to enjoy this time with my father. Isn't that what I'm supposed to do?"

"Of course it is," she said.

"He's happy as hell."

"I'm glad," she said, but sighed again. A clearly audible transatlantic sigh. She was thinking about it much more than Ben was. This was the thing about Lucy. She would take you to where you didn't want to go, even when you'd just told her you didn't. Nevertheless, she repeated that she was glad Ben was enjoying the visit with his father and especially that his father was enjoying it too. "You're doing a great thing, but you and I are different," she said. "I don't know how we found each other, what you see in me."

"Don't project," he said.

"Of course I'm not projecting."

"Then, what I saw in you was everything. Or a lot, let's say. What I could not see in you at first was your tremendous name. Beauregard. That was it. I wanted a wife called Lucille Beauregard. The daughter of Alice and Lester Beauregard. You can't make this stuff up."

"Will you stop?"

"Beauregard. What a great name to hide out in, hide behind, anchor your children's first names with: Bethany Beauregard, Natalie Beauregard, Angela Beauregard, Timothy K. Beauregard."

"What does the *K* stand for?"

"It's silent. It stands for *Knuckle*."

"You really are such a silly beast," she said.

"How many people have mountains named after them? Mount Beauregard?"

"There is no Mount Beauregard."

"But let's say there is one."

She sighed again. "Please look after yourselves. Look after him, but look after yourself too."

Ben drove back to Izabella Street without calling in advance. Mrs. Vukcsics looked relieved to see him if not happy. She invited him into a room he must once have known, one of the first rooms of his life. The house had been subdivided into four units for the families his father had mentioned. He couldn't be sure which part they were in now, what the room corresponded to. It could easily have been the bedroom he'd shared with Frank.

"Look at you," she said to Ben, with her thick accent. "You were so small when you left. I wish we had fled with you."

"You and your daughter and your—"

"My poor Alice was born later. And I have no husband."

So there was a daughter. Mrs. Vukcsics poured Ben some Tokaj wine. It was very sweet but warm and smooth. It took the winter chill right out of him. She lit a cigarette and offered him one too, but he declined. He hadn't smoked since his student days.

"Where is your daughter?" Ben asked.

"She's gone. She was not well. She didn't make it." She blew out smoke wetly.

"And yet—" Ben began.

"Yes, and yet. So this is the life I have left. You like? You want?"

"No, I don't want." Ben took Bela's little notebook out of his pocket and the blond lock of hair Szilvia had sent his father. "I had the hair tested genetically," he said. "There is no link with my father."

She took the lock of hair from Ben and held it up to her nose and took a whiff. "Genetically," she repeated. "What about morally? Your father didn't know if it was or it wasn't. I will keep the hair," she said, and pressed it into a folded napkin.

Ben didn't know what to say. So that was it? Case closed.

"I have something for you," she said. She placed an envelope, marked the Ferenc Liszt Academy, on the table between them. Ben didn't reach for it. He wanted something more to happen—he wanted to press her, but she saved him the trouble. "I had no child with your father," she said. "You had no half-sister. Happy?" Ben nodded faintly. "Open the envelope," she said.

There were two concert tickets inside. "Oh, how nice of you," Ben said.

"Have a look at the tickets," she said.

They were for a recital on Wednesday afternoon, a piano recital featuring Zsofia Beck. Mrs. Vukcsics's eyes were blazing. "But someone did have a child. Feel free to have her tested genetically."

"Is she related to us?" Ben asked.

"Yes, she is. She's Bela's granddaughter."

"My father's Bela? *Our* Bela?"

"*Your* Bela. Your father's brother had a child with Zsofia. Or he left her pregnant."

"Bela *left* her."

"No, he didn't leave her. He died."

It was the first time he'd heard it said. His family had wondered, had guessed at a thousand fates, but the word had never been uttered. "They had a son, or Zsofia had a son. She named him Bela Beck. Poor man, the son. I found him because I was searching for more labor camp survivors, checking them against death certificates, crossing people off the list. Naturally, I recognized the name right away because of the family." She indicated the house they were sitting in. She took a drag of her smoke and exhaled straight at Ben. "But of course, this was not *the* Bela Beck. It was his son. This one died of cancer prematurely, poor, poor man. One of the bad ones," she said. "Pancreatic. Some years ago. Ten at least." She tried to pick a bit of tobacco from the tip of her tongue, and when she couldn't, she spat toward the floor. It was an old ceramic tile floor with a fleur-de-lis pattern. It stirred an ancient memory in Ben. He thought again of Nadinka. How she had driven his cars with him across these tiles, their pattern imprinted on his memory as the path to good and happy things.

"Bela Beck," he repeated.

"Yes, and he had a daughter, Zsofia, named after her grandmother. It's her recital you'll be seeing on Wednesday. She knows you're coming. I told her."

He put his hand over his mouth. He was suddenly nervous. He felt for the folded lump of cash in his front pants pocket to make sure it was there, though he knew it was. He got to his feet. "Please let me pay you for the tickets." He pulled out a couple of hundred dollars.

"Don't be silly," she said. "I've done well enough by you."

"I insist. Let me give you a bit of money."

"Please," she said. "I was so glad to make this connection between you. It feels right to me." She put her hand on her heart, and then she hugged Ben and kissed him on the cheek in a warm, tobacco-y way. Her eyes were glistening.

"Goodbye, Mrs. Vukcsics. I'm glad we met."

She watched as he walked out to his car. He had a last look at the building. She was waving even as he drove away.

18

On Wednesday morning, Ben told his father that this was the day of the surprise he had mentioned. The surprise was bigger even than Ben had thought, much bigger, bigger than anti-Semitism. He was going to relieve his father of the guilt he felt about Szilvia Vukcsics. Zoltan asked what they were doing, and Ben said they were going to a late-afternoon concert.

"Do you have tickets?"

"Yes, I ordered them online from home."

"From home." He didn't look too impressed, but he did say, "They have nice concerts here. They take their music very seriously. At the opera house?" Ben shook his head. "The Budapest Philharmonic? They are very good." No again.

"Let me surprise you," Ben said.

"I don't know if I can stand all the excitement."

"Do you know what, Dad? It will be good."

"I'm sure," he said. "Will it be in a coffee shop or a tavern?"

"It will be at the Liszt Academy."

Now his father sat up. "Really?" Ben took his turn not answering this time. "My brother played there. He *taught* there."

"Yes," Ben replied, but said nothing more.

Zoltan and Ben arrived at the Liszt Academy quite early, as was their wont. It was an impressive late-nineteenth-century building. The freestanding sign outside the door, which was framed by white holiday lights, listed the late-afternoon's piano recital and its player, Zsofia Beck.

His father looked at the sign and then at Ben. "What a name she has," he said.

"Yes."

"Is that why you brought me here—because of this glorious name?"

"Yes it is," Ben said.

"I wonder how old she is."

"Early thirties. Thirty-two, to be exact. I looked her up."

Zoltan searched his son's eyes, then said, "Let's go inside. I'm cold."

They checked their coats and were shown into the old walnut-paneled recital hall. It was here Ferenc Liszt himself—or Franz Liszt, as the rest of the world liked to call him, and as he liked to call himself to avoid the taint of being Hungarian—premiered several of his last works. Some seventy-five or eighty seats were arranged around a Bösendorfer grand piano.

Zoltan took a seat, front and center, while Ben wandered around the hall. Along a side wall, there was a permanent exhibit in glass cases of Liszt paraphernalia. One case held a pair of white gloves with remarkably long fingers. One held his handwritten score to the Hungarian Dances, Number 2. One held his metronome, one a triangle he'd played as a child, one his white tuxedo shirt and black bow tie, one a letter from Clara Schumann to Franz, and another letters from Camille Saint-Saëns and Frédéric Chopin. The last display case Ben looked at contained the composer's childhood diary, opened at the entry for April 13, 1823. The twelve-year-old wrote, in Hungarian, that Ludwig van Beethoven had heard him play in Vienna—or *seen* him, Liszt wrote, since the older man was deaf by then—but Beethoven seemed to know what notes Liszt was playing by watching and imagining—and then he'd taken the young Liszt's face in his hands and kissed him, once on each cheek, once on the mouth. Liszt wrote that Beethoven had tears in his eyes: "I've brought tears to Ludwig van Beethoven's eyes! Onward!" A note from the curator, on a card placed at the foot of the diary, said that in his will Beethoven had left his piano to Liszt and that the instrument was housed in the Hungarian National Museum.

Zoltan had saved the seat beside him by placing his hat and gloves on it; he said he'd not checked these at the coat check because he was still cold. He asked about the exhibits, and Ben mentioned a few, starting with Liszt's white gloves. "Maybe he had a rash too," his father said.

The radiators were ticking. They'd been cranked up for the concert, no doubt. The hall began to fill up. Zoltan asked where they were having supper afterward—he was hungry already—and Ben told him they could eat wherever he wanted. Zoltan mentioned a schnitzel place they had passed on Andrassy—it was an old place he knew—and Ben said sure, wherever.

Within a few minutes, the hall had filled up entirely, especially with young people, students most likely. Zoltan whispered too loudly that Zsofia Beck might be on the faculty here. These might be her students. He seemed to be admiring them, their youth and exuberance.

But there were some older people too—certainly one woman, who was as old as Zoltan. She was dressed in an elegant black dress accented with white pearls. She must have been cold too, because she wore a fur coat draped over her shoulders. She sat in a reserved seat, the last seat to the left in the front row.

A white-haired, elegantly dressed gentleman entered from a side door and stood before them. He welcomed everyone in grand Hungarian manner and enumerated Zsofia Beck's accomplishments. She had won the International Tchaikovsky Competition when she was just nineteen and had not looked back. She had graduated from Juilliard. She was now touring with the Berlin Philharmonic and recording with Deutsche Grammophon. She was the recipient of a dozen international prizes, including a Grammy. She was now to play a program of pieces selected especially for this occasion.

Then out stepped Zsofia Beck. She was a radiant beauty, with white skin, raven-black hair and brown—almost black—eyes, like dark beads of oil on white porcelain. But more striking—far more—was that she was the female incarnation of Zoltan's brother. If Ben had set the two dozen or more photos he'd seen of Bela beside hers, except for the length of hair, one could not distinguish between the living and the dead. Ben didn't once look at his father. In fact, he shielded his left eye with a hand, like a visor. And Zoltan was more silent than anyone could have expected him to be.

In a sweet, clear voice, Zsofia said she would be playing a special program for a very special occasion. Ben could feel his father's eyes on him, but he did not budge. "In honor of the warm building which now shields us from the chilly river wind, I'll start with a Hungarian rhapsody of Ferenc Liszt, his second. It will be followed by a piano adaptation of Ferenc Lehar's "Vilja Song," from *The Merry Widow*. I'll play a little Chopin, and then I'll close with a favorite of my grandmother's, Robert Schumann's *Kinderszenen*."

She was looking right at Zoltan and Ben, never once addressing anyone else in the room, yet the young people shouted hurrahs and applauded boisterously. What a mysterious thing. It took about thirty seconds to swoon for her, for her warmth, for her white hands clasped in front of her black dress, for the white collar like a platter holding up her sculpted neck, face and head, for the entirety of her.

And then she sat and played, softly, tenderly, softening even the rhapsodic lilt of the Liszt and the Lehar. The Schumann she played lovingly, as if she herself had given birth to the children featured in the piece and was calming their fears on a winter afternoon. She played to thunderous approval, the young people whooping and cheering and applauding uproariously. She finished the program, left and returned to play a little more, a little Beethoven, she said, "Für Elise." It was all so pretty, and with such a reception it could have continued much longer, but she brought the performance to a close with the help of the host, who clapped and then held up his hands to halt the proceedings.

This time Zsofia did not leave the room. People filed by her lovingly. She smiled at each of them, hugged many, and thanked them over and over. Ben turned to his father, who had uncharacteristically stayed in his seat and could not take his eyes off the dazzling young woman.

When the last of her fans filed out, Zoltan rose from his seat but looked wobbly. Zsofia walked to where he and Ben were standing. Zoltan took her hands, opened his mouth, but nothing came out.

"Hello," she said. "I am Zsofia Beck, Bela's granddaughter."

"Bela," he said. That was all he could manage.

"Uncle Zoltan," she said warmly, and put her arms around him. She spoke English without an accent. "I'd like you to meet my grandmother Zsofia."

The striking older woman in the fur shook Zoltan's hand. "Zsofia," he repeated.

"It's been a few years," she said in Hungarian. And there were the liquid eyes. "We have a great deal to talk about," the elder Zsofia said, "and you'll come to our home in Buda now for dinner, and we'll catch up."

"Dinner," he repeated. His face emptied of color, pulling all of his vocabulary down with it, past his mouth, past the exit.

"Of course. What do you think?" she said. "We're going to let you sail off now, after all this time?"

She half turned and was about to move off but waited for his answer. Finally, he recovered himself a little. He said, "We tried for years to find you. I tried for years. I didn't know what had happened to all of you. No one said what became of my brother."

"I'll tell you everything tonight."

The younger Zsofia put her arm around her great-uncle's shoulder and kissed him on the cheek. "Please," she said in English. "We're so glad you're here. Finally."

The color had not returned to Zoltan's face. Was it too much for him all at once? Was it too late to be stirring this up in him? Were the Zsofias and Ben pulling him out of his strangeness, the foreignness that had shielded him from the goings-on here, the continuation of his history? Why did people always assume that everyone was the same and had the same impulses and desires? Why did Ben assume? Why did Lucy assume?

"Dad," Ben whispered, "we don't have to go. I'm happy to take you to the schnitzel place."

"Of course we'll go," he said. "I owe it to my brother."

They offered Ben and Zoltan a ride, but Ben told them they had a car and could follow. The ladies gave the gentlemen the address, just in case. But they had a red Audi, and it was a quiet evening, so it was easy to keep up.

Ben's father looked dazed in the car. He hadn't put his hat on straight, and Ben helped to adjust it. "How did you manage all this?" Zoltan asked.

"It wasn't easy. Lucy did most of the legwork. But Mrs. Vukcsics was the key." Ben told his father about the visit to her place—their one-time home. Of course, he left out the part about the lock of blond hair and the daughter.

"But how could it have come together? Zsofia's name was Vad."

"*Was*," Ben said.

His father rubbed his face with his hands. "Oh, my dear lord," he said. "How much of the story do you know?"

"Not all of it, but some. A lot. From Mom. And from your mom."

"Of course you do. You and Lucy. How could I be so naïve?"

They followed the red Audi across the Chain Bridge into Buda.

"Dad, did you know way back then that Zsofia was pregnant?"

He didn't answer, not even to say "I don't have to tell you." For once, Ben wanted him to say it.

"Dad?"

"Please," Zoltan said, without looking at him. "This is too much for me. I didn't know she was pregnant. How could I have known? It means a whole life has grown up over here, a whole branch of the Beck family. Did you see that girl? Did you watch her play music? Did you see her? She was channeling him, I swear, and she was as good as he was—better. She records with Deutsche Grammophon. And look at us now. We're going over there for dinner."

"The beautiful Zsofia."

"Yes, the beautiful Zsofia."

"Like her grandmother. Her grandmother is beautiful."

"Yes," said Zoltan. "But more like her grandfather. *Exactly* like her grandfather. It's eerie, actually. Extraordinary." He rubbed his face again.

"Dad, you're sure you want to go?"

"Of course I want to go." A moment later, he said, "And they have our name. How could they have our name?"

They crossed another small bridge and turned up into a tony community with impressive stone houses, probably over a hundred years old, their rounded stones and hard lines softened by the light of the moon.

Zoltan expelled air. It shivered out of him. Ben didn't want him to feel that the tables had been turned on him, that for once secrets had been kept from him. Nor did Ben want to reinforce his own initial sense that they were for whatever reason returning to the scene of the crime, returning to the garden from which they had been expelled and could never return, must not return, so mythic had the country of their origin become to his father and consequently to all of them, especially to Ben.

Ben wanted for once to be open with his father. But his father was a man of secrets, a man comfortable with secrets, or at least one who'd found a place for secrets, a room for them, the door to which could and would remain closed. And Zoltan equated secrecy with sadness. You hid sad things away, even from yourself, if you could.

Ben hoped this visit would not add to his father's sadness, or deepen his sadness, making him burrow deeper underground. His father didn't like to be turned inside out. He hated when others did it—fled from them. "People do that because they're lonely," he once told Ben. "They think that baring themselves will attract more love, because love is so close to sympathy. But I am not lonely. I am my own best company."

What puzzled Ben most was that his father felt he needed to remain secretive about a history he could largely not have changed, not have influenced, let alone controlled. Or was that the secret he was trying to keep from himself?

What Ben could be sure of about his father, when they met these people, was that he wasn't going to make a show of being someone he wasn't. That might include his saying suddenly that it was time to leave.

They parked on the cobblestone street while the younger Zsofia waited on the curb to take them each by the arm up to the house. And what a house it was. Ben couldn't help but think of the optimistic stones and timbers that were used to assemble this house in an era when Budapest was trying its best to be Paris and London, but especially Paris.

In the big warm dining room, Zoltan and Ben were invited to sit around a grand table. "I'm so happy to be here." This from Zoltan, in Hungarian. In Ben's whole life, he had not heard him say such a thing. "I would never have imagined it. How my brother is still with us. He's found a way to stay with us."

The younger Zsofia, who had taken a seat beside Ben, said she would translate for him if he didn't understand anything, but Ben had been the only one of the three boys who had kept up his Hungarian. He even studied it for a couple of years in university.

An impressive old portrait of a matriarch hung on the wall behind the elder Zsofia's head. The woman had the same eyes. It was remarkable how such features resurfaced in succeeding generations, parts of people, bits of them, random bits washing up in their successors. You didn't have to look far for an afterlife. Here was the afterlife of a multitude of forebears, assembled right in this room.

A freshly opened bottle of champagne sat bubbling excitedly on the table. The younger Zsofia poured. "This is a great cause for celebration, this reunion. At last." She raised her glass and they raised theirs. They drank. Zoltan drank his champagne right down. He looked at the younger Zsofia. "So your father was born in 1945, I'm guessing."

"Yes," she said. "His name was Bela too, like my grandfather."

"Your grandfather," he repeated.

"Yes," she said. "My father died a decade ago. He raised me by himself, or with my grandmother's help, I should say. My mother was an actress who flew off to America not long after I was born. She was in a traveling musical, which landed in New York, and she defected. Even when I was in New York studying music years later, we didn't meet. I'm not sure if she lives, or lived, in New York or if she had another name. My father raised me without her, the way my grandmother had raised him. It's thanks to him we have this lovely house."

"Yes, he was an inventor," the elder Zsofia said in Hungarian.

"An inventor," Zoltan repeated, ever more cheerful. "*My* father was an inventor. Your *great-grandfather* was an inventor!" he said to the younger Zsofia. "I cannot believe what I'm hearing." Zoltan looked directly at Ben across the table. His eyes were gleaming.

"Yes," the elder Zsofia continued, "from the earliest age, my boy marveled at the composition of things, at the way things were put together, at the components of things, whatever they happened to be, anything, everything. Even natural things." She now stood. She was as striking and even more elegant than Iris Danzinger. In fact, where Iris was glamorous, Zsofia had a simple elegance emanating from within rather than applied from without. Ben tried to picture her at eighteen. "I remember my Bela wondering about the contradiction of bees. He couldn't have been two and a half at the time. He told me they make honey and they sting you. Then there are roses. Beautiful. Exquisite but with thorns. He asked, who thought all that up? He marveled at the ingenuity of things, the way screw-top bottles solved so many problems, as did toilet plungers, the simplicity of them, the light bulb, the atom bomb."

"What did he invent?" Ben asked.

"He was a medical engineer," the younger Zsofia said. "He invented a number of devices to be used in surgery, but his greatest claim to fame, and the thing that paid for the house we're sitting in, is a valve used to bolster the aorta, known worldwide as the Beck-Ganz valve. He worked with a Czech cardiologist to design it."

Zoltan was very pleased. "Who'd have thought?" he said. "Maybe he'll end up saving me before long, poor boy, even if he couldn't save himself. What grand irony. So many ironies."

The housekeeper and the chef, both of them quite ample and with remarkably shiny faces, brought in wine, more champagne, *palinka* and soda water, plus platters of all the best the country could offer: mushroom soup with braided bread, followed by hunter's stew with bread dumplings, two kinds of schnitzels, *lecso*, breaded calf's liver, Debrecen *kolbasz*, beets, potatoes and cucumber salad. The housekeeper started a fire in the big fireplace. It was warm very quickly.

As the hosts helped to dish out the feast and fill Zoltan's and Ben's glasses, Zoltan asked the younger Zsofia in Hungarian, "What about you, my dear? Are you"—he searched for the word, then said it in English—"attached?"

"I'm married to my music," she said like a nun, a music nun.

"We're all married to your music," Ben put in, and she hugged him hard from the side. Ben took a happy sip of wine.

His father looked down the length of the table at the elder Zsofia. "I am not my brother," he said. "I am not Bela."

"Of course you're not," she said. "But not even Bela was Bela. Nor was John Kennedy JFK. Nor was Jesus. Each was elevated out of time by their martyrdom, and we have allowed none of them to touch down since. Forever young. Forever dazzling. Bela was dazzling—he really was dazzling."

"Why did you not contact us?" Zoltan said. "You were the mother of Bela's son. Do you know how thrilled our parents would have been, Bela's and mine?" He clapped his hands together.

The elder Zsofia stood up again. She was not tall. Maybe she felt she could be better heard or had gotten used to presiding over a room in this way. Maybe she had some of the colonel, her father, in her after all.

"It would have been an enormous intrusion," she said, and clasped her hands together. "I had been cast out by my own family. I was poor and looking for help. How likely was it that your parents would have believed me? There was no Bela there to substantiate my case."

"I would have believed you," Zoltan said, and the room was still.

"There are to be no recriminations here tonight," the still-standing Zsofia said. "We are here to reunite, to set history straight, to join our histories. So I propose a toast." They all stood and raised their glasses. Ben's father sloshed some wine onto his cabbage roll. "To us," she said. "To the generations to come." She was looking at her granddaughter and Ben.

Zsofia took her seat again. They ate quietly for several minutes, until Zoltan said it. "So tell me. I need to know what happened when my brother and I parted ways and he came looking for you in Szifla."

Zsofia cleared her throat before saying, "Your brother was the only man I ever knew or loved. Ever. When he came to find me after my father himself had come home unexpectedly from the camp, I would have run away with him. I knew he felt the way I did, and I also knew that my father would have shot him on the spot. But my mother and sister saved him the trouble. Before I saw him, they knocked him unconscious when he came to our house. The doctor came, but he said all we could do was wait." Zsofia started crying, and her granddaughter got up to get her a handkerchief out of a sideboard. She was crying too. Ben hadn't started crying yet but was already brackish.

After a moment, the elder Zsofia said, "It all happened so fast. The Russians interrogated my father for days. They thought he knew something that he didn't." She paused to cry some more and then excused herself to go to the bathroom. No one said a word while she was gone, and no one ate. The younger Zsofia looked at each of her guests and tried to smile. It was hard not to smile back, though they were all anxious and apprehensive. Zoltan's hands were trembling as he poked at a morsel on his plate.

The couple with the shiny faces came in to stoke up the fire. Then they filled the Beck boys' glasses and pointed to their plates, urging them to dig in.

When Zsofia returned, she sat, took a drink of her wine and expelled a jittery breath. She had powdered her face, and she looked pale, too pale.

Zoltan said, "I called your house in Szifla not long after I returned home. I spoke to your mother."

"I know you did," she replied. "I was standing with my mother, holding her hand when the call came. But I couldn't bear to speak to you. I couldn't bear to tell you what had happened. All that mattered was the outcome, that Bela was no more."

They waited for her to continue, but another minute passed. The younger Zsofia urged everyone to eat a little before the food got cold, and Zoltan and Ben took a couple of bites and a sip of wine.

Finally, Zsofia stood up again, set aside her handkerchief and again clasped her hands together in front of her. "The Russians burst into our house and started shouting things—in Russian, naturally. My sister, Enek, and I were shoved aside, and Enek was ready to strike back, and she would have if I hadn't gripped her hand as hard as I could and pulled her down to sit with me on a chair. My mother was whimpering, and a soldier swatted at her, knocking her to the floor. They wanted to know about Bela. My father, who was still being detained, must have said something about him. 'Bela Beck,' the Russians kept repeating, as if he had anything to do with anything."

"Your father betrayed my brother."

"Yes, he did." She let the words settle. Finally, it had to be said. "It was the most expedient solution. He could distract the Russians and dispatch the intruder in a single stroke. Except that while the Russians were searching the house, in the shed and garage and the basement, the most obvious hiding places, I dashed upstairs to hide Bela somehow. It was going to be hopeless, but I had to do something. When I got to him, I took his handsome face in my hands, and he was cold. He was gone. He was cold. The pink had gone out of his lips. I kissed his cold lips hard. I tried to breathe warmth and life back into him, but . . . I must have let out a wail, and the Russians came charging upstairs."

"My brother," Zoltan said. It was all he could manage. He blew out a wet breath.

Ben stepped in. "And your father—"

"My father was taken to the local jail to await trial for war crimes. Your brother was loaded onto a hay wagon along with a dozen other men—collaborators, spies—who had been shot. The wagon was wheeled into the center of town, in front of the town hall, in fact, and set on fire. It was a warning to everyone in the town and the region. The Germans were finished. The Hungarian government, which had collaborated with the Third Reich, was finished. The Russians were in charge now.

"Some days passed, a few weeks. My mother couldn't get in to see my father. I was in terrible despair. I never wanted to see my father again. A regional judge who had been known to subvert the previous regime and who had Communist sympathies, a Judge Lengyel, was placed in charge of the region. He was a relative. He was my mother's cousin. She tried to see Lengyel repeatedly, and when he relented, she begged the judge to drop the charges. My father had been charged as a collaborator with the enemy. My mother told him that her husband was just doing his duty—surely he knew that. He had not committed war crimes, as they were suggesting. It was a time of chaos. People were being executed or arrested all over the country. Finally, on the condition that we leave the country and never return, the judge signed a false death certificate for my father, verifying his execution. He also issued travel papers for us under a fictitious name.

"My father knew a Swiss official in Budapest, and for a big fee he issued us temporary travel papers. We had a relative in Bern, my father's cousin, and within twenty-four hours, we were in a car heading toward Switzerland. I was sitting in the back, and I was sick, spiritually sick, wounded, a wounded spirit. My father drove through the night. We hadn't even called or written ahead. Imagine the surprise on our relatives' faces when we arrived."

Zsofia paused before saying, "But I was pregnant. I told my parents right away, as soon as I was sure. Quite boldly. I hadn't spoken a word to my father since the day Bela died. I marched into my parents' bedroom. I cannot tell you what a state I was in. The signs were unmistakable. I had missed my period. The tingling in me. I was triumphant. I was defiant. I spat out the news. 'I am pregnant with Bela Beck's child.' 'You whore,' my father said. 'This man simply will not go away. We'll end the little bastard's development immediately. I can find a doctor.' 'We'll do no such thing,' I told him. 'This child is more important to me than you are. You are nothing to me and never will be again.' And he said, 'And you are nothing to me, you vile creature.'

"My father disowned me right away. I never exchanged another word with him for the rest of his life. He wanted me to leave that instant. Get out of his sight. 'Gladly,' I told him. Enek came rushing in and pleaded with me not to leave her with them. My father told her to go too, but my mother screamed for all of us to stop. Afterward, I told Enek that she would be much better off without me. I would be a poor single mother.

"I had to return to Hungary. I couldn't stay in Switzerland. It was not that difficult. People were not trying to break back into Hungary. My mother's sister helped me. She lived in Budapest. She had never married and had never had a child in the house. And I billed myself as a widow. Why shouldn't I have? I *was* a widow, was I not? I was a war widow! And I changed my name legally to Beck, because that is the husband I would have taken, and he me, and because our Bela was the father of my beautiful child."

"Did he look like his father?" Zoltan asked.

"No, actually. He looked like my father—he seemed a correction to my defiance, a reminder—but this Bela wasn't like my father, not by nature."

Ben expected her to go get a picture, but she didn't. There were no family photographs in the room, only the one portrait in oils.

The housekeeper and cook returned and offered to reheat the food, but the guests declined. There was no need. Zoltan hardly said another word. He did ask, "And where did you live in Budapest with your aunt?"

"On Sziv Street," she said.

"And we were on Izabella, two blocks over from you! We might have passed you in the street or in a shop."

There was so much to digest: the feast, the drinks, the wounded spirit, the wounded years.

Everyone's face around the table glistened in the lamplight and the firelight. Ben stood up and said, "Aunt Zsofia, I have something for you."

"What?" she asked. "What do you mean?"

Ben had wrapped the little notebook in some hotel letterhead, and the concierge had found him a ribbon to tie the package with. His aunt was almost crying again before she opened it, and she did so with the care of someone handling a piece of ancient glass. Then she held the tiny notebook in her hand. "It was written by Bela," Ben said. "There's a poem near the front called 'Zsofia.'"

"You stole that notebook from me!" his father said.

"I did," Ben said. "I hope you don't mind."

Zoltan crossed his arms. And there was the tear again.

Tears were pouring down the elder Zsofia's face too, forging rivulets in the powder on her cheeks. The young Zsofia came to her side to look. She took the notebook from her grandmother and read the poem out loud.

> *As the morning sun*
> *cracks itself like an egg*
> *on the mountaintop*
> *and pours itself into your eyes,*
> *your liquid eyes,*
> *we flow together*
> *unbound by skin and bones,*
> *veins and vessels.*
>
> *I will wait for you*
> *in the lilting palace of the blind*
> *where only the night sun sees,*
> *its nose just below the surface,*
> *its yellow words murmuring*
> *in the bubbles,*
> *blowing over the reflection*
> *of its own silver heart.*

Now everyone was sobbing. After a time, the hosts and their guests straightened themselves out, sat back and sighed, breathed in the aromas of the room, nibbled a bit more, and then the elder Zsofia asked about her new relatives and their families, what everyone did, what life was like in Canada. Zoltan filled her in, though he forgot half the family members. Ben filled in the rest. Then his father said, "We've had a good life, an ordinary life—it's what I always wanted. My adult life began in a royal wedding." He was smiling. "It was in a bombed-out temple not far from here. We had three children, who leave much to be desired, but who have grown up themselves and followed their paths. There have been no horrors in their way. I would forgo all miracles in exchange for a life without horrors, a life without the tale you just told us." He rubbed his face again and shook his head.

"But the miracle is that life has gone on," Zsofia said. "You have had children and grandchildren in a safe and happy place."

"Yes, that is the miracle. Ordinariness is the miracle. Predictability. Enough, enough, not too much. Nobody should be too beautiful or too smart or too rich. Not if they want to enjoy life. You know, it's a strange thing," Zoltan went on. "I never thought about it until this moment. Here we were, in Hungary, for decades, centuries. We prospered here. We flourished. But in all that time, it never occurred to me, or to any of us, not to accept the Hungarians. That they might not accept us was a given. That we might live together but apart, as it were, was a given. But not to accept them—it was unthinkable."

Before the Beck boys left that night, the young Zsofia graced them with a last piece. They had a baby grand piano in their parlor. The walnut-paneled walls of this room were filled with art, vivid landscapes and rhapsodic abstracts. There were but two family pictures, one of the younger Zsofia in graduation gown getting her degree at Juilliard, and a beautiful black-and-white photograph in a gilded frame of the elder Zsofia as a sixteen- or seventeen-year-old. She was striking, stunning. There it all was: the exoticism, the allure, the eyes that followed you everywhere, followed Ben to his seat near the piano.

If there were other family photographs or portraits, they were elsewhere—in a bedroom likely, a private sanctuary.

Zsofia played Brahms, several pieces, but the one that moved Ben most was the Intermezzo in A major. She said that Brahms had written this beautiful piece for Clara Schumann, Robert Schumann's wife, and that Liszt had written pieces for Clara too—so had Wagner—so had Robert himself, of course.

"Clara must have been quite the figure," Zoltan whispered to Ben, or his version of whispering. "I don't get it."

"I do," Ben said, "and so do you." Zoltan looked surprised, found out.

Zsofia went on to say that the intermezzo was close to her heart. In the little time Zoltan and Ben had come to know her, she was able to say something with her playing that passed all understanding.

Finally, trailing warmth out into the Christmas night,

trailing music, Zoltan and Ben got back into their car to head back to the hotel. Both Zsofias had insisted they stay, they had plenty of room and could have beds made up in a jiffy, but the men thought it best to say their goodbyes, promising to be in touch regularly and to visit again as soon as they could. Ben felt another stab as he said it. He had to turn quickly away from his newfound family.

When they were back in their suite, Zoltan stood in front of Ben, who took a seat. Zoltan clasped his hands in front of him the way his sister-in-law had. His knuckles were turning shiny and white. "You can't imagine what it was like," he said. "Seeing my brother sitting with his back up against the wall of a cave, holding forth. It was one of the most glorious nights of my life. It has returned to me a thousand times in dreams, and I look at him hard in those dreams." He let out a long breath. "I keep wanting to say something to him in those dreams, but nothing will come out of my mouth. And I didn't tell my parents or my wife or Nadinka. I wanted to give my mother and father a few months of hope, that was all," he said. "Was that so bad?"

"No, that was not so bad."

"I couldn't tell them for months and then years. I just let the hope run out."

He looked down at his son and asked him, "What was the real reason you and Lucy tried to arrange all this?"

"The *real* reason?" Ben was afraid that his father had, after all, intuited something.

"Yes, tell me the real reason."

"The real reason was so that you could meet family you've never known, *close* family, your brother's family, a family he didn't have a chance to know, and now you do." So now Ben had lied too. He had to. He could see why one had to.

"How kind of you," Zoltan said, "how very kind." He stepped closer and put a hand on his son's shoulder. "I wish your mother could have been here. How she would have loved these people—how they would have loved her. I wish *my* mother could have been here. Goodness." He clapped his hands together. He looked drained, his face emptied out again, the red gone out of it. And then he turned and stormed off to his room.

The *real* reason was that Zoltan's world had become so puny. It was the thought of the constellation that floated above and around him each night as he lay in his bed: his bladder, his rectum, his white gloves, his cataracts, his tiny yellow Speedo, his fish-eating glasses, his snide dentures—all of it like so much space junk that could come crashing down on him in an instant. The real reason was that they wanted to take him out from under it, if only for a little time.

19

Zoltan told Ben, "When you tell the story of your life, just leave me out of it. Like cutting a person out of a picture." He made a snipping motion with his fingers.

"I'll try," Ben told him. "I'll do my best."

These should have been Zoltan's last words, but they were not. They were *among* the last, but his last words actually were "I hate Jell-O."

It was June 15, 2012, the day Nik Wallenda crossed Niagara Falls on a tightrope, about six months after Zoltan and Ben had visited Hungary. Miraculously, the TV installer arrived in his hospital room and had him set up in time for the crossing, but Zoltan didn't want to watch. Lucy and the girls joined Ben—Lucy had left work early—and all of them were urging him to watch with them.

"The crossing won't happen until tonight," Leah said, "but I'm happy to stay to watch with you." She kissed her grandfather on the forehead.

"Why would I want to watch?" he asked. "Why would anyone want to cross the falls?"

"To get to the other side," both girls said simultaneously, and laughed uproariously.

"Because nature made a huge gash in the land," Leah said, more serious now. She was holding her grandfather's hand. "And this guy is saying he is better than this. He's defying the mighty forces! He's defying death!"

"He's feeling alive!" Anna added. "Look at him." She was on her feet on Zoltan's other side.

"I have news for you," said Zoltan. "He's in nature too, like the rest of us. Life. Death. It's a prank. It's egotism. You're better off watching *The Price Is Right*, believe me. At least there's no hiding what you want when you're watching that show." He took Anna's hand. He looked hard at her. "Don't want things too badly," he told her.

With that, Lucy decided it was time to turn off the TV. If they wanted to watch the preparations for the crossing, she told the girls, they should head down to the lounge. But both wanted to stay. "Go to the lounge," their grandfather told them. "There's nothing to see here." And as they went, he said, "But you're much better off watching *The Price Is Right*, trust me."

It was a Friday. Others had come throughout the day. Sammy popped up a couple of times. He was working with his patients in the clinic down on the second floor. He looked distinguished in his white coat, and Zoltan looked extra grateful to have him there and be able to show him off to the two nurses who looked in on him throughout the afternoon. Sammy asked Ben and their father if anyone was going to watch Wallenda cross the falls later. Zoltan rolled his eyes and didn't answer.

Frank came a little later, but he couldn't stand to watch their father staring out the window. "You got the TV," Frank said to Ben, but then he wanted to leave. He asked Ben to keep him posted, no matter what hour. It looked as if he wasn't heading to Las Vegas after all.

After Frank departed, Zoltan looked straight up at the ceiling for the longest time. He looked pale and sunken, the physical weight of the years flattening him out.

Velda Kerbel stopped in. No one knew how she'd heard about Zoltan's condition, but she found him. She kept her jacket on and fully buttoned and had not put on her false eyelashes. She'd also had the good sense not to bring pickles or herring. She'd had more work done on her face, so that now it looked less like a face and more like someone trying to break out of a face from behind.

Zoltan kept his eyes closed throughout the visit. Ben and Lucy tried to back Velda out into the corridor again, but to no avail. This was, after all, the woman who'd had the gumption to paint the Sistine Chapel ceiling in her own house, the audacity first to build a ceiling big enough to accommodate it. Even if it wasn't the original or as good as the original, she and Michelangelo had qualities in common: fortitude, ambition, the kind of confidence—megalomania—to believe that they could impress the world, that the grandness of their work would be preserved and remembered. What difference did it make that he was as close to the creator in human form as anyone ever was, and she was the re-creator? In the end, wasn't he too a re-creator? Both works featured an even greater creation at their heart: life. And both makers were pleasing themselves mostly, even if she was pleasing only herself and he was pleasing himself as well as many others to come. So really what difference did it all make in the end? Weren't such people all on that same spectrum somewhere, between the fervor and passion of a mildly talented artist and the delirium of a genius? Neither of these was ordinary. This was not the spectrum of ordinariness.

But then the trouble began: vanity entered in, the ego spreading out over the ceiling. Wanting the affirmation. Hungry for it. Zoltan was right: don't want it too much; don't want anything too much.

Velda sat beside Zoltan, her face pulled back into her skull and neck, but the eyelashes off, the new breasts concealed, her perkiness dulled to a murmur. She was saying to Zoltan: "My poor dear man. My Saul left me without even a goodbye, and now you're leaving. My Zoltan, my Zoli. You've never even given me a chance to tell you. How I wanted to tell you, grow old with you, but you beat me to the finish line. I keep accompanying the men in my life to the finish line."

Lucy and Ben were not sure how long they could allow the monologue to continue. Anna and Leah were still down in the lounge. Sammy came by again but slipped away when he saw who was visiting.

Velda held Zoltan's hand and sobbed into it, used it as a hankie. Ben cringed. They might as well have been standing in line with Zoltan somewhere, hungry, famished, so great was the tension mounting in Ben and in Lucy.

But one had to live in the world, with whatever the world served up. Sometimes it was all very bad—deadly even—but sometimes it was just unpleasant, like a fridge rumbling. Or Velda.

If Zoltan could be patient, he would soon be off to the land of the mutes, where he could hold forth as much as he wanted. Or maybe he'd be a man between languages. A man without language.

Finally, Velda kissed Zoltan gently on the forehead. Then she applied some red lipstick and slipped out. In the corridor, she told Lucy and Ben that they should call her and come by sometime. She'd be happy to have them for dinner. "Bring the girls," she added. "Your girls are beautiful. Zoltan must be very proud." Then she kissed Ben slightly too close to his lips and hugged Lucy. Lucy had to wipe her husband down once Velda departed.

When they stepped back into the room, Zoltan said, "Please don't tell anyone else. I beg you." And then he closed his eyes again, but he wasn't sleeping. He opened them a minute later to say, "He dug a grave in me, my brother did. And so did your mother, Benny." Lucy sat down beside him on the bed. "I'm sorry to have to do the same to you."

Lucy took his hand and rubbed it. "Will you send me a sign?" she asked him, her voice shaky. "I didn't have a chance to ask my parents . . ."

Zoltan looked annoyed at this first assignment in the hereafter. But it was Lucy who was asking. Here, surely, the ice in him and the fire in him met and cancelled each other out. Few people could solve him in this way: Bela had, certainly, and Hannah, though only sometimes; Lucy, for sure; and now possibly the younger Zsofia, Bela's look-alike.

"Will you?" she asked again. "Will you send me a sign?" She was rubbing his hand more urgently now.

"I will, but you have to look for it."

"Of course I'll look for it."

"But not too attentively," he said, like an expert. "If you're too attentive, it will not come."

She took him at his word. She covered his hand with her hands.

"It's time to move on," he said, chuckling, as if he were making a joke. He was looking more in Ben's direction than Lucy's. (That was where the jokes resided.)

But it was Lucy who answered. "It's far too soon."

"Why *far*?" he said. "It is time for the next new world. I guess there's no such thing as staying put. I'll head out like

Christopher Columbus, the idiot, with his sense of direction, like mine."

He smiled but then closed his eyes again. Lucy was waiting for more. She hated when conversations ended. Why did conversations have to end? "Father," she said to him, but he was sleeping. She checked to see if he was breathing. He was.

Out in the hall, Ben asked Lucy and the girls if they should call their newly found family in Budapest. Lucy thought that they should, but Leah asked what they hoped to achieve by making such a call.

"It's not about achieving anything," Ben said.

She looked over her shoulder at her grandfather. "What would he want? Ask yourself that."

Zoltan might have been pleased to see the two Zsofias. They were guardians of a past he didn't know he had, or at least not entirely. He had loved them immediately. But still— he had made his wishes clear.

So they didn't call Budapest. They went back in to sit with him. At least an hour passed before he stirred. He half opened his eyes and looked ahead, toward the stopped clock on the wall. His eyes seemed to be roaming back and forth across its surface. Ben and Lucy and their girls were all following his gaze, wondering what he was doing. He might have been running memories across the wall with his eyes, or drawing cave pictures.

Lucy started to say something to him, to ask him how they could make him more comfortable, but Zoltan gripped Ben's hand suddenly, as if to say the time for talk was over. Lucy leaned over Zoltan, but Ben shook his head to stop her.

She went to the window and raised the blinds to let in more light; she checked the sad plant she had been over-watering; she picked up Zoltan's book and set it neatly on the nightstand. She took up Zoltan's dinner menu to fill it out, and that was when he said it: "I hate Jell-O."

Two years later, the young Zsofia came to visit from Budapest. She said it was high time she met the rest of her Canadian family. Everyone fell in love with her instantly, just as Ben and his father had. She was someone you could hardly take your eyes off. Ben heard his daughters asking her to stay, to resettle in Canada, pleading with her, actually. She shook her head and said she wasn't sure but was happy to be asked. She said that her life was in Hungary. It was where her grandmother was, as well as her students. And her music. She said again that she was married to her music. It was Frank, of all people, who said that music was lucky to have her as a spouse.

Lucy and Ben drove Zsofia out to Park Lawn to see where Ben's parents lay. The solitary poplar nearby had been cleaved in half by lightning. It struck Ben as strange that lightning should have vandalized the slow and gentle work of the sun and the rain in this way. Of course, it wasn't all about creation but destruction too. To nature, it was all the same.

For a minute or two, Zsofia bobbed rhythmically the way religious people do and seemed to be mouthing something to the stone. Ben couldn't tell if she was praying or if a melody was running through her head. He gave her a couple of stones, one blue and one white, to place on the headstones. He and Lucy wanted especially for her to see that they had her grandfather Bela's name engraved on the back of his father's headstone, but she hadn't come around to the back yet. She wanted to spend a little more time in the front.

There beneath Zoltan's name were the words

Judge Not

Acknowledgments

It is difficult to overstate how grateful I am to Nicole Winstanley, who has shown faith in my work for years. Some time ago, Timothy Findley told me that, once you have a Penguin on your cover, you've arrived. Nicole has pasted Penguins on the covers of three of my books. I also thank my wonderful editors, Lara Hinchberger, Helen Smith and Alex Schultz, who have improved this novel immeasurably.

I thank Julie Stevenson of Massie and McQuilkin for showing faith in me.

I thank readers of parts or all of the manuscript, foremost among them Dan Needles, Ken Ballen and Antanas Sileika, but also John Bourgeois, Andrew Clark, Lorne Frohman, Rob Shapiro and Jordan Sugar.

Dear friends have helped and encouraged me over the years. I thank Ben Labovitch, Vassiliki Daskalaki, Norma Weiner and Hubert Saint-Onge.

I thank my brothers Peter and Bill, and my sister-in-law Eve Shea.

I thank Andrea and Matthew Moniz, as well as Kellie and Jesse Kertes, who promote my work wherever they go.

I am deeply grateful to the Canada Council for the Arts and the Toronto Arts Council, both of whom helped generously with grants for research, travel and time to write this book.

What would I do without my dear Helen, Angela, Natalie, Jordan and Rob?